INTERFACE: IRELAND

INTERFACE: IRELAND

A NOVEL BY
KEVIN
DOWLING

BARRIE & JENKINS
COMMUNICA-EUROPA

First published in 1979 by
Barrie & Jenkins Ltd
24 Highbury Crescent London N5 1RX

ISBN 0 214 20602 5

Printed in Great Britain by The Anchor Press Ltd
and bound by Wm Brendon & Son Ltd
both of Tiptree, Essex

This book was written for my wife

This book is written for my wife

Interface: (Brit. Mil. Jargon); the geo-
graphical no-man's land between ghettos
occupied by hostile pol., relig., or racial
factions: a battlefield, esp. in urban
guerrilla warfare: theatre of conflict.

Part One

I

It was a bright May morning. A tall, redbrick semi-detached house stood with its feet in a fresh-dug garden. The perpetual haze of smoke which hangs over Manchester had lifted a little, and it was possible to glimpse the moors that roll away to the north of the city. Pascal knelt, with his nose pressed against the attic window of the tall red house, and wished he was walking on the windswept moors. A cloud of condensation fogged the glass; he licked it, tasting bitterness and cold. He wiped the condensation with his hand.

It was Sunday. Through the fledged green barrier of branches round St Alfred's Church, Pascal could see a bustle of figures on a gravel drive. The white webbing of the Boys' Brigade members flashed in the spears of sunlight. A parade was forming up. Pascal shuffled away from the window. He was eleven years old. He quickly became engrossed in something else.

An hour went by. The vicar walked, with his chest puffed out like a huge black robin, behind the embroidered banners and the silver band. Boom! boom! boom! went the big bass drum. The trumpets and the flutes played Anglican hymns.

It had been raining for a week, and the pavements of the rainy city were still patched with pools and areas of damp. The sun cast pennies of light to the undernourished poplars. Late daffodils unpursed their lips. The privets in suburban hedgerows spread tender new fingers to catch the changing light.

The vicar had been an Oxford blue. He was barrel-chested, ruddy with health, and had legs which deserved gaiters. He strode the suburban roads, flanked by his pigeon-chested curates, with a condescending smile for those wealthier parishioners he happened to see.

The world went about its Sunday business. The lower middle classes strolled to church or chapel or assembly rooms. In kitchens everywhere the Sunday roast was already in the oven. In the parks the veterans of war played bowls, and elder sisters played with their little brothers. An occasional spectator waved to a Scout or Guide in the church parade. Some of the children smiled, but none would have dared wave back. The curates who flanked the vicar, an anaemic, earnest-looking pair, carefully timed the swing of their furled umbrellas to coincide with his. They were as awkward as tall black geese in their tail-coats and shiny top hats. The parade majestically circled the parish, then equally majestically came back. The flag of St George, who had slain the dragon, beckoned the respectable from the squat, square tower of the church. The wind stirred the flag and puffed the processional banners till they swelled as proudly as the vicar's chest. The marchers tacked along the curve of the road like a convoy of ships under sail.

In the dim hallway of the tall red house a lamp burned before a picture of the Sacred Heart. A smiling Jesus, his face as soft as a woman's, gestured with Latin sweetness to his burning breast. Under his image was a printed panel.

CONSECRATION OF THE FAMILY TO THE SACRED HEART OF JESUS

A prayer followed, dimly lit by the light of a perpetual lamp whose electric filament was a glowing cross. All the members of the Canning family were listed underneath: Pascal; his two small sisters and his younger brother; their mother, Maureen; their father, who was four years dead.

Pascal had sometimes stood on a chair to read the closely written text. 'Filled with gratitude', it said, 'for the honour which Jesus confers on us by coming to take up his abode with us, we humbly and lovingly ask him to dwell forever in our home and in our hearts.'

Pascal's mother was a nurse and owned a lot of anatomy

10

textbooks. He sometimes looked at diagrams of the heart and wondered which of its chambers would be occupied by God.

The Anglicans' procession passed in front of the tall red house. A man stood watching on the other side of the road, staring patiently over the heads of the children and between the tapestried banners. His eyes were unnaturally bright. He looked shabby. He was a curious sight on a Sunday in this locality. One of the curates picked him out at once. Perhaps he was a dustman, or a labourer. He badly needed a shave. His face was grey, and there was something desperate about it, some want which the curate could sense but not imagine.

The curate smiled, for even the badly dressed are in the inscrutable image of God; and besides, it was a pleasant morning and churchmen should be happy on a Sunday.

The strange man caught the curate's eye, started violently, and blushed. The curate frowned mildly as he looked away. Perhaps it was wrong not to have ignored the fellow, whoever he was. The curate sighed. It was sometimes hard to know what to do for the best.

The procession moved on. A group of women were gossiping on the footpath. They paused to watch as the clergymen walked past. The curate studiously gazed at a scarf round the Scoutmaster's neck. Mrs Wainwright was one of the gossips. She was a dreadful woman. Whenever she could, she accosted him alone. She was trying to persuade him to hear her confession, which was most embarrassing. They were High Church at St Alfred's, but not altogether Roman. Besides, everybody knew Mrs Wainwright's favourite little failing. The vicar called her his Scarlet Woman.

The strange man with the grey, pinched face continued to stare at the tall red house. He read the name-plate over the door: BALLYVARREN. He studied the laburnum tree in the garden, and counted the five red steps which led to the porch. His hands were in his pockets, and his back was stooped as though his stomach was giving him trouble.

Inside the house, in a tiny scullery at the back, Mrs Maureen Canning scrubbed at her children's washing. The cramped room, with its stove and cupboards and double drainer, was very dark. The water was very hot. The hot water made her hands red, but her knuckles were white from the clench of her grip on the brush. From time to time she shifted on her feet, half humming, half singing a tuneless air which was hard to recognize at all.

'Some died by the wayside, some died 'mid the stranger,
And wise men have told us their cause was a failure ...'

Suddenly she broke off and lifted her head, listening. The sound of the Boys' Brigade's bugles filtered faintly through the house, dying in the distance. There was a bird in a cage in the kitchen. She could hear him hop from one perch to another. She could hear the ticking of a clock, and the creak of old pipes that were full of water.

'Pascal!' she shouted. 'Pascal? Are you all right?'

She tensed, in the manner of mothers, cocking her head, listening. Nothing changed. She could hear no answer. Awkwardly, for her hands were wet, she half turned round, and considered going to see what her son was up to; looked at the work she still had left to do, and shook her head.

'Pascal? Are you all right?' she called.

There was still no answer.

Pascal was perfectly happy. He was still in the attic. He was making a parachute out of tissue paper and some lengths of wool. He was very careful to make a perfect square, then fold it into a cone and tear a small hole right in the centre.

Outside, the strange man shivered.

Pascal had a Roman legionary made from hard grey plastic. It wasn't very heavy, but he had some metal washers to tie to the parachute as well. He intended to drop the parachute and its burden down the well of the stairs. He was humming too. It was a habit he got from his mother. There was no thought in what he was humming, and not much tune.

The doorbell rang. Pascal didn't notice. He was absorbed in the tying up of knots. He wondered, vaguely, if his father had ever made a parachute descent. There was a picture of his father in the front room. His father was dressed in Royal Air Force blue.

The widow went to answer the door, wiping her hands on her apron, then pausing to take it off. She threw it down on the kitchen table. She thought that the noise at the door had been made by her niece, who had taken all the younger children for a breath of air in the park.

Mrs Canning was in her early forties. Her hair was a very light brown—almost golden—colour. She was attractive in a handsome sort of way, a formidable woman who ruled her household with a strong will and a cutting voice. Her only income was her salary as a district nurse. So she was not surprised when she saw a man's shadow behind the opaque glass panel of the front door. She imagined it was one of her patients' husbands.

'Yes?' she said, opening the door a crack.

The man was pale and dark and young. He wore a cheap brown suit and a nondescript, crumpled, gaberdine coat. She had never seen him before.

'Mrs Canning?' he asked, quickly. She smiled encourage-ment, having registered at once the nasal Dublin accent.

'That's right.'

'Seamus sent me,' the man blurted. 'My name's Costello—Mick Costello.'

Mrs Canning looked blank. 'Seamus?'

'I knew him in Dublin—Seamus. Can I come in?'

The widow hesitated. 'I suppose so.' She smiled. 'Of course you can. But you've caught me by surprise. I wasn't expecting visitors. The place is a bit of a tip—'

He interrupted her. 'It doesn't matter. Let me in.'

'All right.' He brushed rudely past her. 'What's the matter? Is there something wrong?'

Costello turned to face her in the hall. He took a deep breath. 'Mrs Canning, I'm on the run.'

'What?'

'The police is after me.'

She looked at him in silence. 'You're wanted?'

'I busted out of Pentonville last night.'

'God, why did you come here?' She paused, pursing her lips, and he thought how helpless she looked. 'Come on. Get into the kitchen,' she said. 'In there, quick.'

'Thank you, missus.'

'Sit down.'

Mrs Canning could feel her heart pounding, a mixture of fright, excitement and indignation. However, she pretended to be calm. To give herself a moment to think, she took the abandoned apron from the kitchen table and disposed of it in the scullery, folding it neatly and tossing it down beside the pile of washing. She closed the door then, and came back to sit across the table from her visitor.

'You say my nephew sent you?'

The man hesitated. 'Not exactly.' He shook his head. 'He told me you were his aunt, that you lived in Manchester. That's all.' Costello rubbed his face with a grubby hand. 'I wouldn't be here if I wasn't desperate.'

'Tell me what happened.'

'Everything went wrong.' Costello laughed bitterly. 'It usually does.' He looked up, seeming lost in thought. His gaze was taken by a painting on the wall. He stared at the derelict cottage and the twisted tree beside a lake; at blue mountains behind them, and the purple clouds of an approaching storm.

'It was all laid on,' Costello said. 'There was a car, clothes, money . . . there was supposed to be a house. I was to lie low for a while. It was supposed to be all laid on.'

'What happened at the finish?'

Costello looked at her. His mouth twisted in a smile. 'Farce.' He shook his head. 'I still don't know what happened. There were two of us. We got as far as Birmingham by train. Then the other fella said to split. He said the Branch were on to us. He was nervous. He was even more frightened than I was . . .'

'You were followed?'

'No. I don't think so. The Branch wouldn't follow us. They'd pick us up. It was just the other fella. He was nervous.'

'You came here,' said the widow flatly.

'I had nowhere else to go.'

'No.'

There was a long period of silence. The house was quiet. An occasional car passed by on the road outside.

'I don't want you here,' the widow said. 'I'm not like Seamus. I'm against all that.'

'All I want,' Costello said, 'is a couple of hours of a rest.'

'No.'

14

'Just somewhere to sit in a chair.'

The woman stood up and went to stare out of the window into the garden. There was a blackbird pulling worms from the small rectangle of the lawn. 'What would you do then?'

'Move on.'

'You have some money?'

'Three shillings. You could lend me some.'

She turned on him then, as sudden as a cat. 'What did Seamus say about me? Did he say I had money to give away to fools?' She bit her lip. 'I'm a widow. I have no money. All I have is my job. If they find you here I won't have that.'

'No,' Costello said. 'I'm sorry.'

'What about Pascal?' Mrs Canning said. 'What would I say to him? To any of the children? The neighbours will see you, they'll talk . . .'

'Give me fifteen quid,' Costello said quickly. 'I'll get to Liverpool. Take my chance on the boat.'

'They'll be watched,' Mrs Canning said triumphantly. 'All them ports will be watched.' She nodded. 'They'll pick you up and I'll lose my money.'

'The Movement . . .' Costello said, but his voice trailed off.

'The Movement!' scoffed Mrs Canning. 'The true blues! God's shamrock-waving idiots! They'd send it me back, would they? When? When Cromwell's canonized, that's when!'

Costello said nothing. He leaned forward, staring at the table, holding his head in his hands.

'What did you do?' Mrs Canning demanded. 'Did you shoot someone? Or can't you tell me?'

'I couldn't shoot anybody,' Costello said. 'I stole some guns.'

'You couldn't shoot anybody,' said Mrs Canning ironically. 'But you'd steal some guns so some other fecker would! How many guns did you steal?'

'A few tons of them,' said Costello wearily. 'Rifles and automatics. We cleaned out an armoury near London.'

'Tons of guns? Tons? Lord, it's a Hun you've sent me!' She bent over him. 'Tell me the truth!' she scolded. '*You* couldn't steal a purse from a pensioner!'

'No,' said Costello dully. 'But we stole a van and we packed it with stolen guns.'

'And what happened to the guns? Did the fairies get them?'

'We ran out of petrol on the road to London,' Costello said. 'You're right. We were awful bloody fools.'

'I can see that,' said the widow, excited now. 'You and your half-wit friends against the bloody British Empire.'

'It was the van,' Costello said. 'We stole the van. It was an ould rattletrap of a van. The fuel gauge wasn't working.'

'What did you get?'

'Eight years. Beginning last September.'

Mrs Canning laughed.

Costello turned on her hysterically. 'It's very funny, isn't it? Eight years. And now I've lost my remission.'

The widow looked at him bleakly. 'Oh, yes. You certainly have.'

'Well, let me sleep then! An hour, missus, please! I'm shagged. I'm done completely.'

'You better be on your way.'

Costello stood up. 'Seamus said you were hard.'

'He did, did he?'

'He didn't say you were a fucking monster.' Costello ducked his head, avoiding the woman's cold blue eyes. 'I'm sorry.' He looked furtively round the room, at the wallpaper grubbed by her children's hands, at the bookcase, and the used ashtrays, and the carved knicknack in black bog oak which was standing on the mantel. He reached out and picked it up. 'I shouldn't have come.'

'Gunmen,' Mrs Canning said, 'are out of fashion.'

Costello pretended to laugh. 'It was Seamus,' he said. 'He gave me the idea. He used to talk a lot about Ballyvarren.'

'I left it when I was eighteen years of age,' the woman said. 'They painted the post-office green but they couldn't find me a job.' She took the ornament and put it back on the mantel.

'That's nice,' Costello said. 'That carving's nice.'

'There's a poem goes with that.'

'Yes?'

' "The wolfdog lying down," ' she said, ' "And the harp without the crown—" '

' "And the round tower of Ireland between them." '

'That's right.'

'My mother had one like it.' Embarrassed, he looked at his shoes. 'I'll go now, missus.' He paused. 'Can you give me a couple of pound?' She wouldn't answer. 'Please?'

There was a crash above their heads as Pascal jumped down the last few attic stairs and stumbled on the landing. Mrs Canning grabbed Costello's arm. 'Get in the scullery!' she hissed.

Her fingers dug through Costello's coat, and she pushed him bodily into the small back room. 'Keep quiet!'

She rushed across the kitchen and into the hall, standing where she could bar the kitchen door.

'Mammy!' Pascal shouted. 'Watch out! It's coming!'

Something struck her head and slid down her shoulder and hung in a tangle from her hair.

'My parachute!' yelled Pascal. 'Be careful or you'll tear it!'

He skidded down the stairs, jumped, and landed on his knees.

'Pascal!' she scolded. 'Be careful!'

He jumped up. 'Give it me!'

He was blond and sturdy and looked like his father.

'You're ruining the carpet,' she said. 'I had to tack it down again yesterday.'

'I'm sorry.'

'One of these days you'll break your neck.'

'Can I have the parachute?'

'Here.' She handed it over. 'I'm not having you wrecking the house, though. Go to the park and see if you can find Joan. You can play with the parachute there.'

He scowled. 'I want to stay in.'

'Move!' she ordered, hunting him out with a cuff that deliberately went wide. He laughed mockingly and ran to the door, which he slammed behind him. She wished then that she'd tried to kiss him, and sighed with vexation. These days he usually squirmed aside. Since he started grammar school he'd decided affection was soppy.

Mrs Canning went back into the kitchen. 'He's gone. You can come out.'

Costello grinned sheepishly. 'Sounded like a lively little lad.'

He slouched, with his hands in his pockets, to the middle of the kitchen floor. He looked infinitely seedy.

'People probably said the same thing about you.'

'Yes.'

'I hope he turns out better.'

Costello shrugged. 'It's not his problem,' he said. 'Ireland.'

'What do you mean?' demanded Pascal's mother, indignantly. 'He has more sense, that's all. At least, I hope so.'

'I'll be going, then.'

Mrs Canning softened. 'Sit down,' she said. 'They won't be back for a while. Since you're here, I'll get you something to eat.'

For the first time, Costello smiled without bitterness, and she could see how young he was. Slowly, still smiling, he sat down on a kitchen chair.

'You're mad, the whole lot of you,' said Mrs Canning. 'It's all over. It's been over for thirty year or more now.'

Costello nodded. 'The most of the game is the trying.' He was was shaken by a spasm of coughing. 'Can I take me shoes off, missus?'

'Go ahead.' She went to the scullery and lit the stove. 'I suppose you could eat a horse.'

'A little rabbit between two slices of bread.'

She laughed. 'Them socks look very holy.'

'They're as full of water as a font.'

'I'll give you a pair of Paddy's.' She glanced towards the kitchen. 'I still have his things upstairs.'

There was an entry running along the side of the house. The coalmen used it to make deliveries. Both of them heard the sudden clatter of feet.

'Pascal!' gasped the widow. 'He's coming back! Quick, get in here . . . in the scullery. Hurry!'

Costello lunged forward, stumbling over his shoes, but it was too late. Pascal, his face flushed and his hair tousled, banged open the kitchen door and ran cheerfully in.

'I forgot the washers for my parachute!' he shouted. 'There's a wind . . .'

His voice trailed off as he looked at Costello. 'Hello?' he said. 'Who are you?' When nobody answered, he laughed.

18

'Have you got your shoes wet? Look at the holes in your socks!'

The wanted man flung a frightened glance at Mrs Canning. Her face was pale. She looked at her son, and then at him, and closed her eyes in exasperation.

'This is Mr Costello, Pascal,' she said eventually. She paused. 'He's going to stay with us for a little while.'

'Good!' said Pascal. 'He can help me to fly my parachute.'

Mrs Canning went to her son and grabbed his shoulders. 'You must never tell anyone he's here.' Pascal didn't understand. She shook him. 'It's a secret, Pascal. Promise now. Promise you'll never tell.'

'I promise,' said Pascal. He was very frightened. 'I'll never tell anyone, mammy.'

II

Pascal never did betray Costello. The fugitive stayed hidden in the house for almost a fortnight, and every day Pascal went off to school bursting with the knowledge that his mother was sheltering a wanted man. They were thrilling days. The secret ached to get out; Pascal longed to boast of it, but he learned the keener, peculiar pleasure of keeping quiet. It never occurred to him to consider Costello a criminal. The IRA man was quiet almost to the point of shyness, but he was funny and told stories and knew Pascal's cousin Seamus better than Pascal did himself.

Seamus had been shot and wounded in the shoulder during an arms raid several weeks before. That had happened at a place called Omagh, in County Tyrone; one of the six Irish counties still occupied by the British Army. Pascal begged for details, but Costello hadn't been there. He knew enough, however, to satisfy Pascal that Seamus was a hero. The boy looked forward feverishly to summer, when he could go on holiday to Ireland and hear hints about the story here and there; nobody would say anything straight out, he knew that by now.

Holidays in Ireland happened every year. They began with

19

the smell of smoke, as sharp and dry as a biscuit; then the train pulled out and rolled past mile after mile of houses, past crofts full of purple and yellow weeds, past rabbit hutches, washing lines, and rickety trellises overburdened with roses. It was soon in Liverpool or Holyhead, and Pascal was on the deck of the ferry; the gulls wheeling overhead, the steel hawsers striking sparks off the edge of the quay.

There was one holiday he would always remember. He would remember following the plough in his uncle's fields. Two great horses pulled it patiently, spit falling from their mouths, their harness clattering, their hooves sometimes clinking on a washed-out stone.

The young man beside him was urging them on, cursing cheerfully while a roof of cloud rolled down from the dove-grey hills, crows flying before it like survivors from an ambush.

Then the drops of rain began to spatter on Pascal's fore-head, and he opened his mouth in an O to catch them. More and more of the raindrops fell, till his face was streaming and the ploughman shouted an oath and dashed for cover under a hawthorn hedge. It was warm under the hedge, and the man lit a cigarette, offering Pascal a drag and laughing when he refused. They were dry in there, watching raindrops dribble and glitter from the crippled branches and the fresh green leaves. The abandoned horses were aloof, disinterested, stood patiently and made no movement. Their broad backs steamed slowly, like mouldy blankets spread before a fire.

The ploughman gave a snort of satisfaction. 'This is the life,' he said, emphatically. He spat at the soaking grass outside. 'This is the life, now isn't it, Pascal?'

But Pascal said nothing, grunted.

'Them oul' horses over there, the rain falling,' said the ploughman urgently. He sucked on the cigarette. 'Can you smell the land?'

Wind came, and the rain-sheets swirled.

'Us two snug, in under the hedge and havin' a smoke.'

'Do you think it'll rain for long?' asked Pascal.

'If you stay quiet, we might even see a fox,' the ploughman said. 'There's a nest of them in Woods's field.'

Pascal said nothing, hoping a fox might come.

'Even an Englishman like you,' the ploughman said at last. 'Even an Englishman like you has got to admit that this is something!' He sighed. 'You couldn't wish for a better life.'

Pascal regarded him sullenly. 'I'm not English,' he said, in a hostile tone of voice.

'Sure and what else would you be? A bloody Hottentot? A Cree? Weren't you born over there beyond? You were born in England.' He laughed indulgently. 'You're the next best thing to a Prod.'

'I am not!'

'You are so! I bet you wouldn't even go to Mass if you wasn't made to. You weren't at Communion on Sunday.'

'I had my breakfast early,' said Pascal with dignity. 'I'll go next week.'

'There y'are,' said the ploughman cheerfully, grinding out his fag. 'You et your breakfast like a bloody heathen, an' a good Catholic boy wouldn't have done that.' He spat again. 'He'd have left the breakfast till after.'

Pascal didn't bother with explanations. He sank down against the bank at the back of the ditch, sliding till his bottom caught on a sturdy root. He sat on it, propping up his chin, with an elbow on his knee, staring out at the soft outline of terraced hedges rising up the hill. The silence between them lasted for several minutes, so that Pascal started when the ploughman suddenly demanded: 'What age are you, anyway?'

'Seven.'

'You're a very big lad for seven.'

Rain in Ireland falls softly, like so many veils of chiffon, hiding the landscape in muted thicknesses of grey and green. In the velvet silence of deserted country, you can sit relaxed for many minutes, and then suddenly wonder what happened to the time.

'Will you be going to the match?'

'I don't suppose so,' said Pascal gloomily.

'Ah, they don't play hurley in England anyhow.'

Lazily, Pascal studied the man beside him. His name was John. He was almost nineteen, and had a strong, lean body and a stubbled face.

'You could always take me.'

John lit another cigarette, drawing the smoke in deeply and tilting his head upward to exhale.

'We should still finish it today,' he said, nodding at the horses.

Pascal turned and glanced at the field. 'Smoking is bad for you,' he remarked. 'It stunts your growth.'

John laughed. His trousers flapped when he did so. His trousers were too big, a pair of hand-me-downs whose cuffs were tucked out of sight in his boots. He was wearing a shirt which remembered having once been white. The sleeves were rolled up and the two buttons at the neck were open. 'Yer own mammy smokes.'

'It's bad for you all the same.'

'Naw,' said John. 'It's only bad if you live in the city. In the country you get lots of fresh air.'

Pascal gravely considered this statement.

'Would you like to live in the country, Pascal?'

'I would,' he said. 'I like the country.'

'Ah, it's grand,' John sighed. 'I don't suppose you get into the country at all in England.'

'We do a bit.'

'It's not the same, though. Not the same as here.'

'No.'

'Still, I suppose you like it there in England. You'll be missing all the excitement.' John put the cigarette in the corner of his mouth and rolled it comically across to the other side. 'You'll be big soon enough and then you'll have plenty of money.'

'I suppose,' said Pascal.

'You'll be a proper little English fella then. You won't come home any more. You'll forget all the friends you had here.'

Pascal picked up a pebble and threw it as hard as he could. 'I won't forget!' he shouted. 'What makes you think I'd forget?'

The stone struck John a glancing blow on the head, but he only shook it, laughed, and made a shooing gesture with his hands. Then he ducked out of the shelter of the hedgerow and ran, still laughing, across the furrows to the plough.

22

The rain had diminished to a light drizzle, and as Pascal followed his boots sucked and squelched on the newly broken ground.

'Hup!' John yelled at the team, 'ya pair o' lowsers, ya can't stand there all day!'

John was an orphan, and Pascal was tempted to run to the snorting muzzles of the horses and shout to him over their heads.

'Your mother was English!' he wanted to scream. 'She cleaned chamberpots to make a living! Your dad was an English drunk!'

John wouldn't be able to answer, because nobody knew who his father and mother were.

'You aren't even an orphan, just a bastard!' Pascal wanted to shout. 'Sucks to being Irish 'cos you're not!'

But he didn't dare, so he ran after the plough and John rubbed his hand in Pascal's hair and made a fuss of him. He let Pascal help him to steer the plough, and when the boy was tired he picked him up and placed him on top of Betsy, who was one of the mares. She was a placid horse, and didn't seem to mind.

'You have a grand view up there!' John shouted.

Pascal rode up and down the field ten or a dozen times. The rain was replaced by fitful sunshine which threw fleeting shadows on the flanks of the mountains. The sweet scent of the broken earth and the smell of the horses made Pascal almost drunk with happiness.

He saw the roof of a car sweep past, up the narrow lane which led to the house. He turned and shouted back to John:
'Who would that be, John?'

'How the hell do I know?' shouted John.

The car had come from Dublin to fetch Pascal and put him on the ferry to England. His father had died in hospital that morning. Everyone pretended to be shocked, though Pascal realized later that they must have known what was going to happen.

'Isn't he better off in Heaven?' one of the uncles asked him. Pascal nodded, dumbly. His father had been ill for years.

He grew up, the eldest child of four, and his mother called him 'her white hope'. It was banal enough. She said that she had no money, that she couldn't maintain the house, but somehow they never left it. She scrimped, pinched, managed to get by. She leaned on him at first.

'Now you're the man of the house,' she said. 'You've got to help me.'

It was the nearest she would ever come to asking him for anything, but Pascal was too young to understand. He occasionally remembered to fetch the coal or do the washing up. But he was not much help. He was always in trouble. One day he fell out of a tree and limped home, covered in filth and blood, his best pair of pants ripped open from the trouser pocket to the bottom of the leg. She surveyed him, at first in silence, then quoted a poem.

'He's the man from Eldorado, and he's just arrived in town, In moccasins and oily buckskin shirt.'

She had a poem or a ballad for every occasion, and could produce one at a moment's notice while the rest of the company sat stunned. On a famous occasion she captured a burglar single-handed, quoting Dryden to the startled bobbies who came to arrest him. The unfortunate thief had fallen asleep in an armchair after drinking most of a bottle of whisky, and she heard him snoring. She crept downstairs and clouted his head with a poker. He revealed in court that he was whisked, half-stunned, into the widow's kitchen, where she revived him with hot, sweet tea.

Her delight in literature was possibly inherited. Her father, an eccentric but amiable drunk, used to pay her a penny for a morning recital to clear his head. She learned Gray's *Elegy in a Country Churchyard* in a single day, and he was so delighted that he gave her a shilling from her mother's allowance and brought him with her to the local pub, where she stood on the counter and spouted the verses to the astonished generality.

In her widowed state, she was naturally lonely. She brought Pascal into her bed at night, and they would read his comics together. Her favourite strips were *Nobby the Bobby* and *Desperate Dan*, and she continued to pay tuppence for the *Beano* long after Pascal had outgrown it.

He learned Shakespearian soliloquies from her while his friends were still trying to master *The Wide Range Reader*.

" '*If I could pray to move, prayers would move me,*' " she would suddenly say. 'Come on, finish it!'

' "*But I am constant as the northern star / Of whose true-fixed and resting quality / There is no fellow in the firmament.*" '

'Good. For that you can stay up.'

He used to watch her, when the house was quiet, when the babies were asleep and there was nobody there but themselves and the springer spaniel dog she got in Ireland. She did not smile easily, even then, but when she did Pascal would sigh happily and know that some fascinating story would certainly follow. When something angered her—for example, if something got broken—her face would set in a tense, hard, unforgiving mask. She was relentlessly demanding, and equally stubborn.

Before every Parliamentary and local election she went to the local Tory headquarters and came back with a campaign poster. She stuck it on the front-room window where it could be plainly seen by every passer-by. The front room at the Manchester Ballyvarren was always referred to grandly, as the lounge.

YOUR CONSERVATIVE AND UNIONIST CANDIDATE

'Your father was a Socialist, God rest him, but he knew nothing.' She had never lost her musical Irish brogue. 'If we voted them scallywags in, they'd nationalize the land, and we'd certainly lose this house.'

Her job brought her into contact with prosperous people as well as poor ones. She made many friends, but always maintained a certain well-defined distance. She was very proud.

'He's a respectable man,' she would say. 'He sends his children to the convent.'

It was the ultimate accolade. She had herself been educated at a convent, and was always well disposed towards priests and nuns, who she said were the chosen of God. She had a niece who was a nursing nun in Liverpool and they used to go to see her, and drink fragrant tea from delicate little cups.

She refused him a rise when he demanded sixpence a week to spend.

'Thruppence is quite enough,' she decided. 'If you had any more you'd only get chewing gum, which is extremely bad for the teeth.'

There was never any question when the Foreign Missions appealed for money. Twelve days at a penny a day was enough to buy a little black baby. Once you'd bought him, you were permitted to choose his name. Pascal maliciously selected the most eccentric names he could. It was obligatory to bestow Christian names on Christian babies, but there were any number of saints with risible and unpronounceable names.

At Christmas-time she always bought useful presents. Intriguing parcels contained several pairs of knickers or elasticated braces. Fortunately, all the rest of her scattered brothers and sisters were aware of this, and bombarded her children with toys. She never had to pay for a turkey, for one always arrived from the Irish Ballyvarren sewn up inside a sack. The Customs label was festooned with stamps which Pascal immediately tore off.

One Christmas the sack was leaking and a terrible smell came out when she cut it open. Her face turned pale at first, then crimson with the excess of her rage.

'This fecking yoke is maggots up to here!' she said, and rushed to the local post-office, not to complain but to send a telegram.

TURKEY ROTTEN. SEND ANOTHER. MAUREEN.

Another turkey was sent at once. Her pride forbade her to regard the turkeys as either a gift or an obligation. They were rather an inalienable right, a sort of tribute paid by those fortu-

26

nate enough to remain in Ireland, to assuage the guilt of having sent her out into poverty and exile. Pascal unfailingly spent a couple of months each year at Ballyvarren, the beneficiary of a similar arrangement.

The one thing that spoiled Christmas for his mother was his unrespectable uncle, a man called Mick.

This man, her husband's half-brother, she always referred to as, 'That bloody Red, your famous Uncle Mick'. Mick was a Communist and his English wife was a Party official. Maureen Canning disapproved of them both with a scandalized fascination.

'Your Uncle Mick is a godless man,' she would say, pursing her lips in an unforgiving line while Pascal opened his Christmas parcel. 'Your Auntie Josie is a rabid anti-Catholic as well.'

To Mrs Canning's undisguised disgust, the Christmas parcels usually held books, not any old books but expensive volumes from the Moscow Publishing House. They were lavishly illustrated on expensive paper. Pascal's favourite was about a little boy who went with his daddy to build a hydroelectric dam in the snow-bound wastes of Siberia. While he turned the pages he could hear the slice of runners as their sledge sped eastward through the virgin snow. He was filled with awe by the prospect of an endless forest of birch, the trackless haunt of wolf-packs, bears, and tigers. The boy and his dad suffered terrible hardships, but on Christmas Eve at midnight they were safely back in their snug log cabin.

Pascal could clearly visualize the cabin, its eaves hung with huge icicles as thick as a big man's thigh. Inside the cabin was a roaring stove with a hot black chimney, and the doors were hung with parkas thawing out. The boy and his father would stamp their feet and rub their hands. Then they'd sit by the rough table, and a lantern would cast flickering shadows across their faces.

There was a radio on the table—a big one, whose dials glowed in the gloomy dark. When they switched it on the peal of the Kremlin bells chimed for the morning of Christmas.

'I can see the stars on the towers above Red Square,' the

little boy whispered. Outside, the wolves were howling on the frozen tundra. Pascal was lost in a distant dream as he sat by the kitchen fire.

'There are stars on the towers of Moscow,' he murmured to his mother. Then he closed his eyes, and was able to see them too.

When Mick sent books he wrote a little message on the fly-leaf. 'Lots of love for Pascal at Xmas 1957.'

'He does it to aggravate me,' said Pascal's mother.

Pascal helped himself to a Polish chocolate and glanced mildly up. 'What does he do to aggravate you?'

'It isn't Xmas,' Pascal's mother hissed. 'It's Christmas. The day we remember the birth of Christ.'

Mick always signed his name in Irish, for he was an old revolutionary and wanted his country to be free.

'*Micéal Mac Giolla Chriost*,' he wrote, and Pascal savoured it. 'Michael, the son of the servant of Christ.' Eamon Gilchrist had died when Mick was a child, and his mother had married again. That was why he had a different name from Pascal's father.

Pascal went to visit Mick in London, and was given a treasured copy of *Speeches from the Dock*, an out-of-print collection of the defiant words of patriots en route for a nasty end at the hands of a British executioner. Mick was a patriot himself, for he had run away from home to join a Flying Column and fought the British. He was hunted in the valleys and the hills. The Republic was betrayed, his beloved Ireland was partitioned. Mick turned irregular, fighting former comrades and ending up on hunger strike in jail.

'Your mother's people were all Free Staters,' said Uncle Mick. 'They owned their farm and didn't give a rap about the future of the nation.'

Mick fled from Ireland to America, and then enlisted for the Spanish Civil War. He was wounded by the fascists at Madrid, and smuggled into France on a bootlegger's donkey. He got to London in plenty of time to join the RAF, and was a tail-end gunner on the Lancaster bombers which blitzed the Ruhr.

'My mother says that you're out of your mind.'

'Your mother is a wonderful woman,' said Mick. 'But very narrow.'

Mick owned a pearl-grey Stetson, and had a disconcerting habit of turning up at funerals wearing that and a loud American suit. He made things worse by smoking a large cigar. The end came when he arrived at a wake with his mistress, a pale, anaemic girl from Chelsea who said, 'Delighted to be heyah' when introduced to the recently bereaved.

Soon after it was found that Mick had a malignant tumour. He began drinking whisky to deaden the intolerable pain. He died in agony a few months later, but not before telling Pascal a couple of things about his attitude to life.

The first was how he had both loved and hated Michael Collins. While he talked of Collins, Mick became flushed and highly excited. Collins was the brilliant leader whose radical tactics produced the stalemate of the Irish War of Independence. He ultimately sided with the Free State faction which accepted the enforced partition of the country. To Mick and many others, this was his great betrayal. At the Mouth of Flowers in his native county, they caught him up and killed him.

'I was never sorry,' said Uncle Mick.

They sat drinking whisky, which Pascal did not yet like, and Mick outlined his attitude to England.

'It is a great mistake to hate the English.'

England was like a wealthy man who has endless treasure. It didn't realize how much it had, yet it would fight like the devil to keep everything in its grip.

The English language was a universal tongue. The world's greatest poems and dramas and novels were all in English. Her history was a pageant of great adventures. She had led the world in invention, scholarship and business.

'When the grip of England weakened,' argued Mick, 'she gave up continents. One evening while you were in nappies, she abandoned India.'

Pascal sipped his whisky and looked at his uncle's eyes.

'They can't understand a fella like me. They think that because I'm against them I don't admire them.' He shook his head like a baffled animal. 'If England got out of Ireland

29

tomorrow, they wouldn't miss it. They'd still be the people of Francis Drake and Walter Raleigh, Newtonian physics would still be English, they'd still be the people who discovered evolution.'

'You're a funny man,' said Pascal.

'What have we got to put against that?' asked Mick. 'Besides the frigging Yellow Book of Lecan?'

'We had a share in all of it,' said Pascal.

'It's not enough. We have to have something for ourselves.'

What Mick wanted was independence. He said Ireland had nothing else to give up.

'That crowd of bowsers in Leinster House have sold almost everything else.' Leinster House was the Parliament of Ireland.

A little nation, said Uncle Mick, had a little history. Irish history was simply an account of a single battle, which had to be won or else lose its meaning.

'When you fight for your life, you can have no pity.'

He died a few weeks later. Pascal inherited his books.

He was older now, and becoming steadily more unhappy. His mother's possessiveness was overwhelming. It caged him as securely as a prison. Necessity had made her miserly with money, but this trait quickly became a smothering obsession. From being narrow, she became fanatical. She ruled remorselessly, with neither comprehension nor compassion for anyone else.

Pascal attended a grammar school several miles away, on the other side of town. He had few close friends who lived within reasonable distance. Any attempt he made to foster wider acquaintance was ruthlessly resisted by his mother. It was immoral to talk to girls, and dangerous to play with Protestants. Anyone who lived in a smaller house was to be shunned as though carrying disease.

For Pascal, the house became a penitentiary. His mother no longer sang, as she used to do, while she fussed over endless domestic chores. Neither did Pascal offer to help her. He was soon as moody as she was, an introverted boy in deadly danger of becoming bitter.

The years of loneliness and struggle extracted a bitter

price. Mrs Canning was now quick to discover insults in the most innocent everyday incident. She seemed constantly to smart under some intangible humiliation. Her circle of friends had narrowed to a loyal core, yet she was capable of charming a new acquaintance if she chose to. Her character was fitfully lit by brilliant interludes which revealed her former nature. This curious phenomenon only confirmed her sense of power. She was able to use it, to turn it on and off at will. She remained at the centre of her private universe, and saw no good reason to admit the existence of different stars.

She had always been unselfconsciously Irish. She regarded the Irish Ballyvarren as home, and went back there to recuperate from the cares of her English exile. She was gay then, and took full advantage of the kindly myth that exiles who return to the country have invariably struck it rich. For perhaps three weeks in a single year, she could walk in the fields like a queen.

With her children around her, she could tramp the familiar pastures looking for mushrooms, and since she knew where to look it was easy to impress them. When the foraging was done she would imperiously order Pascal to go down the bog and shoot a rabbit, and when he had done so she would cook it with mushrooms for supper.

She was fastest friends with her nephews, fully grown men who lived in Dublin. As her husband had, she came from a double family. His mother and her father had both been married twice.

The nephews were the sons of a half-sister, and when Maureen Canning was a girl at Ballyvarren they were infants. They were sent to the farm, in batches, whenever a new arrival was expected. Her maternal instincts had first been exercised on them.

Now they were men she could twist them round her finger. She insisted one day that Pascal had to be taught how to catch a trout. It was a habit she had practised in adolescence, not a polite one, but a survival from the time when the Catholics in Ireland owned nothing, not even water in their rivers.

She borrowed a pair of her brother's boots and made clumsy

rendezvous beside the river. It was a small river, not much more than a stream, a mile or so away from the house. There she directed operations. It was midnight by the light of electric torches, and she led them away from the road through a cattle-muddy field.

The chosen spot was beneath a majestic stand of trees, a dark place where the current had undercut their roots.

'That place is full of trout,' she said. They lay there, studying the deep, still water where river trout rested before moving to feed in the stream.

The pool smelled strongly of moss and fish, and was encumbered with driftwood broken off in storms. A gravel bank had built up below it, and the water bubbled quietly over the stones towards the shadowed darkness that lay beyond.

'Dam it here,' she said.

'You get two years in jail if they catch you doing this,' Seamus said. Seamus was one of the nephews, Pascal's cousin.

The stream was shallow where it crossed the gravel, and consequently easy enough to dam. The three poachers paddled and splashed as they built up a weeping rampart of stones and sods which would slow the current and deny the fish escape. The whole enterprise was like something out of childhood, eerily lit by a brilliant moon.

'You know why we like this?' Pascal said. 'It combines conspiracy with getting wet.'

'Jesus,' Seamus said, 'I haven't done this for years.'

It was quickly done.

'Empty the sack,' ordered Pascal's mother.

The quicklime was milky even in the dark. The poison was held in by the rampart of the dam. The trout, drowning in their own element, churned up the water in a desperate search for oxygen. When the poachers saw them thrash and swirl they became exalted like actors in a rite.

'Pascal, there's a whopper!'

'Ah, the fecker!'

'He's gone! You have him! Hold that one, Seamus! Throw him out!'

The tormented fish leaped high in the air, flashing like

knives in the silver light, splashing back down in the deathly milk of the poisoned pool.

'We have twenty!'

'Thirty-seven!'

'Sixty!'

It was a Bacchanalia, a *tuerie,* a slaughter. There was something wild and uncalled-for in the way they enjoyed it, something primitive and wrong which welded them together. A spectator, had he seen it, would have felt disgusted. But this was Ireland, there were no spectators, and they were pagans again for the night. The torches counted the dead, and they were outlaws. They were breathless, full of satisfying guilt, and going home in the car they did not resist an invincible urge to sing.

In the kitchen at home they threw down a victim for each of the household cats. They ate five trout each, congratulating their suppers for having fought so well and being so nobly taken.

They were intoxicated, all of them, by things which had little existence. It was the night they talked nonsense in a farmhouse kitchen, in the company of cats.

'You see?' said his mother, triumphant. 'It wasn't you who invented the world.'

'Molly,' said Pascal's cousin, 'for the love of Jesus, will you leave the lad alone for a single evening?'

She turned on him, snarling. 'He thinks that he knows it all.'

But he didn't think that at all. He was completely baffled at the time. Various relations occasionally sidled up.

'She's a great one to have on the holidays, your mammy.'

Pascal nodded.

'But I wouldn't live with her,' the various relations said, 'if you gave me the Peacock Throne.'

IV

There were terrible wars in the English Ballyvarren. Pascal was almost a man. All his frustration boiled over, and he tested his strength with his mother. When he thrust her aside and declared his independence she mauled him and dragged him down. He was clever at school, but constantly in trouble, because it spoiled his mother's pleasure. On occasion he came home drunk. She would lock him out.

When he seethed with hatred she could answer him back with spite. She could keep him poor. She could turn away his friends and deride his dreaming.

As a mushroom dislodges a flagstone, he invincibly grew up. Nothing she could do could stop it, and so she saw herself grow old and become dispensable. There were savage fights and worse reprisals as the links were broken. It bewildered Pascal. Her ferocity bemused him.

In the end, only one thing held them together. This was the experience of Ireland. It was their single neutral issue, the one ground they could share because both of them had lost it. They were fellow-exiles from Tir na nOg, the Irish fairyland where things are forever different because they always remain the same; Pascal's mother was a monarch of the place, and Pascal a prince who had lost his birthright.

'Will you bury me in Ireland?' she begged him, in a fit of melancholy.

'I will,' he said mischievously. 'Provided you pay my expenses.'

Pascal never could decide why it was that he felt himself Irish rather than English. He could have slipped easily into the kindly English world around him. Yet he chose to remain outside. Perhaps it was pride. Perhaps, as he sometimes thought, he had allowed himself to be lost on a rudderless raft of words; poems and fatal histories, and stories told round the fire.

34

The questions he asked himself seemed not to have any answers; and yet posing the questions seemed more important than almost anything else.

It was a complicated way to grow up.

Part Two

I

The wind banged against the wall of corrugated iron. It blew out of the dark and whined in the four chain-link fences which guarded the perimeter. The floodlights, quivering on their gantries, threw wild shadows through the tangles of rusty wire. A flagpole creaked. The regimental flag snapped against its lanyard.

High above the sprawling camp, Private Nelson gazed with expressionless eyes at the life below him. The wind leapt like a dog round his watch-tower. The scaffolding groaned. The wind panted in the sentry's face, chilled him, and he flinched. Then it bowled away, skittishly, gusting towards the motorway, and an ominous calm descended. It was already dark, but a few prisoners were strolling in the cages, simply for the sake of staying out of the huts. The hut doors were open. Lock-up was not till ten.

The bright artificial light which flooded the place gave an unhealthy look to the shabby groups of men who paced the wire. Their long hours were filled with nothing better than conversation. This had long ago lost any hint of originality. Some of the men were farmers, and tended to suffer more than their comrades from the city. There was neither space nor beauty within the confines of the prison, only a numbing sameness which infected every day. The country-bred were particularly prone to claustrophobia.

The scourges of the camp were the papers, and the news bulletins on television or radio. People lived, died or were killed outside. Babies were born, houses were burned, wives wanted money for clothes. Nothing, not even the conversation, ever changed for the prisoners. Many had no idea why they had been held at all, nobody knew how long the imprisonment would last. Men were sometimes released on compassionate leave to attend a funeral. They appeared in the outside world like phantoms, provisionally free; perhaps got drunk, but always had to go back.

Private Nelson studied them. He watched the prisoners who paced alone, in a useless attempt to find a private moment. He could sometimes predict a nervous breakdown days before it happened. He was used to cages. He had guarded, or helped to fill them, on and off for more than thirty years. He was a weatherbeaten, seamed individual, something of a cynic.

Private Nelson felt his nose begin to water. He sniffed noisily, swallowing the sharp, thin liquid. He shrank deeper into his cape.

Private Nelson had soldiered all over the world. He had begun as a boy soldier, and seen action in Italy and France. There had followed a bitter cocktail of savage colonial wars, starting in Palestine, getting worse in Malaya, continuing in Kenya, Cyprus, Aden, and now in Ireland.

Ireland was the oldest colony on earth, the first and last of the major British possessions. Nelson didn't like soldiering here, but he didn't have much choice. He shrugged. You have to do your job.

The enemy here was white. He probably had cousins in the Regiment, more than thirty per cent of whose Other Ranks were Irish immigrants to Birmingham or Coventry. So it was hard to hate him. Didn't you sing his songs? Nelson had a long string of jokes about Paddies. It was the strangest battle he had ever been involved in. It was a British civil war.

But, God, he was bored with it! Tired, baffled. The dogs were howling in their kennels, as they always did before a storm. They could smell the thunderheads gathering in the hills. Private Nelson shivered. He'd once volunteered for a handlers' course, as a means, he thought, of avoiding something else.

'Nearly bit me bloody arm off,' he muttered resentfully, seeing again the Dobermann's yellow teeth.

He looked round, guiltily. First sign of madness, talking to yourself. Sod the Paddies, anyway. What did they think they were doing? A revolution? Making a revolution? Show me a revolution, Private Nelson thought, show me a single one that has ever succeeded. He was getting older, and his thoughts dwelled more and more on the futility of all he'd seen. His father, prating of Churchill and the General Strike. The union men who had fought in Spain. The black, brown and yellow faces peering from behind the wire, staring at inevitable power, inevitable defeat.

India partitioned. Cyprus. Africa in shards and broken pieces, all those lines on a Foreign Office map. Were they free? Was anyone any happier?

The camp was like an island in the night. Against the deep surrounding blackness, it was a smudge, a yellow smear. The nimbus round the floodlights was yellow and orange. In a few minutes the rain would start to fall, evaporating on the lamps, each drop a separate snake. Hiss!

Despite himself, the sentry coughed. He was getting a sore throat. On all his tours in Ireland he caught a cold. James Connolly's revenge. He had never wanted to come here. He understood completely why the Romans stopped at Bristol, retiring inland to take a bath. They were cheesed off with the weather, naturally enough. It was always raining. The drops were finer, there were more of them, they really made you wet. And there was nothing at all to do. Nothing here except bog and heather. He wished he was in Aldershot, blackguarding sergeants, drinking cup after cup of hot, sweet tea.

It was too windy for moths, but they came anyway. They blundered at the searchlights, and then were suddenly puffed away. The storm was rising. The moths fluttered helplessly into the dark. A few struck the roasting lenses of the lamps, and were shrivelled up. They couldn't help it. It was something in their eyes which drew them remorselessly towards flame.

Only the fittest, strongest moths could make it there tonight. Private Nelson smiled. The destruction of the fittest.

Private Nelson's feet ached. Part of him was looking forward to his pension. The rest was not. He was a single man, without a family. His mother and father had been killed in London, by a bomb explosion in the Blitz. There wasn't anybody else. When he came to retire he would join the British Legion. They would give him a fancy cap with a big gold cap-badge and send him to guard a car-park. It would be a change from guarding cages, but he'd miss the Army. The Army was his family. It was a kind of life.

Silently he surveyed the honeycomb of cages spread before him. The thickets of wire round the central avenue were like thorn hedges. Some kind of life! But the only one he knew. War after war after war. It became routine. Detention cages. Internment. Concentration camps. Hostile populations; factions; temporary friends, eternal enemies. All of them, murderers, traitors, a danger to the only life he knew. His country, his family, his Army. Yes, it was quite a life.

This was his third tour of duty in the North of Ireland. The Battalion had never guarded the camp before. They had been on the streets and among the little hills, getting their legs blown off or their heads bashed in with stones.

The men in the camp were all politicals. They had quit the polling booth and taken down the gun. Now, after three months staring down at them, Private Nelson could recite his section's geography in his sleep. He knew the fauna which inhabited every inch of it, and the faces of the men in the nearest compounds were as familiar as the faces of his friends.

To an extent the prisoners were allowed to live their own lives in the cages. They had starved for a while to get this privilege. They did no work, and would sooner go naked in the wet than wear prison clothing. They stank anyway. They stank of poverty, confinement and sweat. They were constantly bored, like him. The Protestants fought boredom with brutal discipline, parades and callisthenics. The Catholics were moodier. They broke out in periodic revolts.

When the soldiers went in, with batons swinging, the cages were swamped with gas. It was technically called a smoke, since gassing people was bad for public relations. These terrible brawls were the only punctuation in months of lassitude. Sometimes the prisoners burned down their huts; sometimes the soldiers wrecked them. Private Nelson had been down among the cages once. The older men looked at him quietly, without hostility. The punks giggled. He wasn't the man to worry about either category. He was frightened of the dark, unpredictable Irish who nursed their hatred as a mother will nurse a child. He thought the only cure for them was death.

A dark expectancy hung over the huddled camp as it knelt before the storm. A long line of poplars ran beside a near-by road, and suddenly they bent before a vicious gust of wind, as though a giant child had run his fingers through them while he was at play.

He squinted. He stared hard through the obscuring wire of two outlying cages. There was something going on. His eyes narrowed. He didn't yet know how or why, but he was aware that something was wrong.

He picked up the telephone beside his hand. There was a crackle on the line. The lance-corporal on duty muttered an obscenity when Nelson asked for the Officers' Mess.

'Gimme Captain Wilkins,' Private Nelson said, when the barman picked up the phone.

The open line picked up the clink of glasses. Private Nelson was still unused to the changes there had been in the Army. Wilkins, the Intelligence officer, was young and keen. He had left instructions; he was to hear what was going on immediately it happened, and in person. Wilkins was thought of as a bit eccentric. But he was good at his job. He was always on duty, even in the Mess.

Private Nelson licked his lips. 'Somethin' happenin' in Cage C for Charlie, Captain,' he said, when the officer came on. 'Some kind of meetin' in the dining hut. All the big lads have gone in there. They've put a bloke outside to guard the door.'

'Well, Nelson?' Wilkins said, a bit too sharply. 'So what? What's the matter with that?'

Private Nelson felt himself redden. Bugger the upper classes, never volunteer. 'It ain't their usual weekly confab, sir. That's not till Tuesday. It don't look right to me.'

'Maybe they're having a Gaelic lesson,' Wilkins said. 'Or a sing-song or something.'

'It ain't that neither, sir. There wouldn't be a guard on the door.'

Wilkins sighed. He paused, thinking for a moment. Then his voice came crisply down the line. 'Very good, Nelson. Watch them. If there's anything new, ring me back at once.'

'Sir.'

Private Nelson resumed his watch. Theories. They fed you theories, and then threw them back in your face. Total information. 'Every soldier,' the instructors said, 'must be the Army's eyes and ears. He must report anything, however small, at all unusual. It may not seem to mean much, but don't worry. Report to your officers at once.'

Wilkins was a stickler for reports. If he caught you out, jankers. And double quick as well. But maybe things get better.

The wind was rising still. The mournful notes of the war dogs were blown away. Suddenly the watch-tower swayed. For a moment it seemed to stagger. Private Nelson's stomach leaped with alarm. The bloody thing was falling! The corrugated-iron sheets of the outer perimeter fence rumbled like thunder. The lights flickered. And then the wind died down.

Something flashed, briefly, in the light between the cages. It caught Nelson's eye as it tumbled in the air. It was the prisoners' telephone, a hollow piece of wood with a note inside it which they threw between the compounds. The message quickly reached Cage C. It was taken to the dining hut and past the guard.

Private Nelson's throat was dry. It was sore and it tickled. He coughed. He bent as the coughing racked him. When the fit subsided his throat felt worse than ever.

He lifted the telephone again. He exchanged unpleasantries with Lance-Corporal Jameson, who was manning the switch. He spoke to Captain Wilkins. 'They've marched a man into the dining hut,' he said. 'I don't know, I think it's McSharry. Three of them hustled him in. I didn't get a look at his face. There was a message stick thrown over.'

'Message? Where did it come from?'

'The other side of the camp, sir,' Private Nelson said. 'I didn't see exactly where.'

'But the message and the other things are all connected?'

'They could be, sir. It looks like that to me.'

'If that man is brought out, tell me at once. Find out his identity for certain. Use your binoculars. Try to see his face. See who is with him. Watch that cage as carefully as you can. Never mind any of the others. I'll see that the rest of the towers are alerted, and I'll be at my office in ten minutes, Nelson. You can ring me there.'

Private Nelson looked at the tall dark shapes of the camp's remaining watch-towers. 'Right, sir!'

'Thank you, Nelson!'

'Sir!'

The rain fell diagonally, chopping at the camp like a flashing blade, then flapping like a furled curtain. The searchlights turned it to gold and silver ticker-tape. It fell relentlessly, silently, prettily, slopping down the gleaming skins of the Nissen huts and coagulating in brown pools in the depressions round the doors. There was a rush for shelter. The rain began to leak through the shrunken timbers of the huts. The prisoners cursed it as it ran in icy dribbles down the inside of the shells, soaking the stacked bunks, sizzling on inadequate heaters, filling the rooms with the smell of must.

Private Nelson's arm began to ache. The tendons which the Dobermann had bitten still suffered in the damp. Below him the handkerchiefs of space inside the cages became rain-tormented mud. The puddles closed their fists round the Nissen huts till each one was separated from its neighbour. The whole camp seemed battened down, silent, deserted.

Except cage C. In cage C, the bruiser stood by the door of the dining hut, a stolid monument, his face streaming. Private Nelson felt a twinge of satisfaction as unpleasant as a pain. He smiled grimly as he studied the man through powerful binoculars. The Provos were like that sometimes. They made no attempt to hide things. It seemed that they didn't care.

He was bored. Hour after hour spent waiting—for nothing

to happen. Nothing ever did. Nothing that made a difference. Private Nelson yawned.

Suddenly, for no particular reason, he began to think of a prostitute he'd bought, ten years ago, in a brothel in Hong Kong. She was not particularly beautiful, but she excited him. She was somehow very different from any other woman he had known.

He remembered her giggle as he advanced on her, following his enormous cock. But it didn't put him off. He thought it was funny as well. She'd cost a lot, though she was as flat in the chest as a boy. She mocked him in her incomprehensible language. She took him away, to some unguessed-at Chinese heaven. Worth every dollar she cost. He remembered her now, while he stood like a god looking down on the streaming camp. All those men, that complexity of motives. He had never known anyone so pretty. The thought of her laughter thrilled him. He suddenly had an erection.

Far away, over the distant hills, the lightning flashed. Thunder muttered after it. Nelson felt lonely. He sometimes wished he had married. The thought of the prostitute tormented him. He could see her now, as clearly as if she were beside him. Her pimp had told him why she was laughing. Her father and brother had succeeded in swimming across from China. They had promised to buy her freedom.

'You lucky,' said the slant-eyed man. 'She finish today. Four more hours, she finished with this work.'

Nelson had tried to buy them, but the girl was booked for the rest of the evening.

He rubbed his groin, which was swollen to bursting. The lightning danced on the distant hills, and the thunder was getting nearer.

The door of the dining hut flew open, throwing a chunk of light like a pale piece of cheese on the seething ground. The guard disappeared inside, and the light was gone. Private Nelson thought that he heard a scream.

He focused his glasses on the dining-hut door. When it reopened the Provisional guard was half carrying, half supporting the figure of a man. The man's jacket hung loose, and his face was a mask of blood.

The rain swept down, imperial, unforgiving. The crippled man was soaked, hung on his indifferent tormentor like dirty washing draped across a clothes prop by the wind. He was dragged to the door of the cage, which the warders would shortly enter when they called to lock up the huts.

Brutally the injured man was flung headlong into the mud. He fell with a splash into a sickly yellow pool. His head lolled, and then he lifted it. Private Nelson knew him. The face streamed with filth and rain, and Liam McSharry tried to crawl. But then he collapsed. The bruiser kicked him. Private Nelson's hand was already reaching for the phone.

II

Liam McSharry had been arrested six weeks earlier.

He was with two other men in a house in Belfast, waiting to meet his brother. But Moss, as usual, was late.

There were lookouts outside. They must have been taken first. It was clear that the Army knew exactly where to find them. When the door was kicked in McSharry ran out through the kitchen and fell straight into the arms of a waiting NCO. He was rushed, helter skelter, down an alley. When they got him to the Saracen they emptied his pockets and took a Polaroid picture.

'What happened to this man?' the officer demanded, shocked by McSharry's appearance.

'He got run over, sir. A motor-car hit him. He ran into the road.'

'Ah,' said the officer. He gave McSharry a pill. He said it would steady his nerves, and maybe stop the bleeding.

At the police station he was made to stand on his toes, with most of his weight on two fingers pressed against the wall. Sometimes a policeman came, sat on the radiator underneath him, and socked him in the belly. He refused to answer questions.

He was taken to Hollywood Barracks at ten o'clock that night. He was given a cup of tea and a small tumbler of white liquid, which they said would settle his stomach. Then he was taken to a hut which was lined with cubicles. They made him sit facing the wall in one of these small cubicles.

He was kept there for forty hours. Each time he moved, he was struck with batons. The cubicle was insulated with white acoustic tiles. There were 354 holes in each of these tiles, as McSharry knew because he was made to count them.

'You are a decent fellow,' they said. 'Why get mixed up in all this? Give us some information and we won't intern you.'

After a while McSharry began to see visions. Horses were running along the margin of the sea. A city street was littered with riddled bodies. There were soldiers, grinning, frothing at the mouth. When McSharry shut his eyes he was struck on the back of the head. He wondered how they knew he had shut his eyes.

He saw the mandibles of enormous insects, the suckers of snails, and strange protozoa which thrashed in water. All the while there was a babble of background noise—screams, grocery-shop gossip, shots and organ music. By the twentieth hour he thought he had gone insane. Wavering stroboscopic colours began flickering round the walls. He could feel his face turning purple and red and green. They gave him another cup of tea, and it tasted of cheese. Then an odourless grey smoke began seeping out of the walls. McSharry became hysterical. He fell off his chair while trying to grab a handful of this strange grey smoke.

He fell off the chair four times, whimpering. On the fifth occasion and at the fortieth hour, he was dragged to the centre of the room by masked figures. Their faces were crushed under nylon stockings. They abused him. One of them pointed a gun, made maniacal clickings, laughed. He was asked innumerable questions.

'Hey, Liam, tell us about Marx.'

When they had gone another man came who was kinder. He brought in another cup of tea, and apologized because it tasted funny. He said the cook must have cleaned the tea-urn.

'Maybe he left some soap in it, hey?'

When he had drunk the tea McSharry felt ten feet tall. He felt a protective love for this mild-mannered stranger. They discussed small intimate matters, for the policeman's wife was dying of cancer. It was a painful way to die. Then they talked about friends, and particularly Liam McSharry's brother. Moss McSharry, the policeman said, was quite a character. Liam McSharry said, yes.

'He'll soon be running the whole shebang?'

'I expect he will.'

Then the men wearing nylon stockings came back, and the nice one left him.

He could not remember everything he told them. They asked him a lot about money. Money was his job. He was the Finance Officer in a Provisional IRA company, a terrorist accountant. He knew lots of secrets, including the structure of several firms which the Provisionals controlled. One had contracts with the Government.

'If we thought you had killed a soldier, we would shoot you now.'

The Provisionals had decided to invest in commerce when funds from the USA looked shaky. All those exiles got worried about the bombings. The rebels had to have money from somewhere. Now, as McSharry knew, the terrorists owned retail outlets, bars and a stake in building.

'Lots of other things as well.'

He refused to sign, hours later, when they handed him a typed-up statement.

'Drugged,' he scrawled, on the piece of paper.

They made him cross that out, and then beat him up.

Later on, he made an appearance in court.

The courtroom was carpeted in scarlet. The walls were covered in scarlet drapes, and the witness stand was concealed by a crimson curtain.

Two policemen led in McSharry. One had a Sterling sub-machine gun, the other a pistol. The first thing he noticed was a brilliant splash of colour—the Royal Coat of Arms, which was fixed on the curtain above the head of the Commissioner.

The Commissioner smiled. He was a benign, balding, bespectacled man in a grey lounge suit. McSharry was placed on a chair in front of him.

'Will you be legally represented, Mr McSharry?' the Commissioner asked, leaning forward across a huge mahogany table, clasping his hands in front of him.

'I was tortured,' McSharry said.

'You must take that up elsewhere. I have no power to deal with it. Will you be represented?'

McSharry sighed. 'I don't recognize this court.' He looked around him. The Commissioner was flanked by a male stenographer at a separate table. On the left was a witness box, and one of the guards sat at a table beside the door. Behind McSharry, on his right, sat the Counsel for the Crown.

'You have a right to be represented,' the Commissioner said. 'You are in a very serious position, as I'm sure you've realized by now.'

'If I don't have a lawyer, is that a proof that I'm guilty?'

'Of course not,' said the man behind the table. 'It is IRA policy not to recognize the court, we all know that. But I'd need further evidence before I could sign an order.'

'Ah.' The lion and the unicorn seemed to be snarling at McSharry. 'It was just that I wondered.'

'We could adjourn,' said the Commissioner gently. 'We are anxious to treat you fairly. We could give you every opportunity to brief your counsel.'

'No.' He gazed at the Commissioner. 'Get stuffed,' he whispered.

The guard on the chair beside him started, and McSharry flinched; but the guard did not follow through. The Commissioner had shaken his head. In a strange sort of way, McSharry felt grateful.

'You have been given a copy of the charge,' the Commissioner said to McSharry.

'No,' said McSharry. 'No charge.'

'I know that you have been given a copy,' said the Commissioner. He squinted beneath his glasses at McSharry. 'I shall read it to you anyway.'

'That's crap,' said McSharry. 'No charge.'

The Commissioner ignored him. 'The charge reads: "That you are an officer in the Provisional Wing of the Irish Republican Army (IRA), which is a proscribed organization using violence for political ends, and therefore it is said that you are concerned in the direction, training and organization of persons for the purpose of terrorism".' He looked at the prisoner. 'Do you understand?'

'I was tortured,' McSharry said.

'I've already told you; I can't deal with that. You must complain elsewhere.'

'It's you who use violence,' McSharry said. 'You drug and torture and kill.'

Apart from the guard, he was completely isolated in a waste of scarlet carpet. His straight-backed chair left him utterly exposed. His brother Moss wasn't there to help him, either. There was nowhere at all to hide, to lie up and wait till the heat went off. Yet the Commissioner seemed kind.

'I can imagine how you must feel,' he said, in a cultured English accent, 'but swearing doesn't help. I'll call the first witness.'

The witness was identified as 'Officer A', a policeman with the Royal Ulster Constabulary. McSharry could see his shoes, which had been highly polished but bore traces of the yellow mud which was everywhere in Long Kesh Camp. He could see dark socks and trouser-bottoms too; but the witness's figure and face were hidden behind the curtain.

The Prosecutor stood up. He directed his questions to the hidden figure behind the curtain. 'Is what you have to say what you have been told as the result of information?'

'It is,' affirmed the voice.

'Can the source be disclosed—the final decision rests, of course, with the learned Commissioner—without prejudice to the safety of a person or persons?'

'There would be a considerable risk if I gave the evidence openly.'

The Commissioner smiled apologetically at McSharry. 'I'm afraid that means you will have to leave the room, Mr McSharry.'

McSharry looked at him bleakly. 'I can't hear the evidence against me?'

'Under paragraph 17 of the Act,' explained the Commissioner, 'I am entitled to exclude you or your representative from hearing any evidence, if I feel it might prejudice anybody's safety for either you or him to hear it, or if I feel that your hearing it might endanger public security. D'you see? That's the law. I'm afraid you'll have to accept it.'

McSharry nodded, not bothering to answer. He stood up, and was led outside. A guard ushered him into a small cubicle which served as a cell, then locked the door. McSharry waited. He was glad of the privacy. He knew that he was going to be interned, but he was worried about what might happen to him when he got inside the Republican cages.

The door opened. 'Here,' said the guard, offering a lighted cigarette.

McSharry took it. He was surprised and grateful. 'Thanks.'

The guard was an Englishman. He seemed to want to talk. 'Listen, mate. It's not so bad inside. You'll get used to it. You won't get shot at in here. You want ter look at it like this: once you're inside, you're safe.'

McSharry shrugged, but said nothing.

'Ah, well,' said the guard. He backed out and closed the door behind him. McSharry leaned in a corner and smoked. He had not had a cigarette since the evening of his arrest. He sucked the smoke deeply into his lungs, gagged, felt dizzy, and shook his head. Poison, he thought. Poison. He smoked more respectfully then, and enjoyed it.

He felt a little light-headed when they led him back in. The Commissioner leaned forward to address him.

'What I have just heard,' the Commissioner said, 'did not relate to any offence you are alleged to have committed. You understand that? It dealt with the source of the information against you, the informant—'

'A tout,' McSharry said. 'A lousy informer.'

'As you say.' The Commissioner nodded. He consulted his papers. 'I can tell you a certain amount. There was a single informer, and he was paid, and the officer has found him reliable before. I won't allow questions—'

'I'm not asking any.'

'Officer—' said Counsel for the Crown.

'I'm guilty already,' McSharry said.

'No,' said the Commissioner. 'I've been told about information which was laid against you. You're in the unfortunate position of not knowing what this information is, or who gave it, don't you see? You weren't here while the officer was giving evidence about the source of his information, therefore you can't know why I have to restrict this evidence about this source. Can you?'

McSharry couldn't.

'I know it's an impossible situation,' the Commissioner said.

The Crown Prosecutor asked, 'Officer, have you a document marked "Document A" before you. Was it compiled by you from information you were given by your informant?'

'Yes.'

'Did you get evidence from this informer about Liam Francis McSharry?'

'Yes.'

'What was the evidence?'

'That he was a senior officer in Pearse Company of the Belfast Brigade of the Provisional IRA.'

'Did he give any other details? Did he say what McSharry's rank was?'

'He said that he thought McSharry might have been Quartermaster of Pearse Company, or possibly something to do with finance.'

'He said that he thought he might have been,' the Commissioner said. 'That's not very definite.'

'But those positions,' said Counsel for the Crown quickly. 'They would be very much in the background, wouldn't they, officer?'

'Yes,' said the witness eagerly, 'the Quartermaster's job is to obtain and account for munitions, and the Finance Officer deals only with money. An ordinary volunteer wouldn't necessarily meet—'

'Quite.' Counsel for the Crown smiled uncomfortably. He looked nervously at McSharry, then back at the Commissioner. 'We are talking about shadowy figures here, men who stay in the background . . . the Press, I believe, have referred to them as Godfather figures . . .'

'Isn't Mr McSharry rather young for that kind of work?' asked the Commissioner.

'The average age of Provisional volunteers is twenty,' said Counsel for the Crown.

'I think you've explained the informer's ambiguity.'

'He was a volunteer, wasn't he?' McSharry shouted. 'Your lousy informer was a volunteer!'

They looked at him. McSharry had made a mistake, shouting that. The moment the words had left him, he knew he had made a mistake.

'I think we can dismiss the witness,' said Counsel for the Crown. 'The defendant refuses to cross-examine. Call the next witness, please.'

'Officer B' of the Royal Ulster Constabulary was the witness behind the curtain. The moment he spoke, McSharry recognized his voice.

'He was one of the torturers!' he shouted, lunging forward. The guard grabbed his jacket and manhandled him back into his seat.

'Sit down, Mr McSharry.' The Commissioner took off his glasses and began to polish them. He blinked at the prisoner. 'Any complaints you have should be made in writing to the appropriate authorities, the police. I will see that you get the opportunity. That is the proper way. I can't deal with these wild allegations of yours, I'm sure you know that.'

McSharry slumped back in his chair. He looked at the ceiling in a mime of dumb insolence. There was no point arguing.

'Officer B,' called the Counsel for the Crown, 'have you a copy of the document marked "Document B" before you?'

'Yes.'

'What does it contain?'

'It is a summary of the results of an interrogation I conducted on Liam Francis McSharry at Hollywood Barracks, Belfast. It has been signed by two other police officers, who assisted me with the interrogation, and by an Army observer.'

'They showed films,' said McSharry loudly. 'They used a back-projector. Monsters, dead children—and screams. There was so much screaming!'

The Commissioner wrote something down.

52

'Can you summarize for us the details of your report?'

'Yes, sir. We believe that Liam Francis McSharry is Finance Officer for Pearse Company of the Provisional IRA—'

'Did he say so?' the Commissioner asked.

'Not in so many words—'

'I didn't think he had,' the Commissioner said. 'It says nothing about that in Document B.'

'Nevertheless,' urged the Counsel for the Crown, 'McSharry displayed knowledge of the workings of his terrorist unit, didn't he, officer?'

'Yes, sir. His brother is the Commanding Officer, sir.'

'That would be Maurice McSharry, wouldn't it? He is a very important Provisional, isn't he, officer?'

McSharry stood up. The guard grabbed his arm, but the Commissioner waved his hand, a gesture that the guard might leave him. 'Mr McSharry?'

'My brother isn't on trial,' McSharry said. 'First I was tortured. Then you used hearsay evidence. Now the Prosecutor is leading the witness.'

'Well?' the Commissioner asked.

'I want the rules of evidence!' McSharry said. The Commissioner studied him.

'There are no rules of evidence here.'

McSharry straightened. 'What?' he asked, defensively.

'There are no rules of evidence here. Sit down.' The Commissioner turned to Crown Counsel. 'Continue.'

'Maurice McSharry,' the Prosecutor said. 'What do you know about him?'

'He is the present commander in the Pearse Company area,' the voice said, loudly. 'He is in the top five on the Army's wanted list.'

'He's never been convicted of a thing!' McSharry shouted.

'Please be silent.'

'And from what the defendant here told you, officer, you believe that Liam McSharry is his brother's lieutenant?'

'I am certain of it,' the witness stated.

'The brother is rather a remarkable man?'

'He is a Communist, sir. He is very dangerous.'

'When you say he is a Communist, isn't that rather an odd

thing to say?' the Prosecutor asked. 'The Provisionals are not a Communist organization, are they?'

'Some of the younger ones are, sir. The older crowd are regular republicans, but the young tigers—that's what I call them, sir—they're all red.'

'Is this really relevant?' asked the Commissioner.

'If you will allow me, sir, I think that I can show that it is.' Counsel for the Crown bowed slightly. 'When you say Communist, officer, you really just mean red—extreme left wing?'

'Don't tell him what he means,' said the Commissioner testily.

'They are Communist extremists, sir,' said the hidden witness. 'The traditional Republican crowd are—I don't know—they're decent people.'

'Really?' said the Commissioner.

'What I mean is,' said the witness hastily, 'you know where you are with them. They're moral people within certain limits. But these younger people will do anything. They want to put bombs in the London Underground, sir.'

'They put bombs into Coventry before the war,' said the Commissioner. 'There's nothing particularly new about that.'

'With your permission, Mr Commissioner,' said the Prosecuting Counsel, 'these people today are capable of much bigger things than they were in the 1930s.'

Continue,' said the Commissioner.

'Officer,' said Counsel for the Crown, 'is Liam McSharry, the defendant here, what you would call a revolutionary socialist?'

'He's an intellectual, sir. For example, he studies Irish history.'

'Has he got a degree?' asked the Commissioner.

'No, sir. But he does read books.'

'What's wrong with that? What kind of books?'

'History, sir. He has an obsessive interest in Irish history.'

'Well?'

'It's a subversive subject, sir.'

McSharry laughed.

'Silence!' the Commissioner rapped. He turned to Counsel. 'Look, I don't know what all this is about, but then you mustn't assume that I would. I don't necessarily know anything about what happens here outside of this camp. Possibly you could explain where your questions are leading?'

Counsel for the Crown bowed. 'Perhaps the officer could help us. It's true, isn't it, officer, that Irish history is not taught in State-controlled schools in this part of Ireland?'

'It is true, sir.'

'Do you know why?'

'It's a very emotive subject, sir.'

'The Republican terrorist organizations draw their pretended justification, in fact, from the unfortunate occurrences which happened here in Ireland in the past?'

'Yes, sir.'

'They deny, in fact, that the State of Northern Ireland has any right to existence?'

'They say it was imposed upon Ireland by the wrongful partition of the country, sir,' said Officer B.

'Quite. And this justifies them—they say it justifies them—in seeking to destroy this state?'

'Yes, sir. Definitely.'

Counsel for the Crown turned to the Commissioner. 'What I have been seeking to demonstrate here, sir, is a balance of probabilities. I would be the first to admit that there are objections to all the evidence you have heard. But if the information the informer laid was false, it was an extremely shrewd choice because there are so many chances of making a mistake about the kind of man who, from the shadows, can help to direct a terrorist campaign.' He paused, looking dramatically in McSharry's direction. 'If the information we have here were false—either deliberately or mistakenly false—the chances of it selecting a man like McSharry are really extremely slim. I would say they were astronomical.

'We have here the brother of one of Northern Ireland's most wanted criminals. He has been named by a reliable informer as an officer of the Irish Republican Army. Three police officers and an observer from the Army have deposed—in Document B, which you will have read in full—that he boasted to them that he planned to help his brother Moss—that's Maurice McSharry, sir—take over the supreme command of the Provisional IRA units in this city of Belfast. He boasted, mind you—'

'He contests the confession,' the Commissioner said.

'They all do, if I may say so with respect. It is a well-known tactic to blacken the police. But I refer you again to the probabilities. We do not claim that McSharry has planted bombs, or shot down British soldiers. Only that he has conspired to help others to do so. As the court can see for itself, he is an intelligent and fluent personality. He may, for all I know, be an idealist. But I say that his fanatical interest in Irish history has led his idealism astray, and that he is guilty as charged.'

The Commissioner agreed, without debating the matter too much. He signed an internment order against Liam Francis McSharry, untroubled by any of the qualms of conscience which sometimes nagged him. He was an intelligent man, and a compassionate one as well. He knew perfectly well that many of the cases brought before him had been trumped up on the flimsiest evidence, and he was growing increasingly disturbed by repeated stories that strange psycho-chemical methods had replaced the more usual strong-arm tactics as a means of extorting confessions. However, when he considered this case the fact of McSharry's guilt seemed patent. The Commissioner thought of himself the Queen's liege-man; while his lawyer's instincts detested the nasty charade of the Long Kesh hearings, his loyalty persuaded him that they were necessary. He therefore condemned McSharry to indefinite confinement without thinking about the matter twice.

A lot of thinking about the case had already been done elsewhere. What had begun as a simple, routine Intelligence operation had been bounced from Battalion level to Brigade, and from there to the highest Intelligence level at Northern Ireland Command.

McSharry had talked a lot under questioning. What he had to say was particularly interesting to Intelligence analysts, since it gave them an insight into the internal politics of the Provisionals' most important fighting unit, the Belfast Brigade.

There was some debate about whether he should be interned at all. If he were delivered into the hands of the 'Fourth

Battalion'—as the Republican prisoners in Long Kesh were called—what would happen? Nobody really knew, but the risks were great.

'It might have been better if he'd tried to escape when we went to arrest him,' said one Intelligence man.

'Why?' he was asked.

'We could have shot him.'

'The Provos will do it for us,' said somebody else. 'What we must do is wait.'

Part of the waiting ended when McSharry was pitched into the mud with a broken leg, his body a mass of bruises.

Part Three

I

Pascal Canning drove his second-hand Vauxhall car to the electronically controlled main gate at Army Headquarters (Northern Ireland), in Lisburn, Co. Antrim. He had an appointment.

He braked and waited patiently for the appearance of the chubby little civilian guard, with his sour face, his sub-machine-gun, and his blue Defence Ministry uniform.

'Pass?' the gateman demanded.

Pascal handed the rectangle of card marked PRESS through the window. 'I'm a reporter,' he said, 'I have an appointment to see Major McDowell.'

The gateman scowled at him as he studied the photograph on the card. He worriedly consulted a list. 'You're expected,' he said, grudgingly. 'I'll have to search the vehicle.' Searchers never called a car a car; it was always a vehicle to them.

Pascal got out and opened the boot and bonnet for the guard's inspection. The gateman glanced into the body of the saloon with a grimace of distaste. 'I see you've got a dog,' he said, pointing to the dried mud-prints of Kelly's paws.

'That's right.'

The gateman's nose turned up. 'I'm a cat man, myself.'

The gateman went back to his lodge and trundled out a mirror mounted on a low trolley. He swung it under the car and carefully examined the chassis.

'You're clean,' he said, again in a grudging voice.

'Thanks,' said Pascal. 'And I hope that your cat has kittens.'

'It's a tom,' said the gateman sourly. 'I already had him neutered.'

Pascal parked behind the main building. He was now in his mid-twenties, and had been reporting from Northern Ireland for the London *Standard Reporter* since shortly after the troubles began again in earnest, in August 1969. He had thought it a great stroke of good luck when the appointment was made permanent in 1970; now he was not so sure.

On this particular day he was in tolerably good humour. The sky was a rich blue, and the air was heavy with the smell of gardens. A few blown roses hung limply on their bushes. The lawns were wet, lime green; but the glory of the place was its conifers, now shadowy and dripping. The British Army's main headquarters in Ireland seemed a long way removed from the miseries of life outside. He gave his name to the armed man in the booth inside the lobby of the principal building. The man asked him to fill in a form.

'If you wait here, sir, Major McDowell will come down to collect you.'

The minutes passed without any sign of McDowell. Pascal tapped his foot impatiently. He looked at the great brown board beside the wicket-gate, with its long list of initials and floors, a military Sanskrit which was gibberish to outsiders.

There was a poster on the wall beside the lift. IS YOUR LINE SECURE? and a picture of a telephone handset, against a background of telegraph poles and question marks. The 'N' had been crossed out and written over, so that the message also had a second reading: IS YOUR LIFE SECURE? Pascal smiled, wryly. He supposed that it was, in here. Time dragged. He hated waiting. There was a display of photographs, stuck on pink card, attached to the lobby wall.

THE PEN IS MIGHTIER THAN THE SWORD (BUT A PICTURE IN THE PAPER IS BETTER THAN EITHER)

Pascal looked at the display. Army Public Relations was now a glamorous speciality. Even the corporals were mad to get in on it. They wanted to learn photography, become cameramen themselves.

Major Bill McDowell was a specialist among specialists. He filled an important niche. He enjoyed the work.

Pascal recognized the Major in several of the photos on display. They were quite old, dating back to the previous Christmas, probably on show to anticipate the next. There was a smiling Santa McDowell, about to climb into a helicopter with a sack of toys in his hand. Here he was again, parachuting down to an orphanage garden, his scarlet robes tucked safely in his belt. And there was his sleigh—a ten-ton armoured personnel carrier, painted white, with sprigs of holly stuck around the gunports. McDowell was grinning beefily and handing out sweets and gifts to some surly urchins, while his jolly attendants stood by with loaded sub-machine-guns to protect him from the urchins' fathers.

There was a tap on Pascal's shoulder.

'Pascal!'

'Major!'

'Do you like our souvenirs?'

Pascal grinned. 'It's early for the season of goodwill.'

'Never too early for goodwill,' McDowell answered heartily. 'We had a jolly good Press out of Christmas last year.' He studied the photos more closely. 'I think the headline I liked best was "Dove among the Ruins".'

'Where was that?' asked Pascal. *'The Guardian?'*

'One of the qualities,' said the Major, with a deprecating smile. 'Makes a change for us, you know, being doves instead of hawks.'

'Different diet,' Pascal said. 'Better image. How are you, anyway?'

'Fine, fine.'

Major McDowell was a short, avuncular man in his middle forties. He was a Scot, but had close family connections in Northern Ireland. His hair was a mass of frizzy black curls, and he affected a pair of heavy horn-rimmed glasses and an air of constant, owlish amazement. McDowell, somebody said, always looked as if he'd just been told a joke and was expecting to hear another at any minute. But it was dangerous to

61

allow appearances to deceive you. McDowell was not to be trifled with.

'I'm glad you were able to come,' said Major McDowell. 'I've been wanting a little chat.'

'No trouble at all. I have a lunch appointment with Colonel Adam.'

'Good. You should come more often.'

'So much work,' said Pascal.

'Yes.'

Major McDowell's colonel, a fleshy-lipped paratrooper called Antony Barnet, held the hieroglyphic title CIPA/GS on the big brown board in the lobby. This made him Chief Information Policy Adviser to the General Staff. He was tipped to get a Brigade. By contrast, Adam Fergusson, the ostensible head of Public Relations, signed all his letters 'Lt-Col.' and was thinking of retiring from the Army. He would never get any further.

This difference in status was readily detectable to anyone who had spent any time at Army Headquarters. It could be explained by military analogy. The Information Policy department was the cannon; Public Relations was merely the shell. Pascal liked Fergusson, and he admired McDowell: but McDowell frightened him a little.

The Major was proud of his physical fitness. Pascal had to hurry to keep up with him. They scorned the elevator and loped easily upstairs. They passed the 'hot' part of the building, the heavily barred gate where an armed soldier stood guarding access to the General and the Operations Room. Soon they were threading through a corridor. The passage led past the main Press Office and was lined with pictures of brawny, photogenic soldiers in a variety of heroic poses. Santa McDowell was among them, in his various incarnations.

'Wait a moment,' said Major McDowell crisply. He stuck his head round the door and then withdrew. 'Looking for Colonel Adam,' he explained, and added needlessly: 'He isn't there.'

Major McDowell was Colonel Barnet's man. The Colonel had a stable of specialist advisers, including an Anglo-Irishman who liaised with the Foreign Office and the British Information Service outlets in foreign embassies.

Army PR was subordinate to Barnet. The newsmen went there for their daily diet of bread-and-butter 'facts'. This was material from the incident logs which described the daily banalities of war. Assassinations, bombings, ambushes, searches, seizures and arrests were chronicled in the logs. So were the itineraries of visiting beauty queens and bigwigs. It was a useful service within certain limits.

However, whenever anything controversial happened, the 'facts' could vary from minute to minute. Five, six or even a dozen versions of a major incident were commonly relayed to newsmen in the form of up-daters and corrections. An important by-product of this was the virtual internment of the city's newsmen in their offices. If they went out to see what had happened they risked missing the single constant of all objective reporting; which was the Army's perception of truth.

When the reporters complained, as they sometimes did, of the contradictions and ambiguities contained in official summaries there was a standard way to placate them. You cited 'difficult communications'. You said you'd had 'fresh reports from the ground'. When some scandalous lie had been planted in millions of minds and was finally uncovered, you blamed the chap who'd gone off duty. You tutted. Perhaps he was only joking. Colonel Barnet's men gave Colonel Fergusson's men the news. They processed it. That was what Information Policy meant. It was an extremely important function.

'I'll have to hunt for an empty office,' Major McDowell said. 'Somebody else is using mine.' They walked down the latest set of corridors, opening doors, peering in, rapidly retreating.

'Ha!' exclaimed McDowell. 'A haven!' He led the way into a tiny office whose only furniture was a desk and telephone, a closed cupboard, two chairs, and an empty noticeboard. 'I'm a displaced person,' Major McDowell grinned.

Pascal grinned back. 'I know the feeling.'

Major McDowell looked at the reporter sharply. 'Sit down,' he said, sitting down himself. Pascal manhandled a straight-backed chair to the front of the desk.

'Well, well, well!' exclaimed a smiling major. 'First things first, eh, Pascal? I'll just phone down and see if the Colonel's back. I won't be a minute.'

'I don't mind waiting at all.'

'Hello,' said Major McDowell. 'Colonel Fergusson in?'

Pascal watched him.

'Yes. McDowell speaking.'

Outside, clutched in the withering branches, a tremendous sky unfolded its glories. Great multi-coloured clouds were drifting over Antrim.

Colonel Fergusson was not back in his office. McDowell chatted to one of the duty officers who manned the Press Room switchboard, did the donkey work with reporters.

Did what?

Made asses of them, of course. Pascal smiled, and was startled by McDowell's grin, which came right on cue, as if to answer him . . . The soldier muttered his farewells, watching Pascal closely. He banged down the handset.

'Well, Pascal?' he said, his eyes twinkling. 'Sorry about that. I've asked them to ring me the moment he gets in.'

'He said he was going to be busy this morning.'

'I wonder why? It's reasonably quiet.'

'Don't know,' said Pascal.

McDowell looked at him closely. 'I've got a good story for you, Pascal.'

Pascal raised his eyebrows. 'They're always welcome.'

'It's unattributable, of course.' McDowell leaned back, making a tent of his fingers and pouting judiciously. 'Hell of a good story, very interesting, not the slightest doubt about that.'

'I'm glad,' said Pascal.

'I've got a letter here.' The Major reached into an inside pocket. 'It should cause a certain mild sensation.' He smiled ironically.

'Yes?' Pascal was interested.

'We've positive proof—I think it's the real positive proof —that the Provo leadership are using this war as an excuse to line their own pockets. You know they do, and I know they do, but it's been a question of proving it.' He waved the letter. 'This is the proof.'

'What is it?' asked Pascal.

'It's a summary of an IRA court martial. Provisionals. Their Camp Commandant tried to get it out of the Maze.' McDowell sniggered. 'His girl friend had it, but I won't say where.'

Pascal watched him finger the flimsy sheets of paper.

'More clap than a round of applause,' said Major McDowell, and glanced expectantly at Pascal.

Pascal smiled.

'We'll call the accused man Billy,' said Major McDowell. He began to read from the letter.

What emerged was extremely confused. At one stage Pascal thought that the charge was the biggest one, of treason. It was never clearly stated, and indeed the whole hearing seemed to have been arranged on orders from outside. It slowly became clear that Billy—whoever he was—was not on trial for his life, but was faced with expulsion from the Provisional movement. He was some kind of dissident. He admitted to spreading rumours.

' "Trying to wreck the Organization," ' McDowell quoted. He looked up at Pascal. 'Listen to this. This bit's important.' He was clearly skipping as he read the letter.

Billy was also an accessary. Another man—

'We'll call him "Mac",' McDowell said. 'That's simplest.'

'Can't you give me their names?'

McDowell laughed. 'You can say we're protecting the guilty.'

Mac, whoever he was, was some kind of *agent provocateur*. He was not on trial at this kangaroo court, but it was clear that the writer only wished that he was.

'What do you think of it?' asked Major McDowell. He had skipped great chunks of the narrative, ending with the verdict on Billy: expulsion.

'It's all a bit vague,' said Pascal. 'I didn't really understand it.'

The Major's face lit up. 'That's 'cos I haven't read the post-script. It's a private message that was with the document.'

'Listen.' McDowell started quoting. ' "Morale here was low already. Since Billy arrived it has hit rock-bottom. We don't know what we're going to do. Expelling him means nothing. The men take his story seriously—" ' McDowell broke off. 'Getting better?'

'Yes,' said Pascal. 'Do go on.'

' "Cash from raids being siphoned off, and private protection given. Officers bought houses, cars, tellys for cash. How can we keep a lid on this one? He spread it around. Men restless. Years in prison for the profit of a few—" '

McDowell grinned at Pascal.

'Strong stuff,' the reporter said.

The soldier continued: ' "We are denying, of course, and have disciplined Billy. We daren't do any more than that, the men won't stand it. Embezzlement stinks. What about Mac? We need answers from Brigade. Pressure to refer the lot to Dublin. Please . . ." ' McDowell paused, sniffing. He looked up. 'That's about it.'

'It's a hell of a story.'

'It's a very big story indeed.'

'This Mac sounds interesting.'

McDowell blinked. 'He is. Oh, he certainly is.' He folded up his papers. 'He's a hothead. A real fanatic. He discovered the jiggery-pokery and he blew his top.' He laughed. 'Someone'll blow the rest off, shortly."

Pascal shifted. 'Dear me.'

'What I thought you could do,' said McDowell, 'is a piece on the graft and corruption angle.' He blinked. 'Should be right up your street. You're very strong on these investigative pieces.'

'I like doing them,' said Pascal.

'That last stuff you brought me was brilliant.'

Pascal smiled. 'They wouldn't use it.'

'All the same,' said McDowell. He chuckled. 'It appeared, though, didn't it?'

'Somewhere else,' said Pascal. 'Coincidence.' It was, like hell, he thought. He felt a stab of alarm that McDowell should know so much.

McDowell beamed. 'You were just unlucky. The *Standard Reporter* will go for this one.'

'Can I see the letter?'

McDowell hesitated. 'I'm not supposed to show anyone this.' He handed it over. Pascal glanced at it. 'It's genuine,' said Major McDowell. 'One hundred per cent.'

'Are you giving it all round?' asked Pascal idly.

The Major smiled. 'It's your exclusive.'

'Ah.' Pascal closed his eyes. Opened them. 'Leaves me a bit exposed.'

'I don't think so. They know we have it. You just bring it out in the open.'

Silence.

'You mustn't read it.'

Pascal looked up. 'I need a couple of names.'

'Check it out,' said McDowell. 'You have your contacts.'

'This Mac fellow, though . . .'

'Give me the letter.' McDowell took it. 'Can't help. I'd like to, but I can't. You can see the reason. If you name the man, he's dead. D'you see?'

'The Provos won't help me on this,' said Pascal. 'They'd be mad to help me.'

McDowell shrugged. 'That's up to them.' There was another silence.

'I'll pass it to the news-desk in London, Bill. They can send across a team.'

McDowell looked disappointed. 'I'd rather you didn't, Pascal.' He smiled. 'Let's keep it in the family, eh? We don't want London grabbing all the glory. Give the local man some kudos for a change.'

'I couldn't do it,' said Pascal.

The major blinked. 'Why not?'

'I have to live here, don't I?'

'They wouldn't dare attack you. They've never harmed a reporter.'

'I'd be frozen out. I'd lose all my contacts. Unless I could talk to Mac.'

Major McDowell sighed.

'This Billy character,' said Pascal. 'They said he'd been disciplined. What happened?'

'He was beaten.'

'Badly?'

'Concussion. Three cracked ribs. One of his knees is up like a football and the other leg is broken.'

'Well, then,' said Pascal.

'It's serious,' McDowell said.

'Certainly seems to be.'

McDowell looked at him. 'You know what they are?' he said. 'Animals. They're thieves and gangsters. That's why you must do the story.'

Pascal frowned. 'How can I?'

'Just write it down and put it in the paper.'

'It's a very good story—'

'Of course it is!'

'Too big for me!' said Pascal. 'You should pass it on to London.'

McDowell folded the letter again and put it in his pocket. 'I can't see your problem.' He paused. 'I suppose I can.'

'There is a problem, Major.'

'I'd still like you to do it for the *Standard Reporter*,' the Major went on. 'There's no immediate hurry. Go away and think about it, Pascal. Come back and see me in another few days. I'm sure that in the end, you'll do it.'

II

McDowell was in a hurry to get away, so he left Pascal in the charge of a corporal whose job was to escort the reporter down to the main Press Office. As they walked through the sterile, institutional corridors, Pascal felt vaguely uneasy. He wondered exactly what McDowell was up to. He didn't trust him.

Like many of the better-connected reporters covering Belfast, Pascal had had regular contact with the Information Policy section. He was well aware that military operations by both the Republican and the Government forces in Northern Ireland were often merely supplementary to their efforts in the fields of political propaganda. The British Army was leading the world in the development of 'psychops', a new branch of military science which relied less on muscle than on political persuasion by the manipulation of the media. It was an imprecise science, however; the political consequences of a particular publicity initiative could not always be predicted exactly. Pascal, and reporters like him, were prepared to take material from dubious sources on both sides without necessarily sub-

68

scribing to either. They often got valuable leads that way.

What worried Pascal in this case was the Major's insistence on exclusivity. It did not fit in with the way he'd expected to be treated. The Army employed extremely skilled political analysts to advise on operations, and they could be very sensitive when a story broke which suggested, however obliquely, that everything was not altogether as it seemed in Northern Ireland. Pascal had had such a story published only recently; so he was surprised at McDowell's apparent generosity.

Lieutenant-Colonel Fergusson drove these lingering anxieties from his mind, for the moment at least. The Press Office was quiet, and Fergusson was relaxed and open.

'Pascal,' he said, holding out his hand. 'I'm delighted to see you.'

'I think I'm late,' said Pascal. 'I was having a chat with Bill McDowell.'

'Doesn't matter,' said the Colonel. 'Listen, I told old Loftus that you were coming, and he suggested that we might all eat together.'

'Fine,' said Pascal. 'I'd love to.'

They left Headquarters to make the short walk to the Officers' Mess, a redbrick Victorian building which reminded Pascal of a vicarage. Major Jack Loftus, who was head of public relations for 39 Brigade—the garrison troops based on Belfast—was already there, and came over to greet them.

'What will you have?' he asked. 'I'm on gin myself.'

'All right,' said Pascal.

'Two gins,' said Colonel Fergusson.

'Doubles, of course,' said Loftus, and went to get them.

'Listen, Pascal, I'm glad you came,' said Colonel Fergusson. 'You're not here often enough, you know.'

'Work . . .' said Pascal.

'I know, but I'm going to insist. I want you to do me a favour. We're having a dance next week—it's 39 Brigade, actually—and I want you to bring your wife.'

'Well,' said Pascal, 'I—'

'You can't keep her locked up all the time, you know. She's a charming lady. I want you both to come as my personal guests.'

69

Embarrassed, Pascal glanced at the garden outside the windows. A low, autumnal sun slanted dispassionately down, dazzling, gilding the sycamores' dead leaves, flaring in the windows' stained-glass borders.

'We'd be glad to come,' he said.

'Splendid,' Colonel Fergusson said. He smiled warmly at Pascal. 'You're honoured, you know. You're the only reporter invited.'

Pascal was startled. 'Oh! Why's that?'

'Private affair,' said the Colonel. 'It's really for the officers' wives. Small sort of thing. But we do admire your work here. You've had some very good stories lately.'

Pascal smiled. 'Thank you.'

'And your wife, of course. She's a smasher.' The Colonel laughed. 'God knows how you got a girl like that.'

Lieutenant-Colonel Fergusson looked the image of a country gentleman. He was a tall, good-looking man with blue eyes and fair hair. He wore a Donegal tweed suit, not new, but not old either. His shoes were hand-made, a homespun tie was knotted discreetly at the faintly checked shirt collar. Pascal envied his style.

Loftus came back, bearing drinks.

'Chin,' he said.

'Cheers.'

'Pascal is coming to the dance,' said Colonel Fergusson triumphantly.

'Oh, jolly good,' said Major Loftus. 'Jolly good.'

'You can solve the baby-sitter problem, Pascal?' the Colonel demanded. His eyes were piercing, and Pascal looked instinctively away.

'I think so,' Pascal said.

'Good show,' said Major Loftus. 'Get that thing out of the way.'

'You have to be careful these days,' Colonel Fergusson said.

The Major signalled emphatic approval by vigorously nodding his head. It was a trait of his. He was universally nicknamed Noddy.

'That's right, too right,' said Noddy.

He was a bachelor, yet he seemed to know all about babysitters. He was a fund of recondite information. He could talk about Communists, infiltrators and conspiracies for hours. His father was something in steel. Pascal smiled politely.

'You have to know who you're inviting into your house these days,' said Major Loftus darkly. He took a generous gulp of gin. 'They get in everywhere if you aren't very careful.'

'You never know who's who,' said Pascal.

Major Loftus looked briefly worried. 'Well, you can't trust anyone, these days, can you, Colonel?'

The Colonel shook his head.

The Mess was crowded. Headquarters looked after its officers well. Both in and out of uniform, they stood chatting casually in groups around the room. There was constant coming and going. The room was high and airy, filled to the ceiling with the hum of conversation.

The predominant colour was red. Portraits of the Queen and her Consort presided calmly over a rosy room. The walls were red plush. The chandeliers which hung from the stuccoed ceiling reflected the colour from a thousand facets; it was repeated in the carpet.

Even the General's face seemed redder than it appeared on television. He roared in his corner of the bar, slapping his knee with exuberant mirth. Heads swivelled to examine the merriment which had suddenly convulsed him. An intensely barbered Brigadier glared at him and frowned.

The Brigadier's tabs lay scarlet on his collar. Pascal watched them as their owner whispered to the Colonel. The Colonel's eyebrows twitched. He seemed very serious. Their indignant gaze seemed to catch the General's eye, for he lifted his glass and presented a mocking toast, at once a boast and a deprecation.

Immediately both the officers looked away. The General's eyes were wet with laughter. His florid face was roasted with a slowly fading smile. His adjutants, who were helplessly laughing too, gazed at his countenance with open admiration.

For no apparent reason the room went suddenly quiet.

The General stared at the Brigadier, who pretended not to notice and went on talking. Pascal's neck felt cold. The General cocked his head like a corner-boy making a quip to his chums, and an aide-de-camp gave a belly-laugh which echoed round the room. Then the General repeated himself, and the rest of his flunkies spluttered in their drinks and hooted. They clustered around the General like worshipping bees who will cluster round a queen. The hum of conversation gradually came back.

Colonel Fergusson coughed politely. 'Jack? Have you met Pascal's wife?'

'I don't believe I have,' Major Loftus said.

'She's his better half, I assure you of that.'

'She has to be prettier,' said Major Loftus. He beamed at Pascal. 'I look forward to it, Pascal, what?'

Pascal nodded. He took another slug of gin. His shoes needed polishing. He felt shabby.

Colonel Fergusson chatted pleasantly, but Pascal's attention wandered. He responded with a certain desperation. He kept looking at the barbered Brigadier, a small, deadly, bullet-headed man.

The crackle of small-arms fire leached into the room like a milky poison leaking from a dam.

'Target practice,' said Colonel Fergusson. Pascal started, ashamed of his lack of manners. Major Loftus stepped into the breach with a declaration.

'Background intelligence,' he said, nodding towards the Brigadier. 'That's the way to win.' He nodded again, beaming. His face was a florid sculpture. 'We must try to know every-thing. Use a computer to remember it. The Intelligence census, and the good old computer, what? We'll beat the bombers. Soon restore peace.'

Pascal returned his smile.

'You newspaper johnnies,' Major Loftus said, 'too pessi-mistic by half. We keep saying we're winning, but you won't believe us.'

'The bombing does go on.'

'Last gasp, old boy. We're making it hot for them now, eh, Colonel?'

'Certainly are,' said Colonel Fergusson.

'More than a third of the population literally taped!' exclaimed Major Loftus. 'Even know the colour of their wallpaper, Pascal. When they redecorate—tap on the walls.' He frowned. 'Secret caches of guns, what?'

'Yes,' said Pascal.

'How many pints of milk do they order? Need extra supplies when you shelter a terrorist gunman . . .'

'It's remarkably ingenious,' said Colonel Fergusson.

'This computer we have in London,' said Major Loftus eagerly, 'any soldier can talk to it now. Fearfully expensive installation. But your squaddie's in touch, by radio. Relay his questions from base.'

'Ministry of Defence,' said Colonel Fergusson.

'And damn useful if we get any trouble at home,' said Major Loftus. 'All these Trotskyists and Commies—'

'I don't expect there will be any,' said Colonel Fergusson. 'Not real trouble.'

Major Loftus frowned. 'Let's just wait and see. You know my opinion.'

Pascal couldn't resist it. 'They get in everywhere,' he said.

Major Loftus nodded. 'Quite.'

Colonel Fergusson, who was lifting his glass, grinned wickedly at Pascal.

'Statistics,' said Major Loftus. 'Traffic flow—' He waved his hand vaguely. 'That sort of thing. Nearly all the Catholics here give passive support. They have to. You can write them off.'

'I wouldn't say that,' Colonel Fergusson protested.

'No. I didn't mean quite that.' Major Loftus became confused. 'Some of them are really quite decent . . . but, you see, it's a question of alertness. Ready for anything, what? We've got forty thousand eyes in Ulster, twenty thousand pairs of feet . . . if you can link them to one big brain . . .'

Pascal nodded. 'Of course.'

Colonel Fergusson laughed. 'You'll find that half your men are peeling spuds, I think, Major. Or pushing pens, or something. We're drowning in bureaucracy.'

'That's true,' said Major Loftus, sadly. He dosed himself with gin.

'Technology *is* important,' said Colonel Fergusson easily. 'You could write a book on the changes that have come since

73

the twenties campaign in Ireland. Think of helicopters, for one thing.'

'Radio,' Pascal suggested.

'Yes. The telephone. In the last Irish war, the population couldn't lay information even if it wanted to. Now all that has to be done is to ring the confidential number.'

'That's very important,' said Major Loftus, sagely. 'That's why the Provisionals have vandalized all the public kiosks, Pascal. You should write about that.' He looked anxiously over his glass. 'They're beginning to crack. We have them on the run.'

'Don't speak too soon,' said Colonel Fergusson. 'The job's not finished.' He smiled at Pascal. 'They're bound to see reason eventually. There's no way they can win.'

Pascal shrugged. 'It's not a question of reason, not entirely. There's a lot of emotion, too—'

'Exactly!' Major Loftus' voice was thick with enthusiasm. 'They're too emotional.' He tapped his head. 'They haven't got enough up here.'

Pascal laughed pleasantly and tried to steer the conversation somewhere else. 'How's old Woodie, Colonel? Is he settling down on the Rhine?'

'Missing us badly,' said Colonel Fergusson laconically. He turned towards Major Loftus. 'You mustn't say these things to Pascal, Jack.' He clapped Pascal on the shoulder. 'We've got him down as a bit of a Bolshie.'

Pascal looked at him quizzically. 'On your fancy computer?'

The Colonel grinned. 'Top of the programme.'

'I'd fuse it.'

'But you have seen how they live?' Major Loftus demanded. He was clearly oblivious of anything the other two might say. 'Thought the bloody wops were dirty till I looked at the Falls Road. Worse than the bloody Casbah.'

'It's the dole, you know,' said Pascal. 'They spend it on horses.'

'What did I tell you, Jack?' laughed Colonel Fergusson. 'He *is* a bolshie.' He flourished his glass delightedly, smiling at the reporter. 'Major Loftus dislikes Belfast.'

'Hate it,' said the Major, nodding. 'Rather be on the Rhine.

It's very good training, of course. Have to say that. But after a while it palls.'

'How long have you been here?' Pascal asked.

'Six months, two weeks, let me see . . . three days.'

'Counting the hours, eh, Pascal?'

Pascal grinned at the Colonel.

'Like the bloody Arabs, they are,' said Major Loftus. 'Stab-you-in-the-back merchants. Hit and run. Natural cowards.'

'Ah, well. It'll end some time.'

'I've heard that one before,' said Pascal.

'You make a joke?' asked Major Loftus, seeing both men smiling.

'No.'

There was silence. 'Do you want another drink?' the Colonel asked, abruptly.

'No, thanks,' said Pascal. He drained his glass.

'If I drink any more gin today, I shall have an abortion,' Major Loftus said.

'Then we'll eat,' said Colonel Fergusson. 'I wonder what they've got for lunch?'

A steaming cartwheel of paella lay on hot-plates in the dining-room. It looked delicious. There was a queue for service. A long, highly polished mahogany table ran the length of the room. It was ranged with flowers along the middle. Scattered at points along it were feeding men. There was some conversation, but not very much. The atmosphere was entirely different from the one inside the bar. Everyone seemed to be hurried.

Pascal and his hosts selected their silver from the sideboard. There was a cut-glass vase there, full of chrysanthemums.

'After you,' said Colonel Fergusson.

'Thanks.'

Dark oil-paintings of long-dead warriors stared down. Pascal fiddled with his cutlery. They waited in line.

'You mustn't mind Loftus,' the Colonel said softly.

Loftus was in front of them, chatting amiably with a brother officer.

'He gets these bees in his bonnet.'

'That's why he nods all the time.'

Colonel Fergusson grinned. 'Everyone's under a strain.' The

queue was a long one and he wanted to talk. 'I even brood occasionally myself.'

'About what?'

The Colonel chuckled. 'The general paralysis of things. Life's complicated, isn't it?'

'Yes.'

'But then,' said the Colonel, 'I suppose it always was.'

Pascal liked him. He wished they could be friends. When Fergusson appeared on television he denounced his enemies with such ringing conviction that Pascal envied him.

'You surprise me.'

'Why?'

Pascal looked at him. 'I didn't think you had doubts.'

They shuffled nearer the hot-plates. The Colonel straightened. He began talking of inconsequential affairs.

The stewards were stolid men in linen jackets. They served liberal helpings. Major Loftus took his and waited cheerfully for Pascal and the Colonel.

'Looks jolly good,' he remarked. Later, when they were eating, he looked up. 'Wonder where they got the mussels?'

'The local market?'

'Probably flew them in from Scotland,' Major Loftus said. 'They're ab-solutely delicious.' He savoured one of his mussels, looking raptly at the ceiling. 'They ran out of kidneys, you know, this morning.'

'Did they?' asked Colonel Fergusson politely.

The Major nodded. 'They did as well! Isn't that scandalous?'

'Terrible,' said Colonel Fergusson. He leaned back, sucking his teeth. 'You should put that in the book. That's a legitimate complaint.'

'No bloody good,' said Major Loftus. He dug into his meal, and came up chewing. 'Never take any notice anyway.'

'Interesting to read it, though.' The Colonel finished his meal. 'Complete social history of the modern army.' He laughed reflectively. 'The Scots on porridge. Fascinating stuff.'

'Yes,' said Pascal.

'Document of the times we live in.' He glanced at Pascal. 'We have a complaints book here in the Mess. You should look at it some time. Make an interesting story.'

76

'Like your tank, eh, Colonel?' Major Loftus glanced slyly down the table. 'Sort of time capsule, what?'

Colonel Fergusson groaned. 'Can't we forget that tank?'

He had once commanded a group of Chieftain tanks during a NATO exercise on Lüneberg Heath. The generals of several countries were in attendance. One of his men, anxious to show initiative, had made an unauthorized detour across a deep peat bog. They had never extracted the tank. It had sunk without trace to join the prehistoric elks, the bronze cauldrons and the strangled men of the Teuton dawn.

'What happened to the driver?' Pascal asked. 'I take it, he did get out.'

'Fined fifty pounds,' said Major Loftus gleefully.

'Ah,' said Pascal.

'That's the way the money goes,' said Loftus. 'The tank cost a million.' He wiped his lips on the serviette. 'Didn't have enough for breakfast. Do you think I could scrounge some more?'

He got up and strode to the top of the room to queue again.

'I don't recommend the cheese,' said Colonel Fergusson. 'Shall we have some coffee?'

'Yes.'

The silver coffee urn was at the bottom end of the room. They left their plates for the stewards to clear and carried the coffee to a spacious lobby outside. In a cool alcove under the massive stairs a carpet had been laid on the smooth flagged floor. There were easy chairs scattered about. The atmosphere was gentleman's club, but for the moment there was nobody there.

The Colonel lowered himself into an armchair. Pascal sat on the settee.

They chatted in desultory fashion and sipped their coffee.

'What's the sensation this week?' asked the Colonel. 'When should I read the paper?'

'Every day,' said Pascal. 'You know our motto: Every day we've got something to say.'

Colonel Fergusson laughed.

'Actually,' said Pascal. He leaned forward. 'There was one thing I meant to mention.'

'What's that?'

'These restricted files.'

'Which ones?'

' "UK Eyes Only",' said Pascal. 'I was talking to a policeman.'

The Colonel nodded. 'The police don't like them.'

'No.'

'Let's not fool ourselves,' said Colonel Fergusson. 'This is sensitive material. If we gave it all to the police, they'd leak it to the Loyalist extremists. Invitation to murder. It'd all end up on the Shankhill Road.'

'I know,' said Pascal. 'I can see the problem. But the Protestant terrorists' files? All the stuff on assassinations?'

'Same difference. The assassins get tipped off before we arrest them.'

'Ah,' said Pascal. He nodded. 'This policeman didn't look at it that way.'

'He wouldn't, would he?'

'He struck me as sincere.'

'Probably was. There's just a few bad hats in the Force.'

'I mean, they want to clean up the city,' said Pascal. 'It is their city.'

'Of course.'

'What he said,' said Pascal hesitantly, 'was that the new classification prevented that. It keeps the police in the dark.'

Colonel Fergusson sipped his coffee. 'Police headquarters is leaking like a sieve. When they plug the leaks they can have the files.'

'He said it was a deliberate Army policy.'

'What?'

'To tolerate counter-terrorism,' Pascal said. 'You know. *Pour décourager les autres.*'

'Nonsense,' said Colonel Fergusson.

'I told him we couldn't suggest such a thing,' said Pascal. 'Not in a British paper.'

III

The exits from the motorway to the ghetto were blocked—there had been a febrile, uneasy air about the town all day—so Pascal was forced to take the long route through town as he came back from Lisburn to check the story. A windowless prison van was inching through the traffic on Donegall Road, and Pascal followed it. It was an old police water-cannon which had been converted to serve as a mobile cell. It was making a run from the Markets to Crumlin Road jail. The prisoners inside hammered with their shoes on the armoured walls, beating time as though on a monstrous drum while they shouted the words of their anthem.

> 'Where are the boys, who stood with me,
> When history was made?
> A gradh, mo criodh, I long to see,
> The Boys of the Old Brigade.'

This was the faction song of the Provisional IRA, who were engaged in slowly blowing the city and its people to bits; and it drifted from the prison van and became just another noise in the bustle of indifferent office-girls and shoppers.

Pascal left the van at the junction of Royal Avenue. While he waited at the lights the shriek of sirens closed on him, and fire engines and ambulances howled their way through on red. There was a bomb alert near the City Hall. The police and Army were there already, but Pascal gambled that it was another false alarm. There had been scores of false ones lately.

It took him ten minutes to get up North Street and cross the interface at Millfield. He was now on Divis. It was a shattered ruin. The Civil Rights Campaign died here, on a night of fire in August 1969. That was the night when the croppies were told to lie down. Hundreds of houses in the Catholic slum were burnt by a furious mob led by uniformed police. Divis Towers, a thin-walled block of overcrowded plebeian apartments, was raked with machine-guns by the forces of the law. There was no one to answer their fire. Everything followed from that.

At Hastings Street Barracks Pascal was forced to slow down. It was a small police-station—they were always called barracks in Ireland—which told the story of unfolding fury.

The steel-shuttered windows had been fortified with bricks (against stones and petrol-bombs). Piles of sandbags and protruding steel deflector plates had spread across the pavement (to protect it from satchel-bombs, blast-bombs and nail-bombs). Huge sheets of corrugated tin topped the wall of the station yard (a precaution against snipers). There were dragons' teeth on the carriageway outside (car bombs). Finally: chicken-wire nets (which would break up rockets) were wrapped round the façade on thirty-foot poles.

That was the story of the war.

Pascal, as he carefully negotiated the series of tarmac ramps outside the building, had seen every stage so far.

He passed farther along the road. Acres of brickfields licked round the base of the beetling tower of flats. They had once been covered by streets of houses, built for the workers in the linen-mills. The majority had been razed or rendered unfit for habitation, officially because the land was needed for an urban motorway. When this solid block of Catholic voters had been shunted to shoddy new estates on the periphery the motorway project was cancelled. What houses survived were occupied by squatters. The city had the worst housing record in Western Europe. The squatters had nowhere else to go. Gangs of armed Provisionals controlled the only estates which could take them, and these were already overcrowded. The price of a house was the approval of a gunman. Those who couldn't pay it had to manage as best they could.

The squatters who lingered here were the lowest of the low. They had failed to adjust to life. The gunmen didn't want them, and the Belfast Corporation didn't want them either.

From time to time teams of soldiers were sent to the slums to evict them. The soldiers usually arrived at night, in armoured bulldozers, scout cars and APCs. They did demolition work till dawn. In statements issued later they revealed that the streets were difficult to patrol and could be used by snipers. Huge heaps of insanitary rubble were left to fester, the playground for scores of thousands of rats. The owners of the rubble, the Belfast Corporation, said that moving it might not be entirely safe.

Visiting photographers flocked to these scenes of urban devastation. They found children playing in a glittering landscape of broken glass, smashed toiletware, and puddles. Some of the children had been bitten by local rodents. The pictures —some of them won awards—told the world what terrorism means. The world misunderstood them.

Like a ramshackle Berlin Wall, the infamous Belfast Peaceline played hopscotch among the little streets on the other side of the road. It was a new partition, the ultimate publicity stunt, erected to separate the sects and proposed as an answer to the problem.

He remembered the headline on one of his earliest stories: THE STREETS WITH THE SHATTERED CHIMNEYS. Snipers employed them for sighting weapons across the Peaceline. A chimney-pot's size is the size of a human head.

Scorch-marks on the roadway punctuated Pascal's route. They had been made by burning barricades, erected against an Army whose only function, it seemed to the men who built them, was upholding the *status quo*. Pascal was able to cross them now. The wheels of the Vauxhall made a juddering sound as they rolled over ancient scars.

He went by Albert Street and puzzled his way round a maze of turnings. He left his car in a narrow street of artisans' houses. Someone had written:

THE NORTH BEGAN. THE NORTH HELD ON. GOD BLESS OUR NORTHERN LAND.

Pascal knew he was being watched. The curtains had twitched the moment he arrived. A woman scrubbing her doorstep stopped work and stared openly till he passed. He was, and would be for ever, a stranger. Then a child ran up.

To discover his accent?

'Gi' us a penny, mister?'

Pascal dug in his pocket. He retrieved a sixpence.

'Ta. Would you know the time?'

Pascal nodded. He showed the boy his watch. The youngster

looked at him strangely, and then skipped off.

The sweetshop was on the corner. The sign over the door said 'Liam Gleeson' in faded, curlicued letters. The owner was a man called Corrigan. He was a bent and faded man, who regarded his visitors from under his eyebrows. Pascal had never seen him smile.

Corrigan's disconcerting habit of wringing his hands together while he waited impatiently for customers to make their choice had led to his nickname, Squeezy. He was not an attractive man, but he was brilliant at making sweets. He made butter-scotch, bulls-eyes and lemon drops, the best to be found in the city. Pascal paused to glance at the window before entering the shop. The jars of humbugs, raspberry splits, caramels, eclairs and bon-bons made a bright and tempting display.

Pascal pushed open the door. The shop was dark and the lino thin. There was a jam-jar containing two spoons on top of the counter. PLEASE RATTLE FOR ATTENTION said a little sign. Feeling as foolish as he usually did, Pascal rattled them. He feared that he had not been heard, but the shopkeeper finally appeared, rubbing his hands and examining Pascal distrustfully.

'You, is it?'

'Yes,' said Pascal. 'It's me.'

'What do ye want, eh?'

'Pound of your peanut brittle,' said Pascal. 'Half a pound of yellow man.'

The shopkeeper sniffed and shook his head. He shuffled to the window and extracted the boxes of candy, then slowly shuffled back.

'It's for my children,' Pascal said. 'They love your toffee.'

Squeezy attacked the yellow man—a sort of hard, golden honeycomb—with a silver hammer. He broke off pieces with short, irritable strokes, and weighed off the required amount.

'Have you Peggy's Leg?' asked Pascal.

'You know I haven't,' said the old man grumpily.

'You should stock it,' said Pascal. 'It could be the thing that finally restores peace. Everyone's jaws would get stuck together. They'd all be speechless.'

'Horrible Free State muck.'

'Have you got any fudge? My wife likes fudge.'

The shopkeeper cracked his knuckles in exasperation. 'What kind of fudge? Chocolate fudge? Milk fudge? What d'you want? Nut fudge? Caramel fudge?'

'Let me see . . . caramel fudge. A quarter. And I want to see Sean Ruadh.'

The shopkeeper turned and examined him slyly. 'What do you want with Sean? A quarter of fudge, did you say?'

'Yes, a quarter will do,' said Pascal. 'I wanted to talk to him, that's all.'

'What for?'

'I heard there was trouble.'

'There's always trouble.'

'That's why I want to talk to Sean. He deals with the Press, after all.'

Squeezy rubbed his hands and cackled.

'He does still deal with the Press?' asked Pascal.

'The Irish papers, yes. He'll talk to them. Or the Swedes, or the Germans, or the Yanks. But not to you. Not to the *Standard Reporter*, saving your presence, Mr Canning. Or to any other durty British paper. There's a war on. He's had new orders.'

'What orders?'

'Nothing for the British.'

Pascal smiled. 'Sean knows me. Besides, it's very important. There's all sorts of rumours, Squeezy.'

'What sort of rumours?' Corrigan asked, looking at Pascal from beneath his eyebrows.

Pascal gestured with his hands. 'Embezzlement of funds. Theft by your officers, to put it shortly.'

'Is there now?' asked Squeezy.

There was a clatter as the door slammed open. A teenager burst in. He was panting. Pascal put his age at about fifteen, but it was hard to tell. He was dressed like a skinhead, in a denim suit and boots. He was carrying a rifle. It was an Armalite AR 180, a sniper's weapon with a tumbling bullet. Glittering new, it hung from a sling at his shoulder. The newcomer glanced at Pascal.

'Give us a slider, Squeezy,' he said.

The old man looked at the boy, and then hard at Pascal. He blinked repeatedly. For a moment he seemed to hesitate between finishing Pascal's order or serving the boy. Then he went to the fridge at the other end of the counter, and made the boy an ice-cream wafer. He handed it over.

'Ta, Squeezy.' The boy unhitched the sling from his shoulder and carefully put his weapon down. One after the other, he searched in his pockets for change. He found some, licked his wafer, and handed the money to Squeezy.

The old man wouldn't take it. 'Put it away. I've got lots of ice cream.'

'I'm payin',' scowled the boy. 'Branco Kane takes nothin' for nothin'.' He looked triumphantly at Pascal.

'Ach, you know I wouldn't mind. You shouldn't.' Squeezy laboriously unlocked the drawer where he kept his money. 'I'll gi' you a wafer any time you want.'

'Don't mind me,' Branco said to Pascal. He took an enormous lick of his wafer, held the ice-cream on his tongue. 'I'm not listenin'.' Then he picked up his gun.

Pascal nodded nervously. He turned to the shopkeeper again. There was nothing else to be done. 'Sean knows me well,' he said softly. 'We've talked together plenty of times before.'

'There's been a change of orders,' the shopkeeper growled.

'But I've got to check a story.'

'I'm sorry, Mr Canning. Can't be done.' Squeezy seemed to be washing his hands of the whole affair. 'No talkin' to the guther Press.' He carefully finished weighing out the fudge, and then returned it to its place on a middle shelf.

Pascal, intensely aware of Branco's interested attention, wondered what else he could say. 'Come on, Squeezy. I thought you didn't believe in censoring the papers? You're always saying how you think it's wrong.'

'Huh!' snorted Branco Kane. 'Tell that to the *Daily Mirror*. We censored that, all right. We blew the fucking plant up.'

There was an uncomfortable silence.

'We should have shot the fucking staff while we was at it.'

Pascal smiled at Squeezy. 'You will try?'

'Waste o' time,' said the old man. 'We had our orders.'

'It's very important.'

'What's important?' the boy demanded.

Pascal made a mistake. He tried to ignore him. 'Squeezy—'

'I said, what's important?' roared Branco Kane. He worked the bolt of the rifle, and pointed it theatrically at Pascal.

Pascal licked his lips. 'Squeezy?'

'When I talk, you answer!' exclaimed the boy, finishing the last soggy fragment of his wafer, returning his sticky index to the trigger of his gun.

Squeezy washed his hands; 'Hush, now, Branco. Hold your whisht. Mr Canning was just on his way.'

Pascal nodded. 'I better be going. What do I owe you?'

'Eight, an' sixteen an' ten, twenty-four, thirty-four pee, Mr Canning. Branco, don't point that gun.'

'Cheap at the price,' said Pascal weakly. He was terrified, but got out his wallet and produced a note.

'Hey, Brit,' said Branco softly, 'put up your hands.'

Pascal didn't believe he was serious. He put the pound note down on the counter. Then he looked at the young man's face, and slowly, very cautiously, as he'd seen them do it in the movies, Pascal put up his hands.

'Step away from that counter.'

Branco Kane had a broken tooth. It showed jagged when he grinned, as he was grinning now. Otherwise he was quite good-looking, or would have been were it not for his staring eyes.

'What paper does this punk work for?'

'The *Standard Reporter*,' Squeezy said nervously. 'Branco, you put down that oul' gun.'

'The *Standard Reporter* stinks. What does he want?'

'He wants to talk to Sean.'

'He wants to talk to Sean?' said Branco sarcastically. 'We were shouting out for fifty frigging years and none of the bastards would listen. Now he wants to talk to Sean.'

'I've got a story I want to check out.'

'How would you like to die?'

There was an old clock, ticking above the bon-bons. 'Not particularly. Not just now.'

The boy said, 'Shall I tell you something? I'm going to kill you.'

The eye of a rifle never blinks. Pascal looked at it, and almost wanted to laugh. This tragic farce couldn't possibly happen to him. He was watching a passage from a badly written play.

'I'm fair. I'll give you a chance to run,' said Branco Kane. 'I don't like shooting a sitting target.'

The boy brought the rifle up to his chest. He edged cautiously round Pascal, gesturing with the muzzle for Pascal to move towards the door. It occurred to the reporter that Branco expected to be attacked, but this merely made Pascal more careful.

'Get out of here!' shouted Branco. 'I'll count to twenty. I just want to see you run.'

Pascal tried to swallow. His mouth was dry, his heart was pounding. He could feel the adrenalin rushing into his veins, getting him ready for instant flight. He forced himself to fight against it. Calm yourself, said his brain. Nothing is this absurd.

There is a great unanswered question, Pascal thought. Do you really feel a bullet in the brain?

The grey slates on all the houses seemed unusually vivid. The dull bricks looked almost scarlet. Pascal thought of all the minor characters in second-feature films whom he'd seen despatched, and wondered why his own end should have to be so ridiculous. Thinking that made it easier not to run. The chickweed growing between broken flagstones seemed as glamorous as orchids. The stitching in homely curtains had been done with a hempen rope. It was an awful long way to the corner.

Pascal's heels crashed, like thunderbolts, along the narrow little street. He wondered how many eyes were watching, waiting to see him run. He dodged round a corner. He couldn't believe his luck. The sadist had followed him, and would murder him now, while he hoped. The reporter broke into a desperate, awkward run, until he realized he was merely running deeper into the ghetto. A new fear struck him. The military post on top of the mill; what if the soldier should shoot him down?

It was distinctly unhealthy to run in a place like this. He passed some women, who looked at him queerly. He made himself slow down. It was absurd to panic, but he felt absurd. Bewildered, he searched around him for a landmark. The street-names had been taken down long before to confuse the Army patrols. The street was familiar, but it might have been anywhere. It was just another street in a smoking stretch of industrial slum.

Pascal stopped. Some children, who were skipping beside a lamp-post, stared at the stranger curiously. Suddenly there was no need at all to be frightened. The whole thing became banal. He remembered what a teacher had told him—it seemed years ago now, when he was young. There were no itineraries, only directions. Trusting himself doubtfully, he chose one. It took him to the car.

Only later did he remember that he'd lost both his money and his sweets. The thought amused him. He liked to bring his children sweets, particularly ones that were so authentically old-fashioned. He shrugged. No point in going back to Squeezy Corrigan's now. He'd avoid it for a while. As for the kids, they'd have to make do with some unauthentic humbugs. He could stroll up North Street any time he liked, and buy a packet from Woolworths.

IV

Pascal was back in the office in time to catch the first-edition deadline. There wasn't much to put over. A body with multiple stab wounds had been found in a back entry in the early hours of the morning, but that story had been written before lunch. Eddie Armstrong, the *Standard Reporter*'s chief photographer, had wired pictures of a billy goat which had been adopted as the mascot of a battalion stationed out in the sticks, near Derry. He seemed happy. Shortly after seven o'clock, the night duty reporter looked in, swapped a few cracks, and went off to have his tea at the office pub. Pascal stayed on.

He tried to convince himself that he ought to go home, but he was tired and feeling a little resentful of his lot. McDowell's story about IRA corruption still troubled him. He didn't doubt

87

that it was true, but then so were a lot of things; he just wondered why this particular parcel of worms had been handed him on a plate.

He knew in advance that if he wrote the story it would make page one. Not just in the Irish editions—which was easy—but throughout the London run. It would fit in well with the paper's line. He ought, perhaps, to have been pleased; instead he felt frustrated, angry with the paper and angrier with himself. It hadn't taken him long to realize that he should not have come here, at least not if he wanted to prove himself in newspaper work; but at the time the opportunity arose things had seemed so much simpler.

Pascal was just beginning a career as a reporter when a whole series of major foreign stories began breaking. The student revolts in Paris which toppled De Gaulle were followed by the arrival of tanks in Prague. The Civil Rights movement in the United States had spawned popular demands for an end to the Vietnam war.

All these dramas, played out as they were on the stage of the global village, became suddenly personal and relevant when the troubles began again in Ireland.

People were shocked. Suburban Britain began to learn things which had been obvious for fifty years, but which had hitherto been passed over in silence. Members of the British Parliament were beaten to their knees by Loyalist ultras in front of television cameras; Protestant terrorists murdered Catholics and planted bombs in order to bring down a Protestant Prime Minister who was soft on Rome. The Special Powers Act—a legal instrument which a South African Minister of Justice said was better than anything he had—was seen to be the mainstay of a provincial dictatorship which had nothing to learn from fascism anywhere.

The British Press was taken by the story. It seemed at the time to have all the glamour which attached to events in the American South; student marchers, downtrodden natives and redneck police. A great deal of liberal ink was spilled before anyone realized that they might pose all the questions they liked; the Government either could not, or would not, answer.

Pascal was young; he had sympathies in the country; he continued to look for answers long after it ceased to be fashionable to do so. It was said that Northern Ireland was a part of Britain—although it was governed quite differently—and that the majority community had a democratic right to continue being British for as long as they wanted. It was also said that this same majority would turn on the Catholics and massacre them all if the British Army pulled out. The two arguments seemed to sit uneasily together. On the one hand, one changed nothing for solid democratic reasons; and on the other, one changed nothing because the democratically constituted majority were a bloodthirsty band of would-be assassins.

Pascal had lived with the stalemate for too long now to imagine that the best reporting in the world could do anything to change it. He saw the fruits of consensus politics—the over-powering inertia which invites trouble by seeking to avoid it—in the streets each day. They were shovelled into plastic bags or stowed neatly away in hastily ordered coffins. They became statistics which were used by one side, or the other, or the other, to prove how barbarous their enemies were; nothing more than that.

The telephone rang. Not Pascal's phone, one of the sets on somebody else's desk. He let it ring. He stared at it and waited for it to stop. When it didn't stop ringing he stood up and picked up the handset.

'*Standard Reporter.*'

'Pascal?' It was Ann, his wife.

'Hello, love.'

'Pascal—listen. Your mother just rang.'

'Yes?'

'She had a call from Ballyvarren. Andy had another heart attack. He's very sick. She's flying into Dublin tonight.'

Pascal grunted.

'You still there?'

'Yes,' said Pascal. 'That's just what we needed, isn't it?'

'I'm sorry, darling.'

'Is he very sick?'

'Your mother thinks he's dying.'

'What should we do? Do you think I should go down?'

'She said not to. She said she'd keep in touch.'

'Hmmh.'

'Are you coming home?'

Pascal hesitated. 'I've a few things to do. I—'

'I'll kiss the kids for you,' said Ann. 'See you later.'

' 'Bye.'

'Don't worry too much,' said Ann. 'He might be all right.'

'Yes,' said Pascal. 'Sure.'

Pascal hung up. He stood where he was for a moment, then sat on the edge of the desk and stared at nothing in particular. The office was dirty. There were papers everywhere. The fluorescent lights were stained with stale cigarette smoke, the walls smeared and covered with graffiti. Even the windows were tapestried with peeling tape, gone dirty at the edges. It kept out the daylight, but it was supposed to protect him from shrapnel.

He went out. It was dark outside. An old tramp had already settled on a bench in the public square. There was little traffic. People were frightened of being kidnapped and murdered if they ventured into the city. The tramp was safe because no one would mourn his loss, and no political cause would be served by killing him.

Pascal had to fumble in his pocket to find keys to unlock the gates which sealed off the car-park. The gates screeched in protest when he opened them. Inside, there was almost total darkness. The car-park was hemmed in on all sides by tall buildings, several of which had been burned out by fire-bombs; all of them were deserted.

He got into the car and sat in the darkness. He thought of the big blond man who was dying sixty miles south of Dublin. He thought of the nights, like this one, when he was a child, when Andy and he had sat in a barn waiting for a roan cow to drop her calf; or walked quietly through the sleeping fields with a fox slung over Pascal's shoulder.

It seemed wrong and ridiculous that Andy should be dying, but Pascal knew that he was. He'd had other attacks, and the doctors said that the next one . . . Pascal shook his head. He put his forehead on the steering-wheel and stayed like that. He was glad it was dark.

Andy was one of the happiest men that Pascal had ever met.

He never seemed to want anything. He was just there, with his big, slow grin and his droll way of talking; and he had been ever since Pascal could remember. He was Pascal's summertime father, the man he looked up to.

The heart attacks had begun shortly after Andy's mother died. She was in her nineties. Her last few years had been spent helplessly in bed. Pascal suspected that it was because of her that his uncle had waited until middle age to marry. He'd been engaged for eleven years. Of course, he didn't have children; his bride was already nearly forty on her wedding day. Like so many Irishmen, Andy had been the passive victim of the love and terror of women. He was both debtor and polluter, the slave of motherhood and the fearful spectator of animal reproduction.

So maybe he wasn't happy; Pascal didn't know. All he knew was that Andy's children were his brother and sister's children; and that they came to the Irish Ballyvarren—most of them from England—and were welcome there in a house without sons of its own.

Pascal started the car. The lights threw eerie shadows in the deserted compound. He drove out into the road and then locked up. He headed for the west of the city, where the ghettos were.

The walls of the slums had been whitewashed by the people who lived in them, so that snipers could kill soldiers more easily at night. The Army had been round with a water-cannon and roughly sprayed the whitewash black. Children who hurled paint bombs at the water-cannon, hoping to blind the driver and make him crash, had added a touch of colour to an abstract frieze whose principal message was hate.

The houses and mills burned by the Loyalists had been partially cleared away. Mallow grew from the cinders. The sites were littered with newer wreckage, like battlefields glimpsed through gaps in a barricade. On the bricks of a smoke-blackened gable someone had scrawled question and answer:

WHO KILLED COCK ROBIN?
WE DID—PROVOS

The car sped through the lightless streets. The stars seemed

91

icy. The houses were battened down, the patrolling Army rifle-men like black phantoms. A mill loomed. The car bucked as it crossed over ramps. There was wire, and wood, and sandbags; bullet-scars in the brickwork, and cold blued steel in the soldiers' hands. An incinerated bus lay wrecked across a pave-ment: a broken lorry rusted on a piece of wasteland. The flag-stones had been looted and broken up to make ammunition.

A soldier was caught in the glare of Pascal's headlights. As Pascal braked the soldier aimed his rifle. He aimed it at Pascal's head. Then the car was skidding, the wheels had mounted the pavement, and—nothing regrettable happened.

Pascal continued his journey. The shattered roadway wound through the Catholic ghetto. He was slowed by ramps while he passed a graveyard. Then he was passing a fort.

Benny McWilliams lived here.

There were two parked cars in the tiny garden in front of McWilliams's house. One was an engineless wreck, the other a battered jalopy. Their purpose was to prevent car bombs from being parked too close. They were not very good for the flowers.

Pascal knocked on his friend's front door. The front-room curtains were drawn, and the windows protected by plastic film and cage of wire. One of the curtains opened, Eilish's face peered out, and then the curtain flapped shut.

He waited. The door was opened, and the reporter was hustled in. 'How're ye, Pascal?' asked Benny's wife. 'The boss is in here. He'll be with ye in a minute. He's just been seein' to Jackie.'

Jackie was Benny's daughter. She was kneeling by the sofa while her father was swabbing her head. There was an ugly gash which had split her eyebrow. Benny looked up. 'Hiya, Pascal.' He gestured at the wound. 'Them wee fuckers at school.'

Benny McWilliams grinned. He was fat and sweaty, a politician whose health had been wrecked by six years' intern-ment on unspecified charges; one of the old IRA of the forties and early fifties.

'Sit yourself down. We were talkin' of you last night.'

Jacqueline, Benny's daughter, was thirteen years old and

frightened. She found civil wars were a strain. Her friends threw stones at the soldiers, but if she did too her daddy got all upset. She was therefore branded, a soldier-lover, a traitor. When the soldiers weren't there her schoolmates got bored, and they sometimes threw stones at her.

Benny, despite the contrary evidence, was a socialist. He believed in the brotherhood of man. He thought the Provisionals the unwitting allies of England's interests, and freedom a complex idea. Not that he was an idealist; he was too old for that, and too ignorant to pretend that he knew the solution. He fixed things, coaxed a few favours, and tried to keep track of the voters and voters' children who disappeared into Army camps in the early hours, almost every morning.

Every party despised him, except his own. Even they became doubtful sometimes. The Loyalists wouldn't kill him, because he made such a splendid satirical figure. They had a strip cartoon, 'Bill and Ben, the IRA men', in which Benny starred.

As for the Provisionals, they sent him a letter bomb which blew off one of his fingers. But they wouldn't kill him, and neither would the Army, for fear of offending his friends. He survived in the twilight, arranging truces, uselessly saying that all the combatants were wrong.

'D'you hear the latest?' asked Benny, delicately swabbing.

Awkwardly, Pascal moved some washing from the cheap grey sofa. James Connolly, who was shot with Pearse, gazed stonily down from the wall.

'A harmless old man and his wife,' said Benny. 'They were sitting at home, watching the telly, and sudden this gunman bursts in.' He paused, stabbing at Jacqueline's wound.

'Daddy!'

' "Fuckit! shouts the gunman",' said Benny. 'Wrong house! Then he shot out the lampshade, turned on his heel, and ran.'

'Turrible.' Eilish chuckled. 'Turrible, ain't it, Pascal?'

'Terrible,' said Pascal.

Benny laughed. 'I thought it was fucking hilarious.'

'C'mon Jackie,' said Eilish briskly. 'We'll go in the back and leave your daddy to talk. You're near finished that bleedin', love.'

'Wait till it stops,' said Pascal.

'Och! She's all right!' said Eilish. 'She's had worse than that.' She picked up the bowl of reddish water from her husband's feet and took the bloodstained rag. 'C'mon, Jackie.' The parlour was Benny's office.

McWilliams brushed vigorously at the lint which clung to his trousers. 'Pascal, oul' son? What can we do for you?'

Pascal lied. 'I was coming from Lisburn, so I thought that I'd call.'

'You'll have a drink?' asked Benny.

'Love one.'

Benny's gross, unhappy body heaved itself up from the chair. He waddled to a cabinet in the corner, clutched a tumbler, half filling it with whiskey.

'Benny? You remember when all this started?'

Benny glanced at him.

'Did you think it would come to this?'

'No,' said Benny, filling the second glass. 'If you'd told me, I'd have said you were talking nonsense.'

'When John sat down on his bottom, that day in Derry—that started it, though?'

Benny came back. 'I suppose so.'

'Then is he responsible?' Pascal took the glass he was offered. 'Are you responsible, Benny?'

Benny looked startled. 'Of course I'm not responsible.'

Pascal smiled, rather desperately. He knew what he wanted to say, but was not quite sure how to put it. 'This place was a powder keg, wasn't it, Benny? And people like you lit the fuse.'

'Balls,' said Benny succinctly.

'Of course you did,' said Pascal.

'They had us tied up in knots.' Benny drank some whiskey. 'There were thousands of people homeless. Some of these ghettos had forty per cent unemployment. What could anyone do? We sat in the streets on our arses.'

'You bucked the system.'

'We wanted a decent life.'

'But you couldn't have one.'

'No,' said Benny. 'We couldn't have one.'

'Look,' said Pascal, 'suppose that the Brits pull out—'

'They will pull out,' interjected Benny. 'They don't want anything to do with this fuckin' hole.'

'Well, you started the process,' said Pascal. 'What you did led to everything else that followed. When you sat down in the street you bucked the system, and that led straight to the bombs; you people are just as responsible as the men who plant them.'

Benny shrugged. 'No. We would have settled for very little. A place to sleep and a job. A little bit of dignity, that's all. We weren't out chasing a Republic.'

'You were,' said Pascal.

'Not this way.'

'But if you get one this way?'

'What do you want me to say?'

'Will it have been worth it?' demanded Pascal. 'That's what I want you to say.'

'Fuck you,' said Bennny. 'No!'

'You're a prig,' said Pascal. 'Your grandchildren will think that it was.' Pascal drank deeply, so that the spirit burned and was hard to swallow. 'I nearly got shot this morning.'

'It might have saved me some whiskey,' said Benny sourly.

'I'm a prig, too,' said Pascal. 'I come into your house and drink your whiskey and try to blame everything on you.' He lay back and put his head against the wall and closed his eyes. When he opened them again, he said: 'I like the danger, Benny, I like surviving. I like them trying to hurt me, because when they don't I can look back on it and feel that I'm some-body special.' There was a picture of Easter Week in Dublin over the mantelpiece, the Easter of ruins and resurrection, the Easter for which Pascal was named. 'I'm sick, Benny. Isn't that sick?'

'You can always leave.'

'You can't though, can you? Everyone can't leave.' Pascal drank more whiskey. 'I'm talking too much. I'm sorry I was rude.'

'It could happen to a bishop.'

'Living here,' said Pascal, 'it's funny. It's like drug abuse. You get hooked on the adrenalin. It's a high. It gets so you need the violence. It gives you that extra charge.'

'For God's sake, Pascal,' said Benny. 'You're either pissed or you think too much. I've always said you should work for the *Daily Mirror*.'

'That's too intellectual,' Pascal said.

'Fuckin' shower,' said Benny. 'Did you see what they wrote this morning?'

'I knew a chap on the *Sunday Express*,' said Pascal, 'who got diarrhoea. He was sitting on the thunder box when a bomb exploded in the building next door. They pulled him out from a welter of rubble and shit, and he blamed it on eating curry.'

Benny laughed heartily, shaking his head.

'Said he'd never eat Indian again,' said Pascal. 'He didn't, either. They blew up the restaurant last week.'

'They want people to buy Irish,' Benny said.

'I'm in trouble, Benny.'

'Drink whiskey. The only reliable cure.'

'You remember all those bombs that went off before they should have gone off?'

'I remember the bombs.'

'There were so many of them, I thought I might do a piece,' said Pascal.

'I never read it.'

'It wasn't published. The Editor didn't like it.'

Benny grinned malignly. 'Not enough sex?'

'I gave the information to a friend. He did a piece for a magazine in London. It annoyed the Army.'

Benny tutted.

'It was about a secret weapon,' said Pascal. 'A thing they can use that can detonate bombs.'

Benny chortled delightedly. 'Jasus,' he said. 'James Bond.'

'Did you ever hear of Radio Frequency Focusing?'

'Never in me life.'

'They can focus radio waves,' said Pascal. 'Like you focus light from a laser.'

'Sounds terrible,' said Benny.

'You can detonate bombs while the bombers are making them.'

96

Benny looked interested. 'Ah.'

'They've been using it here.'

'Well,' said Benny. 'It saves on bullets.'

'But not just the bombers get killed. Anyone gets killed. You do, I do, anyone does. It's your hard luck if you happen to be passing.'

'I didn't say it was right,' said Benny.

'Shall I tell you something?' Pascal leaned forward. 'I met an old lady in hospital. She was in a house near by when a bomb-making factory blew up. She fainted and fell on the hearth and her brain got hot and the poor old lady went mad. She was quite insane.'

'Jesus,' said Benny. 'Was it the Brits?'

'How do I know?' said Pascal. 'How does anyone know? That was the point of the story.'

'What kind of trouble you in?'

Pascal sat back. 'The Army gave me a story, Benny. A big one. I think it's true. They want me to carry it. Not anyone else. Just me.'

'And?' said Benny.

'It's my reward for embarrassing them,' said Pascal. 'They're embarrassing me. They have evidence about thievery among the Provos. It's irrelevant to the political issues here, but it's just what they've wanted for years. From now on out the entire problem is going to be presented as a struggle between sheriffs and outlaws. The incorruptible Brits v. the mobster Irish.'

'If it hurts the Provos, I'm for it.'

'It won't hurt the Provos. It will prolong the conditions which allow the Provos to flourish.'

'That's your complaint?'

Pascal nodded. 'In the long term. In the short term, if I use this story alone, I'm effectively silenced. I wreck my contacts throughout the Catholic ghettos. If I don't use the story, I'm a fellow-traveller. McDowell can call me a traitor and say I cover up for the bombers.'

Benny stood up. 'Finish that drink.' Pascal passed him his empty glass. 'Why do I bother with you?' asked Benny.

Benny shuffled to the gimcrack cabinet in the crowded corner. This time he brought back the bottle. 'You could have been something honest,' he said. He sat down heavily. 'A pimp, or something.'

'It's the easy life. Be buggered to the money.'

Benny's hand trembled as he poured some whiskey. Coughing, he handed the glass to Pascal, then carefully poured his own. 'But you surely know your way round. You've got plenty of contacts.'

'Not any more,' said Pascal, uncomfortably. 'Not on a story like this.'

'Och, you have,' said Benny.

'I used to.' Pascal gulped his drink. 'I had one good man, but he died of cancer. Most of the rest have been shot, or jailed, or run off to Dublin.'

Benny laughed. 'The last is the worst.'

Pascal watched him carefully. 'I haven't got time to go blundering round in the dark. I need to know exactly what's going on.'

'You want me to help?'

'I want to talk to someone who knows just what he's talking about.'

'A Provo?'

'One of the big ones.'

Benny McWilliams farted. 'Sure,' he said carelessly. 'I'll find you a Provo. You'd better tell me the details.'

The reporter told him.

V

Pascal met his Provo the following afternoon. He was in the office playing darts with Louis, the wireman, when the telephone rang. It startled him, and he missed his double top.

'Christ,' said Pascal, 'I'm having that again.'

'No, you're not,' said Louis. 'You ought to have nerves of steel.'

'I'll beat you anyway,' said Pascal. The wireman laughed. Pascal strolled to the telephone and picked it up.

'*Standard Reporter.*'

'Pascal?'

'Who's this?'

'Benny. Listen. I don't want to talk on the phone.'

'Sure.'

'I want you to meet me. About that thing the other day.'

'Where, Benny?'

'That place where we had the sing-song. You remember the place?'

'Where I took my bow?' asked Pascal lightly.

'I'll see you there, half an hour.' The connection was broken. A second later Pascal heard the familiar clicks.

The Broken Bough was a shebeen controlled by the Provisional IRA. There were scores of shebeens in both the confessional ghettos. They were run by the various gangs, and served for both profit and social control. They sold cheaper drink and afforded more security than the licensed bars, which were constantly under attack. Strangers could be vetted easily, mythologies reinforced, and heresies stamped out. Their only drawback, from the terrorists' point of view, was that they made ideal listening posts for police and military informers.

Pascal looked at the wireman, who was standing expectantly with the darts held ready. 'I'll concede that game,' he said. 'I'll beat you next time. I have to go out for a while.'

'What about those assassinations?' the wireman objected. 'You said I'd get early copy.'

'I've nearly finished. You can have it the minute I get back.'

The wireman shrugged expressively.

'I'll see you, then,' said Pascal, putting his coat on.

'What time d'you think you'll be back?'

'An hour or two. 'Bye.'

'See you, Pascal.'

The Broken Bough was an underground warren, the converted strongroom of a burnt-out bank which the Provos had refurbished. Its name referred to the poets' idea of Ireland, a Red Rose Tree which would never flower unless it was watered with blood. Ulster itself was the broken bough.

The shebeen, as Pascal knew, would be dark and dingy, and would still stink of the fire which had swept through the bank. Nevertheless, he was glad to get out of the office. The sky was a cloudless and limitless blue, and the sun did its best to brighten the dismal city, picking out a cornice, or a pane of glass, brightening faded colours, giving all the habitual dullness a decided boost.

First as he walked, then as he drove through the city, Pascal's eyes were drawn to the barrier of hills which sealed off Belfast from the rest of Ireland. Craigantlet, Castlereagh, Collin, Black Mountain, Divis; they were beautiful names, and the hills were indifferent and beautiful. Cave Hill, which lay out of his vision to the north, was his favourite. It had an extraordinary skyline, like the profile of Napoleon sleeping; and a giants' ring; and it was there that the idea of freedom had been born in Ireland.

He felt almost at home; thought of the salmon fishermen drawing blades from the sea two or three hours up the coast. Of the old men, artfully building basalt and limestone into dry stone walls; of the knitting of nets at Strangford, the viking-crack, *strang fjord*. He would like to go there again. He would like to go to Ardboe; to Ringneil, for the wild grey geese in the springtime; to Kesh, Belcoo and Garrison; to Pomeroy, to see that old blind singer; to the banks of the Mourne and the Fairywater, and down to Armagh to eat apples.

He parked near the dark shebeen. There was a man, either idler or guard, near the broken door. He looked sardonically at Pascal. Pascal clattered down the stairs and was soon in a narrow room.

The walls had been roughly painted. They were green and white. There was a stained brown counter and a range of bottles behind it.

McWilliams was reading posters. He glanced at Pascal. 'We must be winnin',' he said. 'You can get tuppence off potatoes at the People's Co-op.'

A fat grey slug with his bright blue eyes, he blinked like a lighthouse in the gloomy, depressing twilight.

'Moss McSharry,' breathed Benny, pointing. 'Lemme buy you a drink.'

Startled, Pascal looked towards the end of the bar. He saw a sombre figure, brooding over a whiskey, the highlights dull in his curly red hair, and his shoulders hunched.

100

Benny made no attempt to go down to McSharry. He lumbered instead to the nearer end of the bar.

'Jameson,' Pascal ordered.

'Three Jameson,' said Benny. He gestured to the barman. 'Fire down the other to your man.' He turned gravely to Pascal. 'I want you to meet this fellow behind me.' He spoke in a grumbling whisper that seemed drawn from the bottom of his belly. Pascal opened his mouth to reply. 'Presently,' Benny interrupted. 'Presently. In a minute.' The barman came back and Benny paid him. 'You know this letter you were telling me about?'

'Yes,' said Pascal.

'The fella the Provos beat up in the camp?'

'Yes?'

'That fucker there behind you is the brother of the man they beat up.'

'You're joking,' said Pascal.

'Yeah,' said Benny. His breath stank of alcohol and age.

Pascal looked away. McSharry—his face angular and bearded, but still, Pascal thought, recognizably himself— ignored the reporter completely.

'Come here, come here,' Benny beckoned. 'The brother is called Liam McSharry. That's the Billy McDowell told you about. This one's Moss. Maurice. Wild, wild, Provo. One of the hard ones. The Army want him bad.'

'Listen—' said Pascal.

Benny held up his hand. He swallowed his tot of whiskey. He beckoned to the barman, who came and silently poured him another. Benny leaned forward so that his mouth was near Pascal's ear. 'The letter's a fake. It was never written. But McSharry wants you to publish what you know about it anyway.'

'He *wants* me to publish?' asked Pascal.

Benny blinked, and smiled knowingly at Pascal. 'Why not?' He shrugged elaborately. 'He wants it published, the Brits want it published, who are you to argue?'

'Why do they want it published?' asked Pascal suspiciously.

'His mother's from a hill at the back of Tyrone. They're

devious people there.' Benny avoided Pascal's eyes. He looked uncomfortable.

'What's happening?' Pascal demanded. 'What is it, Benny?'

'There's a faction fight in the organization. Your man there wants to take over. He wants to be boss.'

'Well?' said Pascal.

'What you have might help him to become boss,' said Benny, 'provided somebody publishes it.' Benny was sweating. 'If it does, he'll start bombing London again. Only badly this time.' The politician glanced nervously over his shoulder. 'I'm not supposed to know this, Pascal. Neither are you.'

Pascal nodded. 'Of course not. I'll be careful.'

'Careful?' wheezed Benny. 'You'd better be.'

Pascal looked at Benny strangely. 'I don't understand,' he said slowly. 'The Army can't know that they're helping McSharry.' A pause. 'McDowell can't know, Benny, can he?'

'I don't give a tinker's curse,' said Benny McWilliams. 'They might do. They might be giving him rope to hang himself with. I wish I didn't know, that's all. I wish that I wasn't involved.'

Benny guzzled another mouthful of whiskey. 'They tried it on in London before,' he said. 'They put in a couple of car bombs. A morning's ration for Belfast, and the Brits screamed blue murder. They'll try different tactics next time. That fella up there has a brain. He's not interested in stunts. He'll use incendiaries. Hundreds of little fires. You know how easy it is. Children can do it. He could cost them millions.'

'Pounds, shillings and pence.'

'Much more valuable than blood.'

'How do you know all this?'

Benny tapped his nose. 'I know it.'

'Christ,' said Pascal. 'What do we do? This isn't journalism, is it?'

Benny leaned on the bar. He sighed. 'It's politics,' he said. 'You're locked in a small dark room with a gang of homicidal maniacs. The madmen are wearing blindfolds, but your hands are tied and they're all carrying daggers.'

'But you can't let it happen. . .'

102

Benny laughed, bitterly. 'It's not your job to stop it,' he said. 'You just try to survive.'

'Maybe we should tell,' said Pascal.

'Tell what? To who?'

Pascal shook his head, as though wanting to clear it, to see things right. 'The Army.'

'Certainly,' said Benny. 'What size do you take in hoods?'

'I mean—'

'The Army don't tell me when they shoot down innocent men,' Benny watched Pascal wearily. 'Make for the door. Get out. Don't get involved with this.'

'How can I not? I already am.'

'All right,' snapped Benny. 'But listen. Remember that small dark room. The maniacs agree. Say yes and they'll leave you alone.'

Pause. Pascal looked at McWilliams hopelessly. 'I tried to tell you at once, but you wouldn't let me. I know McSharry.'

Consternation spread across Benny's features. 'You know McSharry?' McWilliams repeated.

'I haven't seen him for months,' said Pascal. 'I thought he went down to Dublin to hide up, or something.'

'You know the fucker, and you get me involved with this?' said Benny, shrilly. 'Listen. One word—'

'I won't' interrupted Pascal.

'One hint, Pascal, and I'm in trouble.'

'No. Of course not. No.'

'C'mon and meet him then,' said Benny savagely. He looked desperately at Pascal, and then waddled down the bar.

Pascal followed, wishing to God he were dead. When McSharry saw them coming he smiled at Benny. He had a beaked, ascetic face, like a Viking or a Christian monk from some savage island which the Vikings raided.

'Pascal Canning,' said Benny, waving carelessly at Pascal. 'He says that he knows you.'

The tiger's eyes watched Pascal. 'He does.'

'You never told me.'

'You never asked.' McSharry extended his hand. 'Hiya, Pascal.'

The shock of his voice still fascinated Pascal. So did the hard green eyes.

'Moss.'

Pascal was back, he and a photographer, on the wrong side of a barricade in August. Trees had been felled to halt the advance of the Army. Their leaves were brilliantly green in the sunlight, and petrol bombs fell amongst them like enormous, exotic blossoms. McSharry directed. The Army's teargas blew back in the soldiers' faces. They wore goggle-eyed gas masks. They formed phalanxes and fired plastic bullets which came swooping out of the sky. The rioters threw stones.

'I thought you had gone to Dublin.'

'They couldn't do without me.'

He was neatly, almost obsessively dressed. Pascal imagined him installed in a middle-class suburb, perhaps in Malone, while the soldiers scourged the poor in their search for rebels.

'Pascal did stories I gave him before,' McSharry said. Benny nodded. 'I can trust him, see? He's not on the Army's payroll.'

There was nothing that Pascal could say. McSharry had helped him, and he had accepted his help. It was after the car bomb. It was before the assassinations. Was that an excuse?

'So many ghastly things have happened.'

McSharry looked at him quickly. 'The whole fucking country's wrecked.'

'We agree on that.'

It was Benny who broke the silence. 'I told him you wanted that story printed.' He glanced awkwardly at Pascal. 'I'll leave you to it.'

'Benny,' McSharry said. 'Have another drink, will you?'

Benny wheezed. 'I'm rightly.' His fat hand flapped. He lifted his glass to demonstrate its contents, then drained the whiskey. 'We didn't drink enough when the drink was cheap.' He nodded. 'I'm expected somewhere.'

'Thanks for fixing it up.'

'Yeah.' Benny grinned at McSharry. Then he turned to Pascal. 'I'll be seeing you, boy. Remember your Highway Code.'

104

When he had gone McSharry beckoned the barman. 'Give us two more Irish.' He looked curiously at Pascal. 'What did he mean with the Highway Code?'

'Always give way to trains,' said Pascal. 'It's a private joke.'

'Is that in the Highway Code?'

'Yes. But it's not down there as a joke.'

It amused McSharry. The drinks were served, and the barman retreated discreetly out of earshot. They were alone in the bar. Pascal found a stool and planted himself in front of McSharry.

'How has it been with you?' McSharry asked him.

Pascal studied him. 'I'm tired. I feel as if I were filthy.'

'Nobody finds it easy.'

'You?'

'I couldn't stick it in Dublin.'

'I don't want to use this letter.'

McSharry watched him coolly.

'It's bad enough for the Irish to be murderers,' said Pascal. 'Do we have to depict them as thieves?'

'Some of them are.'

Pascal smiled. 'Yes. But this is different.'

McSharry's lip curled up. 'You would only be telling the truth.' He tapped the bar. His fingers were short and blunt. 'Why don't you want to do it?'

'Because I used to believe in Ireland.'

McSharry smiled sarcastically. 'Does it touch your honour?' Pascal nodded, almost imperceptibly. McSharry laughed. 'I want you to blow this scandal open.' He became implacable. 'Print everything they gave you. They got it from my brother. He was working on it for me.'

Pascal looked at him. 'Why?'

'You know the history of the Provisionals, don't you?'

'Yes,' said Pascal quietly.

'Nobody believed that Civil Rights would ever get anywhere up here. I didn't. I lived here. Nobody did.'

'No.'

'But they caused one hell of a fuss when they started marching.' McSharry's face was bitter. 'They alarmed everyone. Even the Government in Dublin.' He hesitated. 'Right?'

105

'Right,' said Pascal.

'The heirs of the free Republic didn't like all that fuss one bit. It might have spread down South.'

'It might.'

'Have you been in the Dublin slums?' When Pascal nodded: 'People might have decided that civil rights weren't the exclusive property of those under British rule.' He studied Pascal. 'They might have wanted a few for themselves, down South.'

'I know,' said Pascal. 'The Cabinet in Dublin created and armed the Provisionals. I accept that. It wasn't a clever thing to do.'

'Of course it was,' McSharry said. 'They provided a distraction. They went off to fight a foreign enemy, and everyone forgot about their enemies at home.'

Pascal said, 'Yes.'

'The trouble was, nobody expected them to be so successful.'

Pascal shook his head.

'They changed, Pascal. The British Army transformed them. They made the Provisionals legitimate again.'

'There were a lot of mistakes.'

McSharry coughed. He seemed to have a catch in his throat, and he coughed repeatedly. He looked embarrassed afterwards, as though weakness shamed him. 'They recruited me.'

'I know,' said Pascal, softly. 'I know exactly.'

'I didn't join this fight,' McSharry said, 'for the sake of killing my neighbours.'

'Moss—'

'I want to unite this country.' He was staring now, at the space over Pascal's shoulder. 'To put a final end to our separate excuses for killing each other.'

'You kill,' said Pascal. 'To do it you have to kill.'

'I didn't get permission from a millionaire in Dublin. Do you think it's easy?'

'No.'

'Of course I'll kill,' McSharry shouted. His voice echoed round the bar of the Broken Bough. 'If I have to kill, then believe me, Pascal, I'll kill Protestant or Catholic or soldier or millionaire!' His fanatic's eyes held a paradoxical innocence. 'I want to end this war.'

'So do we all,' said Pascal.

'That's where you're wrong. Never imagine that.'

'We could have a truce. . .'

'I don't want a truce. I told you, I want a solution.'

'There isn't one. It's gone on too long. There's no way you're going to win.'

'I'll use any weapon.'

'No,' said Pascal. 'Better to stop it now.'

McSharry looked at him sideways. 'Honour again?'

'I'm tired.'

'Leave honour for later on. We'll have to invent one, Pascal. We haven't got any left.'

'I don't believe you.'

'Publish the things that I ask you. Let the Brits make it propaganda. It will help me to get what I want.'

'But what do you want?' asked Pascal urgently. 'What is it, Moss? What do you want?'

McSharry looked at him vaguely. 'It'll all be different. Everything will be different. . .'

'It already is,' said Pascal. 'I can't possibly publish this story.'

Part Four

I

Three days had passed quietly. An uneasy lull had fallen on the city. The latest political dead had been quietly buried, and their places taken on the mortuary slabs by victims of disease or accident.

Moss McSharry was about to launch a co-ordinated operation which would bring a good many extra customers to the city's undertaking trade. It would also, if it succeeded well, confirm his prestige as a sophisticated terrorist tactician.

He was nervous, as he always was before an operation. His pride was invested in success. He was standing, waiting—much of his work was waiting—in the squalid back yard of a ruined house somewhere near the Falls Road. A rat scuffled across a noisome pile of old paper and sodden sacking. McSharry saw it scuttle, and he cursed it under his breath. He looked round for a stone to throw at it, but could see none immediately handy; he'd already thrown them all.

Knuckles were kneaded into palms in a gesture of frustration. 'Get yourself off!'

In civilian life McSharry had been a draughtsman. He worked for a firm of aircraft designers in the east side of the city. He was the only Catholic in his department, and had never felt anything else but popular at work. There was no tradition of violent nationalism in his family, so even after the Emergency started Moss was content to do his job, mind his business, and get drunk every Saturday with Protestant and Catholic friends.

He'd been doing that on the night the Paras picked him up. He was walking towards the city centre along a tree-lined avenue near the university, regretting that the sudden appearance of somebody's wife had put an end to an otherwise promising party. He was counting his change, wondering if he could afford a packet of fags and a taxi.

There was a screech of brakes behind him, a shout, and a flurry of booted feet. Something struck McSharry a violent blow in the kidneys. He woke up twenty minutes later in a washroom, being pissed on. His head reeled, he could still remember the taste of the scalding piss.

He tried to get up, but couldn't. His vision was blurred, he had a blinding headache, and the soldiers above him were singing. He felt dream-like, absent. Reality broke in.

'Oh, me uncle Mick, he had a big stick
In the Battle of the Boiling Water.
He killed ten thousand Irish men
In less than an hour and a quarter.'

He was sure they had made a mistake. For a moment he thought he was dreaming. His nose was bleeding, and he was shackled with handcuffs to the pipes of a urinal.

'Hey. . .'

The blood and piss ran down his chin, soaked his shirt, and collected in his lap. The soldiers, big-chinned, big-handed, were bending down.

'Catholic. . .'

'Andytown address . . .'

'Provo . . .'

'No!' McSharry shouted. 'I done nothing! Let me go!'

There were four of them, one bullock-chested, huge.

'Oh, some lay here and some lay there,
And some lay in a corner,
And one poor soul with a carrot up his hole
Lay gasping there for water.'

110

'Sing, McSharry! You cursed us enough! Tell us about your friends . . .'

'Tell us everything. Everything you know.'

'Sing us "God Save the Queen",' roared the biggest soldier. 'Altogether now, "God Save Our Gracious Queen, God . . ." ' His voice trailed off. 'Why don't you sing, McSharry?' he asked plaintively.

A stinging blow across the face. Somebody stamped on his foot. McSharry screamed. They did it again. They kicked at his legs till he started to sing.

> 'Send her victorious, Happy and Glorious,
> Long to reign over us,
> God Save the Queen.'

'That was great, McSharry. That was reely good.'

'Fucking Frank Sinatra we got here.'

While this was going on, some other soldiers blundered into the washroom and saw him, half lying, half hanging from the row of urinals.

'Sorry, Sarge.' They started to retreat.

'Come here, you lot!'

They sauntered in, big bullish men, superb. 'Sarge?'

'What d'you want here? Why d'you come?'

'Piss, Sarge.'

'Well, piss, then! Don't mind him.'

There had been many of them, throughout that first night-mare of a night. A few didn't want any part of it. Humiliation. Shame. 'What, Sarge? There? In front of the prisoner?'

'Why did you come to a piss-house, you didn't want to piss? Frightened he might come down on you? Scared he might suck you off?'

'Naw, Sarge,' laughing. Sheepishly. 'Nothing like that.'

Since there was nothing they could do, they did nothing. Except piss. He could remember the flaccid cocks of a long procession of soldiers, peeing six inches from his face. Big and little, freckled and hairy, some circumcized, some black. Torrents of urine. Then, shake your willy, Johnny; important to keep dry. As soon as he could, the sergeant came and pissed on him again.

The 'interrogation' lasted forty-eight hours.

McSharry knew that such kidnappings were commonplace, especially in areas quartered by the Parachute Regiment. What happened was not simply gratuitous sadism, but was meant to impress any randomly selected Irish Catholic male with his insignificance, his utter powerlessness when confronted by the agents of the State. The fact that he might be completely innocent was immaterial, for he would carry the word back into his ghetto and his friends would hear it; and perhaps take heed.

He was routinely pumped for information. This was done in a more or less scientific manner. He was asked to explain his own attitude to politics, and to give details of the politics of others. He was required to outline the social relationships between families he knew, what people thought of them, what attitudes they had to others. He had no idea what some of the questions meant.

A clause of the Special Powers Act was mentioned at some stage during the process. He didn't pay much attention because it didn't really matter. The Act permitted the authorities to do, quite literally, anything they liked. Just now, they had made him disappear.

'Yer mam was on, McSharry,' one of them said.

'Brother.'

'Dad.'

'Said you weren't here. Said we'd never seen you.'

'Gave 'em a number to phone. Console 'em.'

'Ian Paisley's Dial-a-Prayer.'

'Belfast Prison.'

'The Ministry of Defence.'

'Number Ten Downing Street. Ask for Mr Wilson.'

Pause.

'Later this evening, McSharry, we'll take you out and shoot you.'

'Or shall we shoot him here?'

'We could always dump his body.'

'Easy to say that the Protestants done it.'

'Tell us about the rebels.'

'The Provos.'

'The IRA. You know them all, McSharry. No good sittin' there bluffing.'

The rat grew bolder, snuffling, wrinkling his nose. McSharry lunged forward and stamped his foot, hoping to frighten it off for good. The rat jumped, peered contemptuously over in his direction, and scratched his ear. It wasn't frightened. This was territory for rats, not men.

They were sharing the small back yard of an abandoned terraced house. The Special Constabulary had fired it, one August night in 1969. The whole little terrace had been gutted. Everyone was shocked at the time.

In those days there had been fewer than a dozen ancient guns to defend the Falls. The IRA had sold the rest to the Free Wales Army, according to the papers. The secret army was moribund then. A few elderly men who spun stories and sang rebel songs after closing time in bars.

All that had changed. Something terrible was born.

Impatiently, McSharry popped his head round the backyard door and looked quickly up the entry. An old, forgotten graffiti was fading into the dusty brickwork.

I.R.A.—I RAN AWAY.

Nobody was running any more.

Or everybody was.

It was not the interrogation itself which finally broke McSharry. The violence in him was buried deep and took a lot of mining. He had never hated anyone before, and he kept telling himself that this was all a mistake, that he'd wake up any minute now.

They made McSharry sign a printed receipt for the return of his personal effects. His watch was missing, but he was more than happy to sign. Then they handed him a handbill. 'Dear fellow-citizen,' he read, 'Our first responsibility is to find the few remaining terrorists and their weapons, and so continue the good progress we are making towards reducing violence within the community . . .'

McSharry darted at the rat, and it scampered, squeaking, into the coal house in the corner of the yard.

What broke him in the end was the branding.

'Give us your hand, McSharry.'

It was a little thing, nothing at all compared to the terror of the first few hours.

'Give us your hand!'

They stamped him with a rubber stamp, using indelible ink to make the impression on the backs and palms of both his hands. It would take a week or so to wear off, they said, perhaps not quite so long as that.

McSharry looked at the marks with loathing. He remembered feeling sick.

'We've got to be able to tell you apart,' the sergeant said. 'Haven't we, McSharry?'

The Loyalist assassination squads had a similar problem; identifying Micks.

McSharry bowed his head and suppressed his hatred. It was a novel sensation. It almost made him drunk. He passed no remark when they let him go. He made no complaint when they gave him back what they termed his freedom. He did not approach a lawyer, or try to see his MP. He avoided ministers of religion.

He bought a bottle of Scotch and drank the lot at a single sitting.

Then he went to see a fellow he knew.

The man was extremely sympathetic.

Was he able to shoot?

No, but he could think.

The man nodded. That was important as well.

All of which had brought him here today. To a ruined terrace whose charred ribs were naked to the sky, whose windows were well bricked up, whose door had been carefully kicked in.

He was thinking about murder, and the smell of desolation, and the superabundance of rats.

McSharry enjoyed being married to violence. She was a cruel lover, she ate her husbands. But while it lasted, she gave marvellous satisfaction. She could solve so many problems, soothe him for all his hurts, slay his enemies, make him feel like a man.

It is important to feel like a man.

Footsteps rang out in the alley. His accomplices were

coming. The sniper was called Whizz—Whizz O'Hanlon. He was a lover of motor-bikes, which was strange, because he was married and had three small children. Whizz was small and fastidiously neat. He came from the country. His face had been tanned by rain and weather, he had sharp brown eyes and a temper like a ferret's.

Whizz was a specialist, and did not often work in Belfast. There were three different wars going on at once in the various parts of the Province. Whizz had done most of his work in Derry, where there was a clear-cut, conventional insurgency. Along the Border there was an easily sustained rural guerrilla, and in Belfast the most modern war; an urban terror which convulsed the city.

McSharry wanted a fourth kind of war, to add to the other three.

He wanted to lead a major campaign in England.

The men at Brigade were suspicious of his motives. It was true that they had authorized a few isolated attacks, but this was done as a negotiating ploy and, within its limits, had worked. In return for calling the dogs back from London, certain important members of the Provisional leadership had been given a degree of immunity for their operations in Northern Ireland. That was enough for them. They were realistic. Every campaign that the IRA had attempted to mount in England had ended in disaster; but they were sure that they could not be beaten at home. Their aim was to make Northern Ireland too expensive, in terms of soldiers' lives and taxpayers' money, for the English to continue to rule. That this meant inflicting suffering on Irish people, they recognized. Suffering, they felt—as fascists will—would only purify the stock. Meanwhile, they kept control, and waited to win a political withdrawal.

McSharry, they knew, was not so cynical. He was an anarchist, more than anything else. He did not see the bigger picture. They debated this. McSharry, whatever he said, was not a political radical. His motives were too personal for that, his rebellion an assertion of himself rather than a calculating effort to free the mass of his people.

He frightened the men from Brigade. Something within him

115

had snapped—something they recognized—and he'd forgotten it was necessary to fight, but all the more necessary to live to enjoy the victory.

'His soul's shrivelled up,' said one.

'He's dangerous. We'll watch him.'

McSharry's shrivelled soul was happy in the company of men like Whizz, dangerous men who could accomplish the things he wanted. The sniper was dressed in a leather jacket and a pair of tight black trousers. He was bandy, and had to hurry to keep up with Branco Kane. Kane was a scout in the Fianna, a half-wild savage who'd grown up in the reek of tear gas and filled Molotov cocktails when he should have been chasing girls. Kane had been given the sniper's rifle as a mark of particular honour. The regular carrier, Dinnie Devlin, was already installed and waiting inside the terrace.

McSharry and the sniper shook hands. 'Did you get a sight of the sentry?'

'Aye. We had a dander past this morning.'

'What do you think?'

Whizz shrugged expressively. 'I don't know.'

'You'll hit him,' McSharry said. 'It shouldn't be a problem for a man like you.'

The sniper still said nothing, but took the rifle from Branco, who looked at McSharry expectantly.

'Get yourself off,' the terrorist said. 'Tell Michael he's here.'

O'Hanlon followed McSharry through the yard and up the dangerously ramshackle stairs. The strong smell of charred wood and ancient filth almost sickened him. He hated Belfast, and would never work here unless specifically ordered.

McSharry's volunteers had knocked holes in the terrace walls, so that all the bedrooms of adjoining houses were now connected. The gloomy passage ran the length of the block, behind bricked-up windows facing the main road. In two places only could light shine through. The roofs of two of the houses had fallen in and the interiors were open to the sky. In one place the bedroom floor was dangerous, and McSharry pointed to the causeway of planks which had been fastened to the strongest joists.

'Walk on the planks.'

'I like a thorough job,' the sniper said.

'Wait till you see,' said McSharry. 'Just wait till you see.'

He led O'Hanlon to the gable house, where Dinnie Devlin was waiting. Dinnie was sitting on a box near the bedroom wall. Whizz nodded to him. The carrier looked like any of the thousands of anonymous, hopeless men who lounged on street corners in the poorest quarters of Irish cities.

He was dressed in a cheap brown suit, with a scarf tucked loosely at the neck. He seemed a humorous man who knew that he was beaten before he'd even started. These were useful attributes, which hid him like a cloak. He had never been near to being captured. He might just as well have been invisible.

Dinnie reached out and took the weapon from the sniper. He studied it carefully to make sure that Branco Kane had not done any damage. He'd been vehemently against entrusting it to Branco. He produced three rounds of appropriate ammunition.

The Armalite AR 180 was a lightweight rifle with a folding stock, which made it ideally suited for irregular operations.

'They've got a lovely plan,' said Dinnie, while he loaded. 'A wheeker.'

McSharry pointed to the gable wall. 'As you saw, the sentry is two hundred yards away, down there.' There was a scarred but serviceable table in the room. McSharry manhandled it into the corner. 'Just watch this,' he said. Lithely, he climbed up. The roof was so low that he had to crouch.

McSharry pulled at a flap of wallpaper, stiff with dirt, which was peeling from the wall. Dust flew as he ripped it off. 'A car jack,' he said. 'You see?'

The jack had been installed in the upper course of brickwork. It was one of the squat, hydraulic kind. McSharry worked the mechanism. With a creak, the entire corner of the flimsy roof began rising slowly. 'Get up and have a look,' said McSharry, jumping down.

The movement of the roof ceased. It had been warped upwards by several inches. The damp, deteriorated lathes which supported the slates had bent, uncomplainingly, when thrust was applied to a load-bearing beam.

A narrow firing-platform had been opened, from which the

sandbagged observation post—sangar—could be clearly seen. From outside, McSharry said, shadow cast by a slight overhang would conceal the sniper, and the buckle in the roof merely made the little house seem more derelict than ever.

Both impressed and sceptical, Whizz gestured to Dinnie. 'Gimme the rifle.' Taking it, he mounted on the table and stared in the direction of the sangar. He peered through the telescopic sight. He frowned. He looked up, peering at the sky, then through the sight again. He shook his head.

'Sorry. Can't be did.' He climbed down off the table, and handed the weapon to Dinnie Devlin.

'Of course it can be done,' McSharry said.

'No.' O'Hanlon's voice was definite. 'The problem is the netting over the sentry's observation slits. It makes everything so dark. I'd have to fire from guesswork, see? I can't see him. Can't even see a shadow—no good, not worth the risk.' He looked directly at McSharry. 'You did all this work for nothing, comrade.'

'It's an easy shot,' said McSharry, grinning.

The sniper snatched the rifle from Devlin and thrust it at McSharry. 'Kill him, then. You couldn't even give him a headache.'

McSharry spat. It was a violent, vicious gesture. 'I said it was easy!'

O'Hanlon was startled by his tone. 'All right. But it isn't easy for me. I won't do it.'

'The net,' McSharry said, tapping the side of his head. 'Think about the net.'

'It's good,' said Dinnie. O'Hanlon glared at him.

'We've been practising for days,' said McSharry. 'Come on, get up.' They both climbed up on the table.

'We've got these two young girls, see? They'll be strolling down there in about fifteen minutes, right? One of them has a cold. She'll be using paper hankies.'

Whizz looked silently at the sangar. Then he turned to stare at McSharry. 'A marker,' he said. 'Fucking hell! A marker?'

McSharry nodded, flushed with pleasurable excitement. 'The sentries all know these girls,' he said. His breath smelled sharp. 'Movement is very restricted inside a sangar. So we've worked

118

it out. They chat him up, and while they're talking, one of the girls twines a hankie in the mesh of the net. It's directly under his head.'

'It's still a difficult shot,' the sniper objected.

'For you? No way.'

'Who will they be? These girls?'

'Republican Girl Guides. The Cummann na Cailini.'

Dinnie cackled. 'Guides is the word.'

O'Hanlon hesitated. 'I don't like using kids.'

McSharry jumped down from the table. 'The Brits shot one of their brothers. He was only buried last month. The other has a father in Long Kesh and an uncle in the Crumlin. Both of them know the score all right.'

'Heh! Heh!' wheezed Dinnie Devlin. 'Two wee Cailini! How can we lose, with the colleens of Ireland fighting on our side?'

It was O'Hanlon's turn to climb down. 'I suppose it's all right,' he said, grudgingly.

McSharry was watching him closely. He licked his lips. 'I want a good job done. I owe that regiment something. It was them that took my brother.'

O'Hanlon looked at him warily. 'You're a clever bastard, McSharry. Devious as hell.'

'That's right.'

'They got your brother, so this is your revenge?'

'Yes.'

'His brother had awful bad luck,' said Dinnie Devlin.

'If luck had anything to do with it.'

The sniper's attention was immediately caught. 'You've got informers in the company? Your brother was betrayed?'

'I'm pretty sure.' McSharry spat.

'Let's hope they don't pick us up too.'

'They won't. Nobody's seen you but me.'

'And that kid.'

'Branco's regular. He's all right.'

'You want to be careful,' said Dinnie. 'They get in everywhere these days. There's no one at all you can trust. No one at-all, at-all.'

'The safer they seem,' said Whizz, 'the less you should trust them.'

McSharry seemed to be studying the floor. 'Maybe,' he said. His voice was cold. 'Anyway, Liam is in hospital now. They took him out of the Kesh.'

'Did they now?' demanded Dinnie. 'What's wrong with him, Moss? Was he taken bad?'

A small vein in McSharry's temple began to throb. 'He got beaten up,' he said. 'The soldiers beat him. They broke a couple of bones.'

'The murderin' bastards!' Dinnie piped. 'Murderin', torturin' bastards!'

Whizz O'Hanlon reached out, and grasped McSharry's emaciated shoulder. 'I'll get you one for Liam,' he said.

The pulse in McSharry's temple had become a tic. His cheeks were suffused with blood. He clasped O'Hanlon's arm.

'You get me one,' he said, in a choking voice. 'Isn't it all for Ireland, Whizz? You get me one for her.'

McSharry turned on his heel and left the room. He picked his way over the bridge of planks and came to the top of the stairs. There were three battered old kitchen chairs there waiting. As he went down McSharry jammed them across the stairs as best he could. They were window dressing. When the soldiers came to this house, as he knew they would, they would expect to see some kind of obstruction on the stairs.

He would give them what they expected.

At the foot of the stairs he squatted down and began making ready something he hoped might come as a complete surprise: a booby trap. He lifted a plank and primed the ten-pound bomb beneath. He used infinite care with the trembler fuse, since mercury inside the fuse would close a circuit and detonate the bomb at the slightest movement.

He stood up carefully and went out into the yard. He looked at his watch.

It was a cheap watch, one of a batch of thirty which the Battalion Quartermaster had bought in the Republic. McSharry had begged the watch from him when he first joined the Provisional movement, because the soldiers had stolen his own.

'Don't you use these for priming bombs?' McSharry asked. 'You can spare one for priming me.'

The man had laughed.

'Don't laugh.'

The man stopped laughing.

McSharry waited. He peered towards the gable house at the end of the terrace. Eventually a head appeared at the bedroom window. It was Dinnie Devlin. He'd prised a hole in the bricks. They'd made their getaway through there.

McSharry hurried through the yard and into the filthy alleyway outside. The fresh air washed the stink of explosive from his nostrils. There was a dog with ragged ears, foraging for food in the narrow alley. It cringed against a wall as McSharry passed, slavering hopelessly, displaying teeth.

He turned the corner and walked to the head of the little street. Almost all of its windows had been boarded up, but a small community still haunted this rat-ridden slum. The main road was an artery feeding a cancer. There was a dingy betting shop. Three or four men were leaning against the window.

When McSharry appeared one of the men looked up. The man nodded, almost imperceptibly, in McSharry's direction. Then he straightened, stretched, and walked quickly away. McSharry struck his pocket, as though annoyed at forgetting something. He glanced at his watch, turned on his heel, and within seconds had disappeared.

The road was quiet. Bursts of traffic roared along it, unconsciously speeding up as though to escape the slums. At the end of every street there was a landscape. Divis Mountain, today brown-tweed, loomed pure and unattainable. The sentry in his sangar stared dully at the view through draughty strips of daylight. The observation post was damp, as it was always damp in every kind of weather. The soldier looked forward to being relieved. The change was due in another twenty minutes. He went over, in his head, a verse he'd written for the regimental magazine.

> 'Here I stand with poise and grace
> Staring over yonder space
> All I want from this rat race
> Is some poor sod who'll take my place.'

He yawned. The minute he got off he intended to flop on his

bunk and kip. He hoped the bastards in Able wouldn't make too much noise. He wondered if Major Yarnold would print his poem. They were always looking for verses for that crummy magazine.

He yawned.

Those two girls. They were small and undernourished and mousy-haired. One of them looked like his sister. They wore dark blazers and sad, creased skirts.

The soldier peered at their peaky faces. He had seen them before, in a hundred drab streets in the slums of Liverpool, while he was growing up and wondering what he'd do. What shall I do, Dad, go on the dole or join the Army? Neither of the girls was much to look at—neither, come to that, was his younger sister—but at least they were judies. The judies would give you a laugh. You never knew what the little beggars would say.

'Hiya, Maureen. Hiya, Pat. You still got the sniffles? Still? Yer ought ter eat more spuds.'

One of the girls glanced quickly over her shoulder. Her face leapt through the cross hairs, straight at Whizz. He sucked in his breath when he saw her face. Then she whipped round, and her unformed body strained as she stood on tiptoe to talk to a lonely soldier.

Whizz O'Hanlon watched her coldly. The telescopic sight pulled her small round head into the centre of his vision. He could see the slides she was wearing, small pink plastic butterflies resting on her hair. He saw her pull a paper handkerchief from her satchel, blow her nose. He saw her shoulders hunch, and she seemed very frail and vulnerable to the sniper.

The sangar was built square and solid against the outer barrack wall. A veil of camouflage netting hung in folds from the steeply pitching corrugated iron roof. The girl casually wove the tissue into the netting, chatting indifferently so as not to alarm the soldier. The marker hung in the net like small white fish. There was no sign that the sentry had noticed its significance, or that anyone else had either.

Whizz O'Hanlon watched and waited. The terrace room was utterly silent, except perhaps for the faintest murmur of Dinnie's breath. Outside it seemed that the city traffic was avoiding the road. The sniper lived for moments like this; he loved to stretch them out, patiently, a creative god pretending creation could last for ever.

Until he pulled the trigger, the sentry had his permission to live.

The girls' pink calves vanished slowly into the distance. The sangar was left alone, with nothing but the flapping piece of paper to show that they had ever been near.

A pigeon fluttered from an unseen roof and settled on the barrack wall. He was composed for a minute, then looked mistrustfully towards Whizz.

O'Hanlon thought briefly of the pale, adolescent face he had seen a short time earlier, peering from the shadows. He wondered if the sentry-go had changed. The soldier he had seen was not much more than a boy. Whizz tried to guess his age. Probably not nineteen. The sniper pushed the mental image of a boy—himself—deep down into a dark subconscious. That boy, perhaps, had been quite different. That boy was Irish, had chosen a recruiting office resentfully, had no alternative but to sign on for the dole.

But this boy—he was hardly a boy at all. He was a target. He represented something, an alien State which oppressed the people. Whizz wouldn't kill him for himself. He didn't feel any personal grudge. He was only going to kill a target, to try to forget that it had acne, looked tired, and at some time or other —probably some forgotten public-house brawl—had suffered a broken nose.

He breathed deeply and regularly, as the finest shots in the British Army had carefully instructed him to do. He nestled his cheek comfortably into the hollow of the stock. The thick collar at the end of the Armalite's barrel moved slowly upwards as the sniper sighted, a first time, then a second, finally a third. Dinnie Devlin patiently watched these meticulous, steady arcs. Dinnie had been given his nickname from his favourite exclamation. 'Din' he do it well? Din' he do it well, thon fella?'

He sat on his box, sucking a hollow tooth, quite silent.

The sniper was taking aim. The sentry was thinking of Irish judies. He had never made love to a girl.

Dinnie was wondering, if he was caught, what on earth he was going to say. Would they beat him up? Hmmh. Din' he do it well, though? O'Hanlon was always good.

Resigned to his future, Dinnie watched and waited.

The explosion from the rooftop and the echoing smash of a bullet striking bone made a single sound. Still holding back the trigger, Whizz O'Hanlon closed his eyes and drew his breath.

'I got the bastard,' he breathed.

'Come on!' said Dinnie, lunging forward to pull his sleeve. 'The gun! Gimme the gun! Come on! Move!'

The CO's driver, who happened to be in the barracks yard as the shot rang out, raced at once to the door which gave access to the sangar. He opened it, and shouted out in anguish. The huddled sentry twitched spasmodically, clutching at his throat. O'Hanlon's bullet had shattered his jaw. It had pierced his windpipe, passed along his collar-bone, and torn tumbling, deep into his lung.

The CO's driver fell on his knees and shouted.

The military machine behind him was set for retaliation. A platoon of soldiers, kept at alert, crashed into transport. Others were told to stand by. With a ringing whine, the six-wheeled Saracen armoured carriers accelerated through the opening barrack gate. Their wheels flickered briefly as they crossed the ramps. The radio net was filled with an urgent chatter.

The road outside was quite unchanged. The slums still festered. The mountain wept above them. The wintry sunlight reflected weakly on a million shards of glass that were strewn across the brickfields.

The machine began looking for its enemy. But its enemy was everywhere. It was nowhere to be seen.

The city itself ignored the outburst. It had been going about its business when the distant crack of the rifle carried plainly through the air. A curious American, over on a visit, looked anxiously at her cousin.

'Was that a backfire?'

The Irishwoman said no.

The city could afford to be incurious, for it was used to shootings. Its people could flinch, perhaps, and continue with

124

their shopping. The truth, the multiple truth, would come racing in under the form of rumour. If the shot had been important, they would know in minutes.

Out in the slums the blunt-nosed, brutal, paint-smeared Saracen cars had invaded the ghetto. A woman who failed to get out of the way was run over. Hostile crowds appeared as quickly as a sudden fog on a windless night. Whistles were blown. Bin-lids clattered. Pavements were broken up. Traffic jams were constructed round the area.

The ritual confrontation developed. A flare was fired into the back of an Army lorry, causing second-degree burns to a Corporal Atkinson, of Summer Grove, Gateshead. An officer ordered rubber bullets to be fired to disperse the crowds. They were, point-blank, into bellies and groins and faces.

There were jeers and groans. The soldiers baton-charged a mob. Somebody fired a hand-gun, missed, and vanished round a corner. An old lady of seventy-two attacked a sergeant, swinging a five-pound sack of potatoes. Teenage girls spat in the soldiers' faces. Housewives screamed. An Alsatian dog was shot.

'They're trying to split you up!' an officer shouted. 'Don't let them jostle you! It's the oldest trick in the book! Don't let yourselves be divided!' The riot screamed defiance in the soldiers' faces. Within minutes it was widespread throughout the district.

A squad of troopers ran helter-skelter down a narrow alley which had slogans painted on its walls. The ragged-eared cur McSharry had seen earlier was still conducting a hopeless forage. When it heard the soldiers it spun round, its teeth bared in a terrified snarl, and crouched against a doorway.

The leader of the section, a Welshman from Prestatyn, burst eagerly into a filthy little yard.

'The bastards were in here!' he cried, plunging forward.

He wondered, later, what instinct warned him to pull up. He barely managed it. His boots slithered in the refuse, and he slid, falling forward, grabbing a doorpost to stop himself falling on the stairs.

McSharry had booby-trapped the stairs.

'There's a bomb!' gasped the burly sergeant. His number

two cannoned into him. The Welshman spun round. The yard was filling up with panting soldiers.

'Cover both ends of this terrace!' the sergeant shouted.

He turned to his number two. 'I'm not going in there.' The corporal looked stupidly at him. 'Go on, fuck you, Jones,' cried the sergeant. 'Radio to base. There's a booby trap in there.'

'You reckon, sergeant?' asked the number two, peering doubtfully round the door.

'Fuck you,' cried the Welshman wildly. 'Can't you smell it? What are you playing—pass the parcel? I'm telling you. I can smell a bomb.'

'Very good, Sarge,' said the other, sniffing. 'No need to take that sort of tone with me.'

There was a long, straight street. The lintels and window sills were bright with the summer's paint. All the little door-steps of the little kitchen houses had been carefully, lovingly whitened.

A different section of soldiers were running along this street, clutching their rifles, looking anxiously from side to side.

'You fucks, you British bastards, you English cunts!' screamed the women who lived in the houses. 'We'll send youse home in boxes, you dirty British fucks!' Somebody was swinging a football rattle, deliberately making a din. From the small back yards came the battering of bin-lids. A girl appeared, a beautiful girl, the soldiers noticed, and the air was split with the shriek of a gas-powered throwaway siren.

And then suddenly the siren stopped and the street became silent again. It emptied of life in the space of a minute. The only thing moving was the patrol of soldiers and a shabby ginger cat. And then the cat left too.

There were five soldiers on one side of the street, two on the other. The street vanished, forwards, backwards, into an empty perspective. An eighth soldier performed a clumsy ballet down the emptiness in the middle of the street. He drifted sideways and joined his crouching companions where they sheltered against the walls.

The sounds of rioting reached them clearly from neighbouring streets. Advancing slowly, the soldiers clung to the walls.

126

They shrank in the slender shelter of hostile doors, not knowing when one of the doors would open, not knowing what would happen, what would suddenly appear.

The soldiers dodged, pirouetting at irregular intervals, swapping places swiftly, from one side to the other of the street. They were completely silent.

The slogans bellowed hatred from the harmless little walls.

LET'S KILL A SOLDIER FOR LENT

Suddenly, a nail-bomb sailed gracefully over a roof. Fatalistic, they knew what it was before it landed. A second, fizzing; they flinched. It had come. It was happening, *now*.

The bombs blew up, almost simultaneously, with a shattering, breathtaking blast. One of the soldiers screamed in the awful silence. 'My leg!' he screamed. 'They got my leg!' For the instant, none of his comrades dared to help him.

Glass from the broken windows tinkled inwards. A blue-grey pall of smoke hung like a drifting veil in the middle of the street. A man with a Thompson sub-machine-gun stepped around a corner. The soldiers instantly dived flat.

He was a tall man, with a scarred face, wearing a black blazer and a black beret. He commenced to fire at once. There was nothing the foot-patrol could do but lunge for shelter. The flames from his gun were accusations, the explosions like hammer-blows.

Bullets from the Thompson mashed into brickwork and sparkled when they hit the pavement. A soldier moaned when one of them broke his arm. The others, clinging for shelter to the insufficient street, tried to bring weapons to bear on the scar-faced man.

Though the gunman fought it, his Thompson inexorably climbed. A line of slugs stitched their way through a series of bedroom windows. Then, as quickly as he'd come, the gunman stepped back around his corner. For an instant, the soldiers found themselves alone.

They were artillerymen, used to handling guided missiles. They had casualties. It was hard to cope with their situation.

'Who's hurt?' the section leader shouted. Till he knew, no question of hot pursuit. In any event, it was almost certainly

127

already too late. 'Close in to me! Cover your heads! Watch those rooftops!'

They leapt up. The whistles and the bin-lids and the rattles were resuming. Poorly dressed women, their faces distorted by passion, appeared at the doors and began to scream abuse.

The gunner lying prone had a six-inch nail protruding from his thigh. It had been blown, flat head first, through the muscle of the lower buttock and was rasping on the bone. It was impossible to pull it out. The man screamed when one of the section tried to. The head of the nail was snagged on the muscle inside. The section leader ripped open the blood-soaked trouser-leg, trying to remember if a tourniquet was called for. The man whose arm was broken was watching, clutching it, ashen.

The gang of skinheads came charging and skipping from the end of the little street. They put the patrol under siege. A hail of missiles came raining down. The soldier with the wounded arm reeled sideways, gashed on the head by a broken bottle. One of his comrades—a nine-year man from Coventry —lost his head and charged blindly at the tormentors.

They whooped, falling back, opening ranks. Then they felled him with a jagged lump of concrete which struck him on his knee. They closed in, hurling new missiles, preparing to lacerate the man with sticks.

BANG!

And the collective shriek was suddenly a grunt. One of the ringleaders—a frail, cadaverous skinhead of about fifteen— was picked up bodily by the bullet and hurled against a lamp-post.

There was an overwhelming silence.

Everybody looked at the youth uncertainly. His face wore an expression of extreme amazement. One of his trouser-legs —the jeans had been bleached and frayed—was rucked, almost to the level of his knee.

The youth carefully leaned forward and attempted to push it straight. The effort was too much. He died.

The parched blue jeans quite suddenly collapsed. They sagged. The boy rolled forward, like an awkward marionette, and landed on his chin in the gutter.

128

The nine-year man began frantically to jack-knife back.

A huge red stain was spreading on the skinhead's jacket.

The nine-year man got up and ran, crouching, back to the circle of his comrades. They shouted threats to the undecided skinheads, a couple of whom were bending over the body.

A loud ululating keening began to sound. The women on their doorsteps howled and sobbed. A soldier spoke urgently to the hand-set of his radio. There was a curious calm, a stillness.

When the Saracen came to relieve the patrol, the skinheads picked up the dead boy's body, shook their fists at the grinning soldiers for a final time, and ran.

II

While McSharry was organizing murder on the Falls Pascal was trying to catch up on his expenses. He had fallen several weeks behind. He had to leaf through back numbers of the papers in order to remind himself of what he'd been doing on any particular day. He gave Clare, the secretary, a couple of blank restaurant receipts to fill in.

'How much?'

'Six quid for the Steak House,' said Pascal. 'About a tenner for the one from the Culloden. And use different pens.'

He went back to the files. He had a bill for some pot-plants in his wallet. He turned up the appropriate edition.

Louie Golden had been very persuasive as he outlined the story. 'They've got this machine-gun nest, Pascal, and they're growing geraniums out of the sandbags.'

'Oh, yes?' said Pascal, politely.

The News Editor chuckled. 'Not so's they'd interfere in an emergency, you understand. But enough to remind the lads of home.'

'Home?' asked Pascal.

'What we want to project,' the News Editor had said, 'is the impression that the lads can still live a normal life over there. What could be more normal than home?'

'What's normal about a machine-gun nest in a shopping precinct, Lou?'

At the other end of the line the News Editor tutted impatiently. 'I know it's not *normal*,' he said. 'Nothing's normal in that mad land of yours. But we want to show the British Army's efforts to *make* it normal, or at least bearable, for twenty thousand front-line troops. It's a question of morale back home. Growing a little garden in a gun emplacement is good for their families' morale. You get me?'

'Yes, Lou. I suppose it's a good idea.'

'I mean, the gun is never actually *used*,' the News Editor said. 'Or not very often. They put it there for show. It's sort of a deterrent. Busy crossroads, all them kids attacking one another—'

'To cover the lollypop patrol.'

'That's right! What a way to live, eh, Pascal? You see what I mean?'

'I know. What do you want me to say?'

'About them bloody kids? Nothing you can say, son. It's all been said. Young savages. Just get me a good strong story and a bloody good picture with lots of geraniums. What we want is the soldier who grew the geraniums, leaning out of his nest to kiss this girl—'

'What girl?' interrupted Pascal.

'There's got to be a girl!' said Lou. 'That's the whole point of the picture! Hire a model. Explain it to the photographer. The Picture Desk will have already told him, but you know how they fuck things up.'

'It's all that changing lenses,' said Pascal.

'Yeah. Drives them off their heads. Anyway, we want some tits. Get the one with the biggest tits you can find.' He chuckled. 'You can measure them yourself! We want plenty of geraniums. If there aren't enough, tell them to buy some more and send us in the chit. And we want the soldier. Try to get a soldier who doesn't squeeze his pimples. They've all got bloody acne over there.'

'You said you talked to the Army already? They've cleared all this?'

'Talked?' said Louie Golden. 'They suggested it!'

130

'Oh,' said Pascal.

'Yeah. We had a Battalion PR man round to see us last week. He was one of Major McDowell's friends. You know McDowell?'

'Yes.'

'Ah, you'd be surprised, young man. I'm getting to know more of the lads from Army PR than you do yourself. They're always popping in. They let me know what you've been up to.' A pause. 'It's a propaganda battle, Pascal. We've got to support the lads out in the field.' Another pause. 'We're not called the Paper With the Great Big Heart for nothing.'

Pascal shuddered, trying to shut out the vision of everything that had happened that day. Every day since, he had had to pass the place where the car-bomb had exploded and see the stains, and the dinge in the tarmac, and the gouges torn in the office façades by shrapnel.

There was a girl, a guy and a garden of geraniums.

'Bally Communists, you know,' said the keen young officer. 'Well, we've got them on the run. They're nearly beaten.'

Then they had heard the explosion, like distant thunder. The officer very decently let them listen on the net.

'It sounds like a big one,' he said, regretfully. 'I suppose that you'd better go.'

'I'll just snap a few little quickies first,' said Pascal's companion, the photographer. He was a frugal man. He hated wasting petrol.

They were held up in the traffic coming back.

'News is cats' whiskers. A device for measuring gaps.'

Appearance and reality: appearance, a gun emplacement artfully planted with geraniums by a clever PR who knew a major in Information Policy. Reality is altogether different. A ribbon of intestines swinging from the phone lines. An ambulanceman standing on a borrowed kitchen chair, trying to fish them down with the end of a borrowed brush. Reality is ambiguous and full of lies, uncertainties and double meanings. The bombers issue a statement. 'Our warning was ignored. This was done to discredit the Movement.'

Reality is not daring to believe them.

Pascal always crossed the road before he got to the little

dinge. Seeing it made him shiver. He could still remember the smell.

There were screams of pain and a woman was crying, pointing up at a roof. The crows were fighting for scraps of a shattered arm, bits of tattered clothing still hanging from it.

There were eight dead bodies in the street, another dead on his way to hospital, fifty injured, a dozen amputated limbs.

The photographer. 'Story? Ireland? See Ireland? Ireland's fucking finished. Ireland's a lunatic asylum. Nobody gives a fuck what happens to us here.' The photographer was English.

Nevertheless, he was wrong. At least they published his pictures. Bomb-shock horror. CITY BLAST KILLS NINE. And the footnote: More Ulster News—Page Three.

THE BIRD IN TOMMY ATKINS' GARDEN.

'Lou, why did you do it?'

'Do what?'

'Put that—that obscenity in the paper?'

'What are you talking about?'

'Page Three.'

'We want plenty more stories like that, young lad. You mustn't forget there's a war on.'

Horror.

'I'll tell you this,' said Louie Golden. 'If we pulled out now, there'd be civil war.'

What could you say to that?

Right now, they were living through a lull. Nothing had happened for days. 'We want to project some *happiness*, Pascal.'

'Yes, Lou, sure.'

'You've got carte blanche,' said the magnanimous Lou. 'Go anywhere you like. Get out of that crazy city. And stay away from Derry as well! We want happy stories, Pascal. You know, lad, it costs a helluva lot to run an operation like the one you've got in Ulster.'

'Yes, it's very expensive.'

'There's a recession coming. All the advertising's down. There'll be redundancies. We'll have to fight to keep our *jobs*, Pascal. No more shaking the golden money tree for us. None

132

of the papers will make profits this year, none.' One of the Golden pauses. You weren't supposed to interrupt. 'We want a *drive* in Ulster. We need *circulation*. For that we want *happy stories*, Pascal. We've got to project a little bit of *life*.'

'There is no happiness, Lou. At least, not in Ulster.'

'Nonsense! I don't believe it. Find somebody *normal*. You get good expenses. Whack 'em in. Get out there in the sticks. Find me some funny Paddies, Pascal. The Editor expects it. We've had a talk. I know he's relying on you.'

There was a man in the mountains somewhere who panned for gold. After ten years' searching he had enough gold for a cap on two of his teeth.

THE MAN WITH THE GOLDEN SMILE (Weekend Murders in Ulster—Page 16).

The lulls were the loneliest times, when the television screens went dark and there were seven hours between you and morning. There was nothing to do but wait. All over the city the small platoons were active. Guns were being smuggled past checkpoints. Bombs were patiently manufactured. The police were on edge. The young Tommies were frightened. The partisans were starving themselves, on hunger strikes, in jails.

The only thing lulls were good for was doing expenses. And even then you had to go back over past events that you'd rather forget. The more dead there were in a week, the more stuff you got in the paper; and the more you could charge on expenses.

'Clare,' said Pascal. 'I'm going out for a drink.'

'Where will you be if they want you?'

'Sammy's. Sammy Slevin's.'

Sammy's was near the car-park. When Pascal got there Christopher Strickland was already installed at the bar.

'I've just ordered soup,' he said. 'You fancy some?'

'Yes,' said Pascal. Sammy's was famous for soup. 'Cream of tomato,' he ordered. 'And a Jameson.'

The whiskey came first.

'I hate these bloody lulls,' said Pascal.

'What lulls?' Strickland said. 'The lull's over. They've started again. That bomb this morning.'

'What bomb this morning?'

Strickland wagged his finger. 'You haven't been doing your calls.'

'I went shopping,' Pascal admitted. 'I wanted to buy some toys for my little boy. It's his birthday soon.'

'How are the kids?'

'Fine,' said Pascal. 'Helen is cutting a tooth.'

'The Green Jackets shot a Prod,' said Strickland. 'It was late last night—early this morning, really—the bastard was carrying a bomb.'

'Ah.' Pascal knew about that. He had been to the dead man's house. The man's brother had a farm near Lurgan. He'd visited town, and they'd both got drunk. The 'bomb' was a present, a goose wrapped up in a sack. They hadn't heard when the Army had called them to halt.

'There's bound to be trouble,' said Strickland. 'The Prods won't like it at all.'

The mirrors at Slevin's, and the bar's location in a narrow side-street, made the midday light seem eccentric and unnatural. They rendered the daylight somehow disgraceful, a usurper who had taken the place of night, which was when Slevin's came into its own. At night, even empty, the bar could be warm and cheerful. During the day its scars were obvious; the cigarette burns on the bar, the threadbare carpet, the initials carved on the surfaces of tables.

Pascal hiccuped. 'I needed this soup.'

'It's a day that was out all night,' said Sammy Slevin.

Sammy was a small, round man. He looked like a mole, or a solicitor. What drew his clients was his lunchtime soup and his cellarful of whiskey. Sammy's soup was the warmest thing in the city that wasn't bottled. He also had stocks of rare old Irish whiskey from defunct distilleries; poets, artists and journalists fed on these twin ambrosias. Sammy watched their posturings with fey, understanding eyes. He never extended credit.

He was a natural conservative, a Catholic who voted for the Unionist ticket, but seemed to like the company of boastful and blasphemous men. They knew it all; they might let him into the secret.

'Give us that roll,' said Strickland, snatching the roll from

134

Pascal's fingers. 'You haven't touched it.' He broke the bread, and mixed it with his tomato soup. 'Did you hear the one about the Irish kidnapper?'

'I'm going to,' said Pascal.

'Kidnapped this little Belfast lad, you see,' said Strickland. 'Sent him home with a ransom note for his mother.' Pascal laughed. Strickland stared, offended. 'The mother sent him back with the money.'

Ha ha ha.

Strickland used to be Pascal's friend. When the troubles started, he was working in a tourist office, selling holidays in Ireland to foreigners. He was sacked for drunkenness, and drifted into journalism. His natural ebullience was coupled with a love of intrigue, and exactly suited the times. Pascal helped to support him as a struggling freelance, and when he got a job on a Dublin paper the relationship continued. They swapped stories and tittle-tattle. Chris was sacked for offending the Cardinal, went back to freelancing, and finally ended up on the *British Tribune*, a sensational broadsheet in the quality end of the market.

'We had a malicious phone call to the office the other day,' said Pascal.

'Yeah?'

'They said: "This is a bomb hoax",' said Pascal.

'D'you hear that, Sammy?' guffawed Strickland excitedly. 'D'you get it? "This is a bomb hoax." This is a—fucking **bomb HOAX.**'

The publican blinked at them both from behind the barricade of his gold-rimmed spectacles.

'I like a joke,' said Strickland. 'But fuck a pantomime.' He pushed his soup-bowl across the counter. 'Why are Irish jokes all stupid?'

'So the English can understand them,' said Sammy, blinking.

Pascal laughed. 'Give us some whiskey, Sammy?'

'Irish, Mr Canning?' asked Sammy complacently. Pascal nodded. He finished the soup he had left. Sammy put the drinks on the bar and extracted payment.

Pascal and Strickland were rivals now. They both chased the same kind of stories, but Strickland had rather more licence since his readership was 'quality'. The edge made him condescending.

'Here's villainy.' Strickland toasted. He smacked his lips. 'What are you doing, these days? You got very much?'

'Not much,' said Pascal.

'Maybe the Prods'll go mad this evening. I can do an analysis, or something.'

'You never know,' said Pascal.

'Nobody wants to know,' said Strickland, gloomily. 'Can't get anything in.' He examined his finger-nails glumly, then started to pick them. 'There used to be a time when they couldn't get enough.'

'The papers are bored with Ulster.'

Strickland looked morosely at Pascal. 'The peace is worse than the war, luv,' he said, comically. 'At least when they're killing each other we can justify our salaries.'

'There'll be killing enough done soon,' said Sammy Slevin complacently. He was polishing tumblers. He glanced at them wryly, his spectacles catching the light. 'Another couple of days, they'll be killing their own mothers. Just you see.'

'I don't know why you should be cheerful,' said Pascal irritably. 'They could bomb this bar as easily as anywhere else.'

Strickland rubbed his thumb with his first two fingers. 'Sammy Slevin's? Sammy keeps his nose clean, don't you, Sammy?'

The publican smiled enigmatically. 'We've been lucky so far.'

'What is it?' Strickland demanded. 'Fifty a week? A hundred?' He shook his head. 'No. It's more than that.' He laughed. 'You canny fucker.'

'What's more than what?' asked Sammy, dangerously.

'The protection money,' insisted Strickland, grinning. 'Do you pay both sides?'

Sammy, after a moment's thought, continued polishing. 'You've an awful big mouth, Mr Strickland.'

'I'm not afraid to ask questions.'

'Don't you mind?' asked Pascal eventually. 'You know, having to pay to these men?'

Sammy looked at him. 'Bulls eat grass, Mr Canning. A lion,

136

now, a lion is partial to meat. I pay my taxes. I'm a trades-man. I mind my business.'

'You're mad, luv,' Strickland said.

Sammy polished. 'I don't think so.'

'All the Irish are mad,' said Strickland.

The door opened, squeaking on the coloured tiled floor. Sammy shrugged, and moved up the bar to serve the new-comer. It was a burly labourer in a navy-blue donkey jacket. He wanted some soup.

'You know what they said about the corpse,' said Strickland. 'Sensible to the last, and he died raving.' He dug in his pocket for cigarettes.

'Smoke?'

'I gave them up,' said Pascal.

'They are mad,' Strickland said.

'What can they do but pay?'

'Turn the bastards in,' said Strickland fiercely. 'I'm sick of it. I'm bored.' He thought about this for a minute. 'What have you got, Pascal? I need ideas. At the moment I've sweet fuck all.'

'What about the mortars?' Pascal said. 'If you worked it up a bit, you could probably make it a story.'

'Sod technology. Who the hell cares any more?'

'Go and see McDowell.'

'McDowell's a load of shit. I wouldn't believe him if he said good morning.'

'There aren't any stories here,' said Pascal helplessly. 'All that there is, is the war.'

Strickland glanced at him. 'You shouldn't have joined if you can't take a joke,' he sneered. Repenting that, he gave a playful punch to Pascal's shoulder. 'You shouldn't take it seriously, luv.'

'Sure.'

'First principle. Got to remain detached.'

'Too many detachments in Ulster.'

Christopher Strickland yawned and shrugged. 'I've stopped worrying. What's the difference? We'll all be dead in a hun-dred years.' A grin split his plump, ironic features. 'Come on, then, Pascal! What the hell does it matter?'

'Whether we die of natural causes.' Pascal drained his glass and set it down on the counter. 'Tell you the truth, Chris, I—'

He never finished his sentence. There was a loud BOOM! outside, and both men flinched. The windows rattled fiercely. They ducked. One of the panes had cracked, but it didn't break.

They lifted their heads, stared at the window, then looked at each other.

'That was a bang,' said Pascal.

'Back to the war!' the publican shouted, from the other end of the bar.

'Fuck the bloody war!' said Strickland. 'I'm not in any condition to handle a war. I need another drink. Give us an Irish, Sammy.'

Pascal and Strickland looked cautiously at one another. 'I wonder was there a warning?' Pascal said.

Strickland bolted down what was left of his drink. 'C'mon Sammy, two more Jameson here.' He shook his head, making a shivering sound with his fleshy lips. 'They could have waited till after lunch.'

'It would have been dark by then,' said Sammy Slevin dryly.

Pascal took the fresh glass of whiskey and sipped it reflectively. Sammy, watching them both, began polishing tumblers with a spotless linen cloth.

'We'd better take a look, I suppose,' said Pascal.

Strickland wrinkled his nose. 'Fuck it, it's only a bomb. We can get it from the Army.'

'I think we ought to go,' said Pascal.

'For a paragraph or two? Sod that.'

'All right,' said Pascal. The whiskey burned in his throat. 'I'll see you later.'

'You're bomb-bloody-happy,' Strickland shouted after him. 'Like a fucking vampire. Bloody unhealthy, it is.'

138

III

Pascal walked out. The rawness of the day was tempered by the golden light of early winter. As he reached the main road a fire-engine shrieked past him, then another. Traffic was backing up. He followed the sound of the sirens.

He didn't hurry. As Strickland had said, an explosion was merely routine. A coil of thick black smoke was rising over Smithfield. Pascal walked idly, letting the cold air ventilate the whiskey he'd just drunk, wondering—recognized indifference—if anyone had just been killed.

Smithfield was Belfast's flea-market. The most prosperous businesses were pawnshops and discothèques. The second-hand stalls were mostly Catholic-owned. The roadway leading into it was littered with dead canaries. They looked like dirty lollipops, abandoned among the glass. Smoke was pouring from a ruined pet shop, but the firemen had already put out the fire and had only to damp down the embers. Pascal picked his way to a small red car. His foot caught on something soft; a headless Alsatian puppy.

'What happened?' He showed his Press card.

'Couple of lads on a motorbike,' said the fire officer. 'Bomb in a shopping bag. Two pounds, only a small one. Everything under control.'

'Hell of a mess,' said Pascal.

The fire officer said, 'Look over there.'

A fireman was adding to a pile of cages on the sidewalk. The birds inside were cheeping piteously.

'All either blind or deaf,' said the man in the bright white helmet.

Pascal walked on. He saw a parrot lying dead in the window display of a shop selling radios and televisions. Glass from the shattered window had blown through the shop like shrapnel, ripping partitions, breaking television tubes, scarring expensive hi-fis.

Smoke had almost stopped coming from the pet-shop. A

139

fat black rabbit lolloped helplessly through the charred doorway, obviously blind. A child who had been standing with a
crowd of urchins saw the rabbit emerge, and swooped after it.
He caught it easily, and ran off, shouting exultantly. A fireman
started to give chase, but he soon came back.

'Wee fucker.' He glared at Pascal angrily. 'Taken it home
for his tea.'

By some freak of the explosion, the façade of the hairdress-
ing saloon next door to the pet-shop had collapsed outwards. It
lay almost entire in the roadway. The buildings here were extremely old, and the frontage of this one was wooden. The
shop was undamaged inside, and reminded Pascal of an open-
fronted model from a child's toy village.

The barber, a middle-aged man in a white coat, was enticing
back one of his customers, who had evidently been having a
shampoo. There was great play-acting in this. The dishevelled
client was obviously shocked, and wanted nothing better than
to get back home. He shuffled reluctantly forward, dragging
his feet among the glass, stepping gingerly round the jagged
nails on the ripped-out boards.

Pascal couldn't hear what was said, but the barber was a
mime of enormous talent. His facial contortions expressed
sympathy, resignation, and, more than anything else, righteous
horror at the thought that his friend should go home with
bubbles in his hair. He eventually steered the man back to his
padded chair, and talking volubly, began the work of com-
pleting his rinse.

Pascal felt a surge of affection for this city of valiant bar-
bers. How could these people be beaten? The street re-echoed
with the sound of their running repairs. Glaziers and carpen-
ters were kept on permanent stand-by to cope with incidents
like this. A loud hammering, and the cracked carillon of
broken glass being swept into piles in the gutters; they seemed
to Pascal like an affirmation of life.

He turned back to the pet-shop. A television crew had
established itself by the pile of cages, so Pascal idly walked
over.

'Hello, Reg,' said Pascal.

Reg was the sound engineer, an enormous man in his middle

fifties with a thin silver-grey moustache. When he saw Pascal he beamed with pleasure.

'Hiya, Pascal. Bloody good story, eh?'

'Yes,' said Pascal, grinning. 'How are you doin', Reg?'

'You arsked me that 'alf an hour ago,' said Reg, confidentially, 'I'd have said we was goin' to shoot ourselves. Boy, were we up a gum tree! But this saved our bacon, this did! Doin' fine, fine. How are you doin' yourself?'

'I'm fine, too,' said Pascal. 'What was the trouble?'

'Trouble?' said Reg. 'Trouble? 'Aven't you heard? Trouble? The Falls is goin' bananas, mate. First, they shot a soldier. Then our lot run over an old lady. Then there was a fuckin' riot, the fuckin' shots started flying, there's soldier's lyin' round all over the landscape shot, some kid's bin killed what was a livin' saint, Pascal, a *livin'* saint up in his own area, you ask me what was the trouble?'

'Jesus,' said Pascal. 'When?'

'An hour ago, when *you* was havin' a drink, I'll betcha.' Reg winked at Pascal. 'Matter o' fact, so were we. Jack over there's three-quarters pissed. We wasn't expectin' nothin', see? Then, fumph! Fuckin' Editor screamin' for film—'s 'appenin' all over, Pascal, not just here in Belfast—sent a team up the Falls, gets cut off in the fuckin' riot, cameraman injured, all of 'em trapped in the barricks—no film. Not an inch o' film. We got two teams on the road, on specials. Everythin' up to us.' He looked gratefully over his shoulder. 'Fuckin' miracle, this was.' He laughed, banging Pascal's chest with a massive paw. 'Fuckin' miracle, Pascal!'

'It's very . . . um . . . telegenic,' Pascal said, trying to control his amusement.

'See Jack, there? Jack!' Reg bellowed to the reporter, who had just finished talking to a policeman. 'Pissed?' he whispered to Pascal. 'He had five whiskies what I know of, an' Wally says he had gin.' Then his face grew grave. 'But a true professional, Pascal. He's pulled us out o' the fire. They din' want to send us. Said this was a crummy story.'

Jack Graham, the television reporter, stepped fastidiously across a flapping goldfish in the gutter. He was followed by his cameraman, Wally.

'Oh, hello, Pascal,' he said.

He was a small, well-tailored man, who reminded Pascal irresistibly of a parson defrocked for his attentions to choir-boys. He was, he would often say, 'in his middle thirsties'. When Pascal saw him he was wearing a mohair suit, blue shirt and a tie with a large Windsor knot. He was carrying, rather disdainfully, the body of a pigeon.

'Hello, Jack,' said Pascal. He nodded at the pigeon. 'You been studying local colour?'

Graham looked at the pigeon as if for a moment he'd forgotten it was there. 'Oh, this?' He smiled serenely at Pascal. 'Poor thing—it had a broken wing. Imagine those nasty bombers. I found it flapping about in the street. I thought it was kinder to wring its neck.' He looked anxiously at Pascal. 'Don't you agree it was kinder?'

'Yes,' said Pascal. He nodded to Wally. 'Nice to see you, but I'll have to go. I better get up the Falls and see what's happening.'

'Terrible, dear boy. Terrible.' Jack swayed slightly, but made a quick recovery. 'Perhaps we'll see you at the pub quite soon,' he said. 'You must call in, one of these days.'

'I'd love to,' Pascal said. 'If you want any more livestock, by the way, there's a splendid parrot in the window over there.'

'Deadstock, dear boy,' said Jack. He smiled weakly up at Pascal. 'Any more deadstock would be a bit *de trop*.'

Pascal hurried back from Smithfield to the office. He was going in by the street door when Eddie Armstrong, the *Standard Reporter*'s chief photographer, came clattering down the stairs.

'Eddie,' said Pascal. 'They've blown up a pet-shop in Smithfield. If you dash across you might get some pictures.'

'We'll pick 'em up from the *Telegraph*,' Eddie said. 'Forget Smithfield.'

'Right. There's a riot on the Falls. I was just going up there.'

'Forget that, too,' said Eddie impatiently. 'The Prods just blew up a bar at Whiterock. There's bodies all over the place. That's the story.'

'Christ,' said Pascal.

'Christ wasn't there when it happened,' Eddie said.

Pascal and Eddie half ran, half walked to the office car-park. They decided to go in Pascal's battered second-hand Vauxhall because—as Eddie pointed out—his XJ-6 would look out of place in a rebel slum.

'It's half crocked anyway,' said Eddie, obviously pleased to have Pascal to keep him company. 'My garageman's a crook.'

'You're the crook,' said Pascal, switching on the ignition. 'You don't give a damn about the Provos—you're going to claim my mileage on your expenses.'

'Maybe I am,' said Eddie, grinning. 'But we won't get hijacked in this old wreck.'

Eddie was in his forties. He was an ex-RAF corporal who had fallen on prosperous times. He owned a luxurious split-level villa at Cultra, on the hills overlooking Belfast Lough, but he lived—at least, he spent most of his time—in Mc-Glades's Old Vic Lounge and Bar, round the corner from the office.

They were into traffic before Pascal remembered the riot; the Lower Falls would be blocked to traffic.

'Go up the Grosvenor Road.'

'No,' said Pascal. 'If it's on the Falls, it will have spread to Aggro Corner. That'll be blocked as well.'

'Christ,' said Eddie. 'Get on the motorway. We can work our way round from there.'

Pascal blew his horn at a delivery van. He swore softly under his breath.

'We should be equipped with sirens.'

'You've passed him,' Eddie looked back. 'Bloody silly bastard.'

'Do you know what happened?'

'Woman phoned in,' said Eddie, succinctly. 'Half hysterical. She said the Prods had thrown in a beer keg.'

'When?'

'A minute before I saw you.'

Pascal looked at his watch. 'It always happens just on the bloody edition.'

'We've missed the Irish,' Eddie replied. 'We'll never get back in time.'

'I haven't filed on Smithfield yet.'

'Sod Smithfield,' Eddie said. 'This is more important.'

The bombed bar was out in the west of the city, where the new estates lapped like a tide round the ankles of the mountains. They reached it quickly, coming off the motorway at Milltown Cemetery, driving recklessly and dangerously because they knew there were no police to stop them.

What was left of the pub looked like a child's sandcastle that had been smashed by an incoming wave. It was a shapeless mound of rubble. A few scorched fingers of wood thrust out of the wreckage. The massive pile of brick and timber was swarming with people who were digging furiously to extricate survivors. They formed human chains which wavered like trains of ants on a heap of dirt. The chains passed handfuls of rubble from top to bottom. Eddie Armstrong moved off to get his pictures, and Pascal went to try to find out what happened.

It seemed that the bar had been almost full. There had been a European soccer match on television which people wanted to see. News had come in that another British soldier had been shot, and that bombs were exploding in several parts of town. An old man, one of the local characters, apparently remarked that they'd have to watch out for Protestant reprisals. It was an easy, obvious thing to say. Nobody took any notice. There was a guard on the door, and everyone assumed that the pub would be reasonably safe while daylight lasted.

They had the common illusion that nothing could happen to them.

The drinkers in the pub were caught flat-footed. The 'guard' was an elderly pensioner, and when the Loyalist squad leapt out of a stolen blue Cortina they pushed him scornfully aside.

'I got the number, mister,' a woman shouted to Pascal. 'You just write it down.'

'Away with you!' screamed another woman. 'The car's dumped and burned by now. They'll never get them.'

'It was a blue Cortina, mister.'

'It was stolen on the Shankhill.'

'It was stolen on top of the Crumlin Road.'

'They ajaxed it in Tiger Bay.'

Four men had made up the squad, three gunmen and a

144

driver. They all wore nylon stockings pulled down over their faces. The women said that they all looked young.

They kicked open the door of the bar and flung in a beer barrel with a sparking fuse. One of the gang sprayed the room with machine-gun fire. The customers panicked and dived for the floor.

'It was a reprisal, mister. For that poor young soldier.'

'Poor young soldier my foot.'

'The bastard was British, wasn't he?'

They all seemed agreed on that.

The sinister barrel rolled fizzing among a crush of bodies. Protestant fuses were less sophisticated than Catholic fuses. There was a frantic, hysterical rush for the doors. They were jammed when the barrel exploded. It disintegrated in a white-hot flash. Aluminium shrapnel slashed its way through the air. A brief high-pressure zone built up. It blew the building round it outwards. The bar was split open like a pod, and the roof collapsed on the ruin.

Brutal shockwaves had rushed down people's ears and noses and frantic mouths. They were deafened in an instant. Their throats were seared. Their lungs and stomachs exploded. The blast swirled into their skulls and blew their heads off. Their torsos were ripped from their limbs.

It took less than a second for it all to happen.

Pascal could see the remains of a body on a sidewalk. Eddie Armstrong was taking pictures. A distressed ambulanceman rushed up and tried to wave him away. People were frightened to learn that a human body has thirty feet of guts. They hated to know how naked they looked when badly slaughtered, like so much beef.

Pascal wanted to shout to Eddie and ask him why he bothered. Some pictures were too disgusting to show the customers while they ate their breakfasts. The newspapers kept them on file. The public preferred something nice and anaesthetic. A massacre was best suggested in a safe, nostalgic way; perhaps an open family bible resting on a blackened pile of bricks. Pictures like that won prizes. The other kind of pictures were likely to make you spew.

Pascal wondered mildly what might be delaying the Army.

They would sometimes arrive at the scene in seconds, at most in minutes.

A shot rang out. One of the labouring ants on the hill of rubble threw up his arms and suddenly died. Then there was a deadly volley. Bullets cracked and whistled into the ruin. Pascal saw a man lose the back of his skull. It came away in a gout of brain.

Pascal did not believe that any of this could possibly be happening. Hysterical faces hung screaming in the air. Arms were flung out, fingers pointed wildly towards the mountain. Shouts and curses were curdled in the bullet-tormented air. People flung themselves down in grotesque positions wherever they stood. Pascal threw himself flat on his belly.

A bullet clanged, a foot away, on the stem of a metal lamp-post. It ricocheted off with a loud whirr. The lamp-post quivered like a struck fork. Pascal rolled and fell and hid behind a kerb-stone. A tried nostrum for times of disaster. When the Bomb goes off or your neighbours start to shoot you make for the nearest gutter. He had never been so frightened in his life.

Far away, and yet so near you could almost touch, the Black Mountain was tranquil and cool and blue. The sun was preparing a magnificent exit. In the rose-coloured sky an Army helicopter pirouetted, looking frail and graceful as the sunset glittered on its shell.

The light glittered redly from the windows of a grey estate of houses. The houses looked down on the camp of the Catholics on the boggy bottom land. From some of those blood-red windows came the crack of rifles, the bark of a heavy machine-gun.

The bomb had been nothing more than a lure to draw a crowd out into the open. Gunmen established on the hillside estate were firing hundreds of rounds, at leisure, into the pack of rescue workers. Cautiously Pascal glanced around him. There was a body, its heels spasmodically kicking, lying in the middle of the road. The rest of the carriageway was clear. People were huddled, staring fixedly up towards the hillside, behind garden walls, behind whatever cover they could find.

After several minutes there was a pause in firing. Two brave

146

volunteer ambulancemen in the uniform of the Knights of Malta ran to the kicking man who lay gasping in the middle of the road.

They picked him up and hurried to the ambulance they'd arrived in. Pascal saw Eddie stand up cautiously and follow them, his camera seeming glued in place on his eye. Eddie was often brave, got extraordinary pictures when he decided to be bothered. There was more gunfire. The ambulance was hit, but the two volunteers manhandled their burden in. One of them waved urgently to the photographer, who was now exposed. He leapt in after the body. Eddie deserved his luck. The doors slammed. Swiftly the vehicle moved off.

A battered car passed it, roaring up the deserted road towards the shattered bar as the ambulance drove away. There were six men in the car, all of them armed, two with rifles sticking out of the windows. They spilled on to the roadway and fanned out to take positions on the other side of the junction where the bar had stood.

They began to pour fire in the direction of the occasional figures who could be seen moving about on the Protestant estate above them.

Pascal, seeing the coloured mountain, the red windows, and the helicopter clattering in a rose-and-cobalt sky, had more than ever an impression of total unreality. He was living a scene from a film, but the scene was real.

An unshaven, thick-necked man in a dirty shirt and a worn black suit ducked across the road and stumbled towards him. The man half knelt, half squatted beside the reporter.

'You a newspaper reporter?' he demanded.

He would never have asked the question unless he already knew. Pascal looked at him. 'Yes,' he said.

'Which paper?'

'The *Standard Reporter*.'

'You better get outa here, fella.'

Pascal looked at the patient face and the ignorant eyes, and knew it would be worse than useless to argue. But he could be stupid too.

'I'm only doing my job,' he protested stubbornly.

'Look, fella. Nobody's goin' to tell you twice. Fuck off.'

The man put his hand inside his jacket and brought out a revolver. It looked like an old one to Pascal. The butt was chipped, and the metal was very scratched. The man did not point the gun at Pascal, but simply showed it him in an intimate way; as though he were displaying a wound.

'Get out.'

'Why?' demanded Pascal. 'Don't you think people need to be told?'

'Look, friend. I told you to fuck off. We got a short way with spies round here.'

'I'm not a spy.'

'You've got till I count to three.'

Pascal ran, half crouched, until he reached the Vauxhall. More armed men were pouring into the district. In the absence of the law, the outlaws gathered to protect the people. He was almost knocked down by a car, horn blaring, taking more of them in to join the battle.

Shivering with delayed-reaction shock, Pascal put the car in gear. Guns were hammering away outside. He was sure that this was his greatest moment of danger. He decided that to do a U-turn would be suicidal. It would expose him for far too long to the Loyalist fire. If he accelerated towards it and turned right down the hill at the pub, he stood a chance of slipping safely between the two opposing forces.

He drove like a maniac, crouching in his seat to minimize the target. His tyres squealed as he skidded round the bend. Within a minute he was more or less safe, knowing that the guerrillas had ignored him, or missed him if they hadn't.

A quarter of a mile further on, he was able to look at himself more calmly. The familiar flood of relief at escaping from an awkward situation made him almost jolly. Around him, life was continuing as normal. The echo of gunfire rattled down from the mountains, but the local housewives ignored it as they carried their shopping bags home with the family tea. A tricolour painted on a wall. The starry plough of Connolly's lost Republic of Labour.

JOIN YOUR LOCAL UNIT OGLAIG NA h-EIREANN.
UP THE REPUBLIC!

148

The black-faced soldiers who came in galoshes and hid in the gardens at night had been painting too:

GOD IS A PARA.
SO IS POPE PAUL.

With a catch of relief, he noticed an Army barricade ahead. The badlands were falling behind him; civilization ahead. A long column of Saracen and Humber armoured cars was parked beside the road. A traffic jam had built up behind an Army barricade. The workers coming home had been stopped for their own safety. They sat waiting behind the wheel, got out and stretched their legs or stood leaning on their cars.

Pascal stopped at the barricade. A young soldier in a dark beret asked him for his licence. Pascal smiled and handed it over. The man glanced at the document, noting the English address. A small dishonesty; he hadn't changed his licence because it got him through checkpoints quicker.

'Manchester, er?' said the soldier, looking curiously at Pascal. 'I'm from Delph.'

'Other side of Oldham?'

The soldier's face cleared. 'Yeah. Never get this trouble with sheep.'

'You've got a lot of sheep in Delph.'

'God's own country,' the soldier said. 'Will you open your boot and bonnet, sir?'

Pascal got out. While the soldier was searching he glanced at the column of armour. Every car held at least eight men. He began to count them.

'Sign me docket, sir?' asked the soldier. He handed Pascal a mimeographed indemnity form. Pascal looked at it uncertainly. The sound of renewed gunplay helped to make up his mind.

'I want to see an officer,' he said.

'Oh, yes?' said the soldier, sharply. 'What for, sir? Isn't everything all right?'

'I'm a reporter.'

'Yes, sir. Will you sign me docket?'

'Yes,' said Pascal. 'After you've fetched an officer.'

'Charlie!' shouted the soldier to a mate on the barricade.

149

'Fetch Major Lloyd. Bloke here won't sign me paper.'

Pascal waited. When he tried to look at him, the soldier looked away. It was evening now, growing chilly. It seemed likely that it might rain.

'What's this?' Major Lloyd strolled jauntily towards Pascal, an ingratiating smile on his face. 'Good evening, sir. This is just a formal document, but it has to be signed. To say you're satisfied we haven't damaged your car or personal belongings.'

Pascal handed him his Press card. 'I'm a newspaperman.'

'Ah,' said the Major. He examined the card. 'Pleased to meet you, Mr Canning.'

'Why have your men stopped here?'

'To man the barricade,' the officer said. 'There's a bit of trouble further along. If you listen you can hear them firing.'

'I know,' said Pascal. 'Why don't you do something about it?'

The officer seemed genuinely surprised. He looked up at the darkening sky. 'Why bother?' he asked. 'They'll have to stop when it's dark.'

'Listen, Major,' shouted Pascal angrily. 'People are getting killed up there! I nearly got killed myself!'

The officer's expression at once became sympathetic. He shook his head. 'I'm sorry. Is it very bad?'

'It's terrible. They were firing on ambulances, man.'

Major Lloyd grinned ironically. He looked to his attendant privates for support. 'You'd be surprised what we find in ambulances, Mr Canning. They use them to carry guns.'

'This one carried a dying man.'

'Oh. Well, what do you want me to do? At the moment they're just shooting each other, Mr Canning. If I tried to stop them they might shoot some of my men.' The tone was cheerfully hearty, the kind one uses to recalcitrant children. 'We wouldn't want that, now, would we?'

'You must have more than a hundred fully armed soldiers here,' said Pascal, fuming.

'Well, what about it?' the officer interrupted sharply. 'We will go in, Mr Canning. As soon as it gets dark.'

'You will,' said Pascal. 'Won't you? And search the Catholic estate for guns.'

150

'They *are* using them, Mr Canning,' said the officer reasonably.

'So are the Protestants.'

'That's not our area, Mr Canning. That's another unit's responsibility.'

'Listen to that!' shouted Pascal. 'That's a heavy machine-gun they've got up there. It's firing down on the bar those bastards bombed. They couldn't do it if you'd gone at once to help at the rescue.'

The officer's face had stiffened. 'I didn't have orders about a bomb,' he said. 'I didn't know that a bomb had gone off.'

'Well, it has, Major Lloyd. There are several people dead.' The reporter waved angrily towards the mountain. 'And you *do* know. There was a spotter helicopter up there immediately after it happened.'

'That's an outrageous suggestion!'

'This is an outrageous situation. But I'll withdraw it, Major; if you send your men to protect the wounded.'

'I have to follow orders,' the Major blustered. 'It is not for me to question dispositions.' They stared at each other. 'Now, would you kindly move your car? You can see that it's blocking the road.'

'Nobody's using the road.'

'If you won't move it, we'll move it for you.'

Pascal pleaded, 'Won't you do anything at all?'

'I expect that I'll get my orders.'

Pascal got back in his car. The soldier stepped forward to hand him the indemnity docket, but Major Lloyd made an irritable sign and the man stepped back.

There was a road junction a few yards past the military barricade. The road on the left swept up to the heart of the Protestant estate where the firing came from. Impulsively, Pascal decided to take it and see for himself. He started the engine, engaged the gears, and began to move off. He indicated for turning left.

There was a shout, and running footsteps behind the car. Pascal stopped. The officer's face appeared at the driver's window.

'Where do you think you're going?'

'Up there,' pointed Pascal.

'You can't.'

'Why not? I'm just doing my job.'

'You can't go up there,' the officer said.

'I'm going anyway.' Pascal pulled away, almost knocking the Major over. A soldier intercepted the car and hammered on the roof.

'Stop this man!' he shouted. 'Stop him!'

Two more soldiers were standing behind the checkpoint. One of them sprinted across Pascal's course, dragging what looked like heavy chains in front of the wheels. Pascal knew what they were—caltraps, four-pointed spikes which would puncture his tyres.

He braked as hard as he could. The officer ran in front of him, holding up his hand. The two men glared at each other. Pascal finally dropped his eyes. The officer gave an order, and two soldiers stationed themselves in front of the car, holding their rifles easily across their bodies, staring curiously at Pascal. The shallow bend which led to the estate was now blocked. The Major sauntered towards Pascal.

'Drive on, Mr Canning,' he said. 'I don't want to have to arrest you.'

Pascal savagely twisted the wheel, moved quickly into second, and with screeching tyres shot away towards town.

Several bombs had exploded by the time he got there. There were bomb alerts in a dozen different places.

IV

Pascal drank more than usual that evening. He went to McGlades's Bar with Eddie, and met up with a man from the *Daily Mail* and some others from the *Belfast Telegraph*. They drank steadily, told stories, and criticized absent friends. Every half-hour or so one of them left the group and rang the Army and Police Press Offices to see if anyone else had been killed. Nobody had. There were several calls for Pascal, but he refused to take them.

'Tell them I'm not here,' he shouted over the din of conversation. 'You haven't seen me all night.'

When he left the bar the city centre was deserted. The broken glass had all been swept up, the last of the fires put out, and the victims carted off to hospitals or morgues. The city was left to lick its wounds in the darkness. There was nobody about but the patrols of Army and police.

Pascal shook his head, trying to clear it, thinking that he was drunk and no longer caring. It was a cold night, and it had been raining heavily, but the worst of the rain was over now. He walked down to the car-park and got the machine out. He headed east towards the Markets. The tyres swished on the streaming, gleaming tarmac. His eyes hurt. He was tired, full of aches and pains, and desperately unhappy. He wanted to get to bed.

He drove by the Cenotaph and the City Hall, past the eyeless buildings, scorched ruins, spiked blue gates. A tangle of barbed wire lay stretched across the steps of the Royal Courts of Justice. It had long since gone rusty in the rain.

Pascal stopped at the lights beside the Markets. Yawned. Tapped his fingers on the wheel. He thought idly of his wife's casual description of Belfast: Warsaw and Jarrow, all mixed up. The eternal, infernal, indomitable slum.

'The lights are long tonight,' he muttered, absently. Then he started. His wife wasn't with him. He had forgotten, thinking of her, that he was quite alone.

First sign of madness, talking to yourself.

Guiltily, Pascal drew off while the lights were still on red. As if going through lights on red could possibly matter on a night like this, in a town like this one. His headlights drilled through the gloom; he accelerated, chasing them home.

Then all at once he was standing desperately on the brakes. A soldier was skewered in the headlights' beam. The soldier urgently signalled that Pascal stop. I'm drunk, thought Pascal. The car skidded wildly. The bridge over the Lagan was blocked.

'Get your lights off!' the soldier yelled.

The car was drifting, sliding down upon the soldier.

'Get 'em off!'

The soldier's mouth was a great red pit.

A Scot, thought Pascal stupidly, convinced he was going to run him over. Not one, two Scots. Two Scottish soldiers.

The car ploughed to a halt. He'd stalled it. He immediately heard the sound of gunfire. The nerveless crack of Armalites. American M1 carbines. Garrands, barking. Gunfire from the rooftops on the other side of the river.

The car's door was wrenched open. A fist punched his arm, knocking him sideways out of the way. A soldier leaned in and swiftly extinguished the lights.

Both the soldiers accused him. 'Why din' you switch yer lights oot?'

'Yer daft, or somethin'?'

'Wann get shot?'

'I didn't hear,' said Pascal defensively. 'I didn't understand—'

'Doan hang aboot! Come on, mon. Oot. Get oot!'

Pascal almost fell through the open door. He ran half crouched across the roadway to the shelter of the parapet. The two soldiers split up, one ducking behind Pascal's car, the other running after its driver, launching himself, landing with a clatter and a curse on the greasy wet pavement.

Pascal and the soldier sized each other up. They were both panting. Suddenly the rifleman grinned. 'At least it's stoppen rainin',' he said.

CRACK! The shot had been shockingly near.

'If you 'ear 'em,' observed the soldier, 'yer know they dinna hit you.'

Pascal forced himself to sound calm. 'Is it an ambush?'

The soldier spluttered. 'Naw, a bacon tree!' His teeth gleamed briefly from his blackened-up face. 'I always wanted some birk to ask me that. Wha' d'you think it is if it ain't an ambush?' He spat. 'Bluidy civic reception?'

'I didn't think,' said Pascal. He pulled his lapels round his throat. 'I've been drinking. I was half asleep at the wheel.'

'Is it an ambush?' repeated the soldier. 'Fuckin' right it's a fuckin' ambush! It's nothin' fuckin' else!'

Pascal peered round the drab green bulk of the soldier's body. He noticed the sweaty smell.

154

'How many of them are there, then?' he asked, apparently casual.

' 'Bout twenty,' said the soldier indifferently. The bridge was blocked by an armoured Humber 'pig' and a couple of jeeps that had run into the first of the fire. More than a dozen soldiers had taken up battle positions under cover.

'Bluidy Irish,' the soldier said. He looked at Pascal. 'You're no Irish?'

'Sort of,' Pascal admitted.

'Yer are, or yer not?'

'Sort of,' Pascal repeated. 'Through my mum and dad. I was born on the other side.'

'Shit,' said the soldier. 'See the Irish? See Ireland? They should tow it away and sink it.'

They both flinched this time as some more ammunition came over.

The soldier was a square, blockish man. His nose was too big and his eyebrows were like ginger exclamations.

'Shower a' cunts,' the soldier said, cheerfully. 'Cannae shoot straight, even.' A tremendous fusillade raked the end of the bridge. 'They had us cold,' said the soldier. 'They didn't even scratch us.'

Pascal, terrified of ricochets, buried his face in his hands and shuddered.

'Doan worry, son,' said the soldier. 'You wait here. Doan move.'

He started crawling along the pavement towards the armoured car, his chunky bottom protruding high in the air.

CRACK!

Pascal, sweating despite the cold, decided he'd had more than enough for today. He had to get out or he'd go insane. On his hands and knees, he began crawling across the road. He wanted to get back in the car, restart the engine, and reverse away. He'd completely forgotten the second soldier.

'Get yerself doon!' a hoarse voice shouted. The soldier's head popped up from behind the bonnet.

'I'm a newspaper reporter!' Pascal bellowed.

'Guid fer you!' the Scotsman shouted back. 'If they hit yer head they might miss yer brain!'

155

'I have to get to a phone,' yelled Pascal, lifting his head like a pantomime horse: 'To report about this for an English paper!'

'I have tae get back to the barricks,' shouted the soldier. 'The Sargent gets upset if ma tea gets cold.'

'I have to phone the OFFICE!' Pascal shouted. 'I just want to let them KNOW!'

'STAY THERE!'

Ignoring him, Pascal stood up and made a dash for his car. The ignition was still switched on, and the wipers were thrashing dryly. It had indeed stopped raining.

'Yer fou!' the remaining soldier screamed, stepping reluctantly out of cover. He grabbed Pascal and started to wrestle. 'Cuckoo, y'are! Mad! Get back on that fucking bridge! Quick! Get back!'

'Reporter,' gasped Pascal. 'Got to get to a phone.'

Another car came skidding over the brow of the hill which ended on the roadway of the bridge. In mutual terror, Pascal and the soldier turned from their quarrel and tried to wave it down.

'Cut them lights!'

'Get your lights off!' Pascal screamed.

The car waltzed, tyres squealing, to a standstill. In what seemed only an instant, Pascal and a well-dressed stranger were huddled side by side beneath the granite parapet, ducking their heads as bullets came whizzing overhead.

'Is it an ambush?' gasped the panting stranger.

'No,' said Pascal sarcastically, 'it's—' He drew his breath, sharply. 'Yes,' he said. 'We've stumbled into an ambush.'

'Good God!' The stranger pulled his coat tighter around him. 'I see you're English as well.' He grunted. 'From your accent.'

'Sort of,' Pascal admitted.

'Where are you from?'

'Manchester.'

'I'm London, myself. Croydon. Henderson.'

'Canning.'

'Very pleased to meet you.' He extended his hand.

Pascal grasped it. 'My pleasure,' he muttered, weakly.

CRASH!

'I say!' said Henderson.

CRASH!

'They're shooting out the lights!'

CRASH!

'Yes,' shouted Pascal. 'So the snipers won't see them.'

'Good Lord!' exclaimed Henderson. 'That's public property!'

Pascal looked sourly at his companion in distress. He settled himself as comfortably as possible against the parapet wall.

'I've never been in anything like *this* before,' said Henderson. 'Have you?'

'Yes,' said Pascal. He was shivering violently. He knew too much to blame it on the cold.

'Often?' ventured Henderson at last.

'I'm a reporter,' Pascal said, as if this were an explanation. 'It happens all the time.'

Henderson accepted that reporters knew about these things. 'I'm a Civil Servant, myself. Lawyer actually.' He made a noise halfway between a cough and a giggle. 'Over here on secondment from the Ministry. Just arrived. I'm supposed to help lock fellers like that lot up.' He wagged a manicured thumb over his shoulder. 'Evidently not succeeding, eh?'

They both watched, their conversation forgotten, while the red-haired soldier Pascal had talked with earlier scrambled hastily back from the direction of the Army vehicles. He held an unintelligible conference with his comrade behind Pascal's car. The two soldiers disappeared together, making for the Markets, presumably to warn off any other traffic.

Then the flares went up.

They rose all along the river, with a series of whooshes, like giant Roman candles.

CRASH! CRASH! CRASH!

Henderson gasped, looked wildly at Pascal.

'They're trying to shoot down the flares,' said Pascal. He nestled back. The bridge, the vehicles, the soldiers, themselves; everything lit as brightly as day.

'Does this sort of thing normally last a long time?'

Pascal looked at his friend the lawyer. 'It's lasted since

Strongbow,' he said. 'About seven hundred years.'

Henderson was glum. He was not in the mood for humour. They sat together in silence, listening to their thoughts and the crackle of the guns.

Henderson jumped. 'What's that?'

'What?'

'I swear I heard somebody singing.'

'No,' said Pascal. He listened.

Thinly, punctuated by the crash and crackle of weaponry, a drunken singing was drifting towards them.

Pascal smiled thinly. 'He's singing the Tantum Ergo,' he said. 'Off key.'

'What's that?'

'A Latin hymn.'

'Good God!' said Henderson. 'Then he must be one of them?'

'So am I,' said Pascal.

'You're a Catholic?' Henderson asked defensively. 'But I mean, it's different, isn't it? Everyone's loyal in England.'

'Certainly,' said Pascal. 'Don't worry.'

'I didn't mean to suggest. . .'

'I know.'

The drunk finally reeled into view on the crest of the hill that hid their view of the Market's quarter. He was staggering from side to side as he sang his hymn.

'*Genitori, genitorque, laus et* . . . be jabers,' said the drunk. 'What are them lovely stars?'

CRASH!

CRACK!

'Here, you'd better get down!' shouted Henderson.

'What? What's this? What's that you say? What're them stars?'

CRACK!

'You're going to get shot!' Henderson exclaimed.

The drunk ignored this prediction. His mouth fell open. A dribble ran unnoticed down his chin. He was wearing an old brown suit, a yellow shirt and a dirty white scarf tucked in at the neck. It was obviously days since he'd shaved. He shut his mouth, looked benignly and knowingly at Pascal and Hender-

158

son, and said: 'Look! Will youse look at them lovely stars?'

Volley after volley of rifle fire rang out. The Provos in the spitting slums across the river were being lavish with ammunition.

'Aren't they beautiful?' demanded the drunk, staring vacantly up at the flares.

'Hey, get down!' shouted Pascal. 'Come on! They'll shoot you if you stand up there.'

The drunk swayed. 'They won't shoot me, the boys,' he said. 'Dinnie Devlin won't get shot. They all know me, you see. They all know old Dinnie. Wouldn't harm a single hair on me head.' He swayed. He almost toppled. 'Up the Republic!' he suddenly shouted. 'Up the rebels! Up the Republic!' It seemed to help him to keep his balance.

The flares were dying now. The dark was returning to slumland.

'We ruz at Easter,' cried the drunk. 'We're a Risen People. We ruz at Easter like Our Lord.' He was silent for a moment while his fuddled brain groped to express his feelings. He returned to the refuge of an off-key Tantum Ergo.

Pascal wanted to pull him down behind the parapet, but Henderson wouldn't help him.

'He might turn nasty,' Henderson said.

Behind the open door of the armoured pig a thin, short soldier had taken up position. He was standing on an ammunition box. He had a rifle in his hands and was aiming it through the open port of the heavy metal door.

'Is he a sniper?' Henderson hissed.

'Yes,' said Pascal.

'What's he got on his gun?'

'An image intensifier,' Pascal whispered. 'It magnifies the available light. You can see as clear as day with no other light but the stars.'

'I hope he shoots them,' Henderson said.

CRASH!

'Did he shoot one?' Henderson's voice was boyishly eager.

CRASH!

'Fuck youse, stop shootin'!' cried the drunk. 'Get on outa that to England!'

But his voice sounded reedy against the darkness of the night, and the sound of the guns which continued to crash.

'We'll match ye!' howled the drunk, waving his fist defiantly towards the soldiers. 'We're up off our knees at last! Yez'll be thravellin' home in boxes, see!'

Pascal looked up at the sky. The clouds had thinned, and the constellation of the Bear glittered dispassionately above the leprous town.

CRASH!

There was a sudden halt to the shooting. Everybody present had caught the different impact, the sound of lead as it smacks on bone.

'What's happening?' asked Henderson, rising.

Pascal too rose quickly to his feet. Above the Short Strand skyline a building bigger than the rest stood out. It dominated the riverside kitchen houses, but not by much. It was a Nonconformist chapel. On the roof was a neon sign, the only light showing across the river. The sign was in tall red letters.

JESUS LOVES ME.

The sign was juddering, as though shaken by a wind.

An unmistakable scraping of metal against slate, the accelerating pummet of a rifle down a roof. A moment later it clattered on the pavement and the soldiers trapped on the bridge gave a sudden, ragged cheer.

'They've GOT one!' Henderson shouted.

A body pitched after the rifle and fell with a dead thump on the street below.

One of the soldiers whooped.

'For Christ's sake, get his weapon!' The officer's voice sounded incongruously cultured as it echoed around the slum and along the silent river.

The drunk rocked on his feet and wiped his sleeve across his mouth. A look of puzzlement and hurt settled like a fever on his face.

'Mister?' he asked. 'What happened? For the love o'God, what happened?'

Pascal hesitated, not knowing what to say.

The drunk's voice was pleading, urgent, plaintive. 'Mister,

160

dear,' he said. 'For the love of God and his Blessed Mother Mary, will youse please tell us what's after happenin'? Did one of our lads get shot?'

CRASH! said the Army sniper's Lee-Enfield. The shooting started again.

'Do you know is he dead?' begged the drunk, bending to where Pascal had taken shelter. He looked at the young reporter, swayed on his feet, straightened eventually. Then he pulled a bottle of cheap red wine from his pocket. It was called Red Biddy. He gasped and he sucked a drink. 'Tatey bread . . . dead . . . ah, mister!' Once more he swabbed at his mouth. 'We've another poor widda, mister.'

'Yes,' said Pascal. 'Get down.'

'One of your friends might kill you,' Henderson said.

The drunk snarled.

'Maybe he was only wounded,' Pascal said.

'Wounded?' The drunk seemed puzzled, philosophical. 'Did youse not hear the fella falling? D'youse think I'm stupid? I know what's wounded. And I know what's dead. . .'

'Get down anyway,' Pascal invited.

The drunk, grey-faced, stared grimly at the crouched young man. 'Get on me knees?' He shook his head. 'Am prayin' for his soul. Am doin' it standin' up.'

Pascal searched in his head for a name. 'Your name's Dinnie,' he said. 'Come on, Dinnie. If you kneel down, I'll kneel with you. We'll pray for his soul together.'

The drunk shook his head contemptuously. He took a deep breath, crossed himself unevenly, and struck his breast. 'De profundish clamavi ad te Domine,' he began.

CRASH!

The gun-battle continued, more cautiously now. They heard running boots, the crack of a pistol.

'They've gone in to get the rifle.'

The drunk's voice quavered as he finished praying. He stood silently, his head sunk on his chest as though fallen asleep. He began suddenly roaring the verses of a ballad.

With mingled horror and pity, Pascal looked at the swaying figure. The ballad was one he had often sung, in the kitchen at Ballyvarren. Where had it led him to? He buried his face in

161

his hands. The drunk sang on. Was he even drunk?

'Canning,' Henderson whispered. 'We'll grab his legs. You're right. We're going to have to get him to shelter.'

Pascal looked up. He saw puzzlement on Henderson's face. 'No,' said Pascal.

'But they'll shoot him,' Henderson protested.

'Touch him,' said Pascal thickly, 'and I'll break your neck.'

Devlin was killed about ten minutes later, when the gun-battle was almost over. A last fusillade pocked the coping stones on the parapet of the bridge, and a stray bullet sliced into Dinnie's chest. Pascal shuffled across to lift him.

Pascal looked at him helplessly. The man's face was rigid, his eyes open, his breathing shallow. A soldier had come back to see what had happened.

Dinnie looked at the soldier, and then at Pascal. Pascal bent down, as though he could not bear it. He began to whisper the Confiteor. Dinnie died at the moment he finished.

'He's gone,' screamed Henderson. 'You killed him.'

Pascal looked at the soldier. 'He committed suicide.'

'No,' cried Henderson. 'No!'

'I killed him,' acknowledged Pascal.

V

When Pascal reached home Ann was at the door before he could turn the key in the lock. Wordlessly, he shambled in. She looked at him in horror. His hair was wild and his clothes were filthy and soaking wet.

'You've got blood on your coat.' He could hear the shock in her voice.

'Have you got any coffee?'

'Pascal! What happened? Are you all right?'

'Oh, it's not my blood.' He stared at her. 'There was trouble in town.'

'Come in. Get into the kitchen.'

He staggered. 'I want some coffee, and some whiskey, quick.'

She rushed into the living-room. 'I'll get the whiskey. Get in

162

the kitchen and sit down.' She called the words over her shoulder. They were hardly said before she was back in the kitchen beside him.

'You look ghastly,' she said, bustling about, finding a glass, slopping it full of too much whiskey. 'Ghastly, ghastly.' She was almost sobbing.

Pascal had slumped on a chair, rested his head on the table.

'A man died in my arms.' She was filling a kettle, lighting the gas. 'The trouble with these sort of wars,' said Pascal, dully, 'you get blood on your hands.'

Ann put on the kettle to boil. He wanted to laugh, with bitterness, frustration, at the anxious way she confronted him. 'What happened?' his wife demanded. 'How did you get like this?'

'A gun-battle. A man got killed. Also an under-man. A terrorist.' He looked up at her. 'Are you any wiser?'

Ann tried to smile. She hesitated. 'Drink up your whiskey. You can put the rest in your coffee.'

'I will if you make it with milk.'

'But the kettle's on . . .' She stopped, looking at her husband with hopeless love. 'All right.' She smiled. 'You sure that you didn't get hurt?'

Pascal rubbed his eyes.

'Of course you got hurt.' Ann touched him lightly.

'I'm tired,' said Pascal.

When the coffee was ready she added whiskey. 'Take off that coat.' She seemed so vulnerable that Pascal was forced to obey. 'You're wet through. Take off your jacket. Drink that coffee. It'll make you warm.'

Pascal grunted with irritation. He wished she would leave him alone.

She was intuitive. She crossed the kitchen and pretended to search in a cupboard. 'The office has been on and off the phone all night.' She thought that she sounded casual, but her voice was as brittle as stone gone rotten. 'They were looking for you. They want you to ring them back.'

'I won't. It's after midnight. I've got three days off.'

'Pascal, it's something to do with the Editor,' said Ann. 'It's very urgent. You're supposed to phone them the minute you

163

get in.' He could see her again at last, her face very pale. 'They were looking for you all over town.'

'I was at McGlades's,' said Pascal.

'They said they phoned there.'

'I told Ian to say that I hadn't been in.'

'I phoned there looking for you too,' said Ann.

'I know,' said Pascal viciously. 'I've had a rotten day. I didn't want anybody bothering me.'

'Not even me?'

'No.'

'Well, shall I tell you why I wanted to bother you? I had a call from Dublin. Your Uncle Andy died this evening. They want us to go down.'

'Oh,' said Pascal. He looked at his wife. She was staring at him as though he were a stranger. Her eyes were glittering. He knew she was going to cry. 'I'm sorry. I'm not myself.'

'No, Pascal, you're not. I don't know you any more. I don't know what's come over you.' She hurried out of the kitchen.

'Ann—' Pascal started to say. 'Thank you for the coffee,' he shouted after her. His stomach was twisted in a cold, hard knot. He felt sick. Why did everything have to happen at once?

He heard rather than saw her come back. She must have been gone five minutes.

'Was it really good coffee?'

'Lovely,' he said. 'Like you.'

'Finish it, then.' He finished it. 'You and I shouldn't quarrel.'

'I suppose I should phone the office.'

'Get out of those clothes. You'll catch pneumonia.' She looked small and fragile and tired. 'You can phone them later.'

'I'm sorry for what I said.' She shrugged. It was rather a desperate gesture. 'I'm a mess,' said Pascal. 'Poor Ann.'

'Your coat's all bloody,' she said. She looked downwards into her lap. 'You couldn't wear it again. Not ever.'

She looked so piteous that Pascal groaned. 'No,' he said. 'What are we going to do?'

Ann's face came up. She had softened slightly. 'Go and get changed now, love.'

'Were the kids all right today?'

'Yes. We went shopping in Bangor.'

'It's good for shopping.'

'It's safe,' said Ann. 'It's got fences round it.' Her voice had become bitter. 'Go and get changed.'

Pascal nodded. He got up and went to the door. 'I'll see you in a few minutes, then.'

'I'll be in the bathroom. I'm having a shower.'

Pascal washed in the handbasin in the corner of the bedroom. He swabbed his face with hot water. He pressed his fingers hard against closed eyelids. It took a moment for his vision to come right. His face stared back from the mirror. He looked away.

Ann was relieved when he left her. She wanted to be alone. She began washing the pan she'd used to heat up the milk for his coffee. A feeling of sick despair, of nausea, stopped her working. She stared sightlessly at the pan and its milky water. She went to the whiskey bottle and stopped. She never normally drank, but she picked up the bottle and gulped half a mouthful. She gagged. She felt worse than ever.

Pascal and his wars. His interminable filthy wars.

She stepped across to the kitchen unit and seized the blood-stained coat, which was lying where he'd dropped it. The thought of it made her dizzy. Quickly, in case she should faint, she opened the door and flung the coat out into the garden.

When she had slammed the door, locked it, and leaned against it she felt slightly better. She looked numbly up at the ceiling. Every day Pascal was getting worse. Now he brought blood back with him.

She looked at her hands, helplessly, feeling sick with horror. All the questions he asked, all the arguments, the fights; how could she get them clean?

She rushed to the bathroom and locked herself in. She stopped. She found she was panting. She resolved that whatever happened, she would force herself to be calm. She took all her clothes off. The contact with blood had soiled them. Then she sat down on the edge of the bath.

She could feel that her fists were clenched, that her elbows were drawn in tightly, that her feet and knees were pressed

165

hard together. It was cold. She shivered and could not stop. Finally she sighed, letting all the foul air rush out of her body, drawing new air in. She began to breathe more normally, but her face was tense and her spirit trembling.

Pascal could not run away. Lots of reporters got their news from the bar of the Europa Hotel, but Pascal didn't. Pascal had to live on his precious interface. He had to see the dead, to bring back their filth on his clothes. What did he see in this city of blood and fire? He came home one night, and the pattern of his vest had been scorched on his shirt by some burning building. She could not believe it, but he hadn't so much as noticed.

She wanted to cry, but she wasn't able. She climbed into the bath and drew the curtain. She started to run the shower. At first the water was as cold as punishment, but later it was hot. She had some special soap by Chanel. A birthday present from Pascal, who had no imagination when it came to presents. She rubbed herself with the soap. At first it made no difference, but the scent of the soap on her skin, the incessant water, helped her at last to relax.

Now she was able to think. The bathroom was tiled in black and pink. She hated the colours, but they came with the house. She had to accept them. She sat down in the black tub and let water cascade through her hair, streaming over her folded body, foetal, hunched up, familiar.

At last she was able to weep. She did so with heaving sobs which shook her body, bumping her forehead repeatedly on the rampart of her knees. The shower beat down and absolved her, dissolving her tears in the floods of its own, letting them drain off her breasts and thighs, coursing them over her belly, finally flushing them out.

Her thoughts came back always to Pascal. She loved him. She loved his talk, his impulsiveness, his sorrows. She loved his helplessness, his strength, the way he always came back for more. She loved Ireland for him. Did he love her as much?

She sat quietly and stared at her toes. The water rilled round them, and flowed away down the plug-hole, and gave no answer. At length she got up and switched off the shower.

Drying herself, she carefully studied her body. She wiped

166

the steam from the bathroom mirror. Three months gone and nothing to show. Gently she felt her belly. Little spaceman in there, floating in water. The firm pink flesh came back. She felt better after a cry, more resolute, stronger. Her face was flushed from the shower, perhaps also from carrying a child. She had not told Pascal.

For a moment despair returned. They had not meant to have a baby. The last one had left her exhausted. Three would be one too many. The tops of her thighs and her lower belly were scarred already. She was ashamed by her stretchmarks. They frightened her. They made her feel old and used. Her waist had thickened. Her body was not a girl's. It was pain and a terrible pleasure. When she looked in the mirror her nipples were glazed, like the eyes of a baby. Some drug in the milk that made babies forgetful, some wonderful, natural drug.

She would not think about that. She would not think of her body's ageing, or of decay, or of accepting pain. Men didn't think like that. They didn't have to. Not until very much later. It had not been coded for them.

She slipped on a nightdress, a fresh one from the airing cupboard. Her chin was firm. She was determined to be cheerful. She wrapped a towel round her hair. She felt clean and scented. She left her abandoned clothes in the corner where she'd thrown them.

When she left the bathroom and went into the hall outside Pascal was on the phone. He was in his pyjamas and dressing gown. She ignored him and went to the bedroom. He was arguing with the operator on the local telephone exchange. He wanted to call England collect, but was having problems.

Ann brushed her teeth at the basin in the corner of the bedroom. The subdued light from the bedside lamps flattered her mirrored image. Watching her own reflection, she felt a moment's ridiculous guilt, a relic of girlish modesty. Should it delight her so much, so impossibly much, to know she was still attractive? But she felt attractive. She felt and she looked like a highly desirable woman.

She was soon established in bed. She found a woman's magazine and peered at it, half interested, distracted. She unrolled the turban and began drying her long brown hair. The

167

warmth and the hum of the hair dryer were comfortable, familiar. So were the strokes of the brush.

She was twenty-six. Pink, freckled, pretty. Her eyes were as green as grass. She'd grown up in an English slum not unlike the warrens off the Falls or the Shankhill Road. Her father was a steelman who'd been badly burned in the back-blast from a furnace. Clever. A grammar-school girl, then later a teacher. Ann. A flower that grew from a patch of society's weeds.

She was fed and watered on the best that her parents had. Taken into the sunlight, her points discussed, her colouring praised like a tulip entered for the local Annual Show. Perhaps in the end they would hang a label on her, they could stand there proudly.

BEST IN EXHIBITION.

She grew up laughing. Perhaps—she sometimes thought so —it was a system of defence, a device that denied she was lonely. Few of her friends had a chance in the exhibition. She was lonely often, and frightened too. Worried what would happen when the Annual Show was over and her parents trudged back to the slums.

Home was the shadow of the winding gear and the howl of the siren at the pit. Home was the smell of dyeworks, old men who spat yellow phlegm into rusty grates and talked of defeated strikes. Home was pigeon racing, streets full of bunting for the Coronation; the acres of demolition.

All sorts of things were home. Fear was the tribes of gypsies, who broke up the pubs in their drunken riot. Joy was a trip to Southport. Hate was the butcher's son, in his father's Rover, pleading to touch her breasts.

Nobody touched her till Pascal. They were married by the priest who had always heard her Confession. The priest's eyes danced when he saw her later. He asked if she liked being married.

Education had helped them to move up a class. They were part of suburbia's dream. They saw Peter Sellers as Doctor Strangelove, ate in Chinese restaurants, and had a child in a better district. There were fogs in autumn, and rain whenever. The starlings came home to roost.

The phone tinkled. There was an extension beside the bed.

On an impulse, Ann switched off the dryer and picked it up.

'. . . nothing but that on TV all night,' the deskman in Manchester said. Manchester dealt with the Irish news because London thought it provincial. 'Top spot on every news. The bombers slaughter the Dove of Peace.'

Pascal was laughing. He sounded nervous. 'Did you know that Graham was drunk?'

'Could have been on drugs, mate. Shot himself full of dope. The Old Man loved it. Said it was the most moving broadcast he'd ever seen. He's been pissing his pants since the Nine O'Clock News. Everyone's getting wet.'

'Well,' said Pascal, comfortably. 'After that soldier, you know, the attack on the pub, the . . .'

'That's a couple of pars,' said the deskman coldly. 'We've been looking for you all night. What the hell were you doing?'

'I got caught in an ambush.'

'You could have phoned in.'

Pascal said nothing.

'What happened?'

'They killed a Provo. The Provos killed a civilian. I've got blood all over my coat.'

'Put the cleaning bill on expenses,' said the deskman mildly.

'Do you want a story?'

'Naw. Too late. We wouldn't use it.'

'It was big,' said Pascal. 'About twenty gunmen.'

'We'll look at it on agency. Might make a par with a blob. What the Old Man wants is this Dove of Peace. It looked smashin' on television.'

'It was a pigeon,' Pascal said. 'It was only a bloody pigeon.'

'The Dove of Peace,' said the deskman wistfully. 'It's a great little symbol, Pascal. We want a really colourful description. Something to tug at our readers' heartstrings. Pile it all on. Miss nothing. We want a dramatic, eye-witness story, like on television. Make the readers see it. You know. The bombed-out pet-shop, the bodies of the slaughtered pets, and the Dead Dove. The Dead Dove, Pascal. Lyin' there, in the broken glass.'

'The bomb didn't kill that pigeon.'

'What?' The deskman in Manchester laughed. 'It looked dead enough to me.'

'Its neck was wrung by a drunken reporter.'

'Naw!' said the deskman, thoroughly intrigued.

'It had a broken wing,' said Pascal. 'He was trying to help.'

'You know,' said the deskman, 'I thought that its head looked funny.' He hesitated. 'Anyway, I'll put you to copy. Remember to make it vivid.'

Pascal said, 'No.'

'Whatdyamean, no? It's one of the Old Man's specials.'

'I've had it,' said Pascal. 'He can sack me if he wants to.'

'Pascal!' the deskman exclaimed. 'Don't be silly, lad. Stop playin' prima donna. I'll put you over to copy.'

'I'm off duty. I'm on my day off. You can take it up with the union.'

'You'll regret this, Pascal. The Editor's going to be mad.'

'Stuff the Editor,' said Pascal, succinctly. 'I'm going to bed. Goodnight.'

Ann put the telephone down. She wanted to laugh. Poor Pascal. She could hear him thumping around in the kitchen, trying to get rid of his temper. He wouldn't know what to do. He'd be thinking of money and security, regretting everything he'd said and wondering how to get out of it. She could imagine his shoulders slumping as he thought the consequences out. She could almost see the woebegone look on his face.

When he came to bed Ann had the light out and was pretending to be asleep. She thought he'd feel better in the morning. He got in clumsily, as always, but she didn't stir when he kissed the back of her neck.

'Ann?' She refused to answer. 'Ann—'

When he shook her shoulder she turned sleepily round in the darkness.

'Will you make love to me, Ann?'

Part Five

I

It was winter, or almost winter: the graveyard was crowded. The murmured prayers sounded quite unreal. They fluttered like butterflies over graveyard grass and the stale yellow marble of tombs, the exhausted survivors of faith in a better time.

To Pascal the scene was unreal. He felt lonely outside it. He might have been watching an old tableau in a painted landscape. It meant nothing at all to him.

The graveyard had been placed high on a windy knoll, as if the dead when they wakened might wish for a view of the country. It was encircled on two sides by the protective arms of a scarp of hills. The third side of the triangle fell to a pleasant river. On the other side of the river were mountains that rose like stairs.

Ballyvarren farm lay a mile away across the fields, and Pascal could see it clearly. The new hay-barn glinted bluely above a blackened stand of elms. A wisp of smoke climbed from the chimney. Above the farm hung a threatening bank of cloud.

He shivered. Whether it was from cold or nostalgia, he had no way of telling. Ann must have felt it happen, because she told him to button his coat, smiled encouragement, then put her arm round his waist.

A thin wind stirred in the wreck of the brambles around the

graveyard. On the other side of a dry stone wall the bruised land was dun and violet, seamed by ditches, scarred by patches of bog.

This was childhood country, the landscape of Peter Pan. Usheen wandered it, come back from the dead like Lazarus, finding priests enthroned where the Fenian bands had feasted. A surviving bard made a verse out of Usheen's anger.

'If my son Osgar and God
Wrestled it out on the hill,
And I saw Osgar go down,
I'd say that your God fought well.'

Osgar and God were wrestling still, and Patrick rattling his staff. The pagan place, where parallel faiths collided, was no longer innocent. Did Pascal himself not live at the end of the world?

Pascal turned and studied his wife. She was watching the ceremony with close attention. A wisp of her hair, caught by the wind, was floating above her forehead.

'Ann?'

'Mmmh?'

'Do you think that my uncle has gone to Hell?'

She looked at him, amused. 'I don't expect so.'

'If he isn't there, he'll eventually get to Heaven.'

She nodded.

'Then why are we all so sorry?'

The sky was filled with multicoloured clouds that seemed to move across it like trains. When the sun broke through a sudden spotlight was thrown on a jaded field or a patch of gorse, so they blazed on the sombre hills. The valley had never seemed lovelier, or wilder. While the people were gathering for Requiem Mass a rainbow appeared in the skies over Bally-varren. It seemed to plunge and vanish in the roof of the distant farm.

It was an unbearably sentimental moment. A Franciscan monk had known how to take full advantage. He said the rainbow showed that Andy had gone to Heaven. Pascal wondered if it would rain, if the Franciscan monk and the throng of mourners would be soaked by the tears of God.

172

He refused to stand near the grave. They were well apart from the wall of people defining its open mouth. His father had been buried in rainy weather, and the coffin splashed when the bearers lowered it in.

They remained near the dry stone wall, knowing the grave-digger sat in the ditch on the other side, watching the hills and smoking a battered pipe.

Beyond the ridge lay Kilkenny, his father's county; Castlecomer, his father's town. In Castlecomer they threw quicklime in Parnell's eyes. His grandmother saw it happen. The priests had said that he sinned. Had Andy sinned? They were throwing down clay in his eyes.

The turbulent sky made the mourners seem spots of darkness, toiling ants flinging clods which crashed on the coffin. A white-backed ant with a hollow stick was flailing the grave with his holy water; for water healeth.

The farm was a dark whale's back amid sage-green fields. Andy would see it no more. There would never be another sodden Sunday morning, when the townland was winding to Mass, when Andy could riddle Pascal:

'Won't the Protestants laugh, if they get to Heaven, and they spending Sundays in bed?' A laugh. 'And us all crawling to Mass?'

It was all absurd. Life was a tragic farce. Pascal started to pray but was soon distracted. A blackbird was singing clearly. A skylark rose, burbled and fell away in the direction of the village. His eyes followed it, naming every field in a patchwork of fields, knowing every roof on every one of the houses.

Ann nudged him. 'They've finished, Pascal.'

A slow tributary vortex milled round the lips of the pit. Religion was represented. There were monks and brothers and nuns and priests. Science had sent Tuomy, the doctor, and the chemist Brennan, and Francis O'Hara, the vet.

Pascal watched them. There were lawyers, policemen, and soldiers. Labourers, shopkeepers, publicans, farmers. Men from the Old IRA. Some who belonged to the new. They threw in the earth, which fell with a cold, dead thump. Some of the women were weeping. Pascal's mother was one. Mary, the widow, stood at the head of the grave.

'I'm cold,' said Pascal, but Ann said nothing.

The dead man's family took up separate stations among the gravestones or along the cindered path. The gravedigger reappeared. People talked to the recently bereaved, patting them on the shoulder or shaking hands or kissing. The blackbird still sang, and the rooks reconnoitred the stubble.

In a little while the mourners began to relax. They had done their duty. The airs, and the views, and the company called them back. Pipes were produced and lighted. Hankies were put away. They were all in their Sunday clothes, so the talk to begin with was formal. It soon went on to all the perennial topics: the weather, rheumatism, how much a bullock would bring.

Some tinkers were there, and were fawning after the priest. He broke away like a renegade calf, and blustered off with his soutane flying, tramping the tussocks of reeds. The altar boys slunk after him. One pushed the iron trolley which had carried the coffin from church. The other was smoking furtively, clutching the little envelope, a gratuity from Jack, which had money in it to buy more fags.

'There's a good big crowd here,' said Pascal.

'Yes,' said Ann.

'Do you know what we're having for dinner?'

They leaned on the wall and waited to see what happened. There were a few sheep grazing in the field on the other side. Eddie Maguire, a landless labourer, came and kissed Ann gravely.

'More beautiful you're getting.'

He took Pascal's hand. 'Pascal, I'm awful sorry.'

Eddie was forty or forty-five. He used to hunt rabbits with Pascal. He had often helped Andy out.

Pascal said, 'We'll miss him badly.'

Eddie shook his head. 'Och, he was a great man, Pascal. A gentleman. He went awful sudden.' He looked doubtfully at Ann. 'When Mrs O'Loughlin went, Andy went straight away after.' He was talking of Andy's mother.

'He loved her an awful lot. Too much.'

'Aye.'

There followed a minute of silence. Everyone thought about

174

Andy. Then Eddie looked up. 'It won't be the same without Andy and Mrs O'Loughlin.' His face was tanned and his eyes were the clearest blue. 'How're ye doin', Pascal? Is it bad up there in the North?'

'Ach,' said Pascal. 'It's much as ever.'

'I get the impression it's worse.'

'It's pretty bad in Belfast.'

'It's terrible, terrible,' said Eddie, sanctimoniously. His face lit up like a sudden sunburst. 'We'll bate the fuckers yet, hey, Pascal? Ould Ireland will have her own.'

'Ould Ireland will have her own,' mimicked Pascal, grinning. Eddie went away, looking highly pleased.

More people came. Few of them mentioned the North. They preferred to talk about greyhounds, or Ann's trim figure, or Pascal's coat. Pascal had bought a new one in Dublin, and thought it looked well.

He was talking to Ann when a figure came towards them from the crowd round his mother and Mary.

'Who is it?' whispered Ann. 'What's wrong?'

Before he could answer, the man was smiling and offering his hand. 'Do you know who I am?' asked the man, as Pascal shook it.

'I do,' said Pascal.

The newcomer beamed delightedly. 'Your mammy said you wouldn't.'

'You're Mick,' said Pascal. 'Mick Costello.'

He was smartly dressed in a new grey suit and a black rain-coat. 'It's years since you saw me. You were only a kid.'

'You haven't changed very much.'

'He has,' Costello said warmly to Ann. 'Last time I saw him, Pascal was playing with a paper parachute and a tin soldier. He was a noisy little gurrier.' Ann smiled. 'I heard from Seamus, Pascal, that's why I came.'

'It was nice of you.'

'I owe a lot to your family. I couldn't have stuck it in that oul' jail.'

'Everything worked out well.'

'I have me own little garage, Pascal, up in the Midlands.' He looked modestly at Ann, seemed secretly delighted. 'A breakdown van, me own business . . . a couple of lads to help me.'

'Are you married?' asked Ann politely.

'I am. I have a houseful of girls.'

'Not involved any more?' asked Pascal.

'I dunno if I was ever really involved,' said Costello. 'You know how it is when you're young.' He said it easily, as though talking of having had measles. 'I'm keepin' the oul' nose to the grindstone, now. Makin' a bit of money.'

'That's best,' said Pascal.

'Talkin' of money, though. You know that I saw your mammy?'

'So you said.'

'You know when I came to stay with you? Half the police in England after me? She lent me fifteen quid to get home. She's just after askin' for it back.'

'That's her,' said Pascal, smiling.

'She's a character, yer mammy.'

'You never had to live with her,' grinned Pascal.

'One of the best.'

'Do you remember the day you left?'

'No,' said Costello. 'What?'

'You gave me half a crown when you came downstairs from the attic. I always remembered. It was the first big money I had.'

All of them laughed. Costello was no longer the pale young fugitive whom Pascal remembered. He had a country tan, and his eyes were dancing. 'You're a journalist, now,' he said. 'A writer.'

'That's it.'

'Above in the North,' said Costello, shaking his head. 'Me with me garage in Meath and yourself up above in the North.'

'It's not so bad,' said Pascal. 'I'm a non-combatant.'

'It's a funny oul' world,' Costello said. 'An awful funny oul' world.'

'Isn't it?' said Pascal.

'Isn't it?' Costello repeated. 'Isn't it, all the same?'

After they'd eaten, most of the men went to talk and drink in the parlour. Pascal lingered a while in the farmhouse kitchen. It was a high, dark room, thinly scattered with damaged or broken furniture of the utmost plainness. The floor was of stone —rather of polished concrete, black with age—easily swept. The hob and bellows by which Pascal used to sit had been taken out, replaced by a coal-burning range. A television, piled high with Andy's greyhound papers and programmes, was incongruously perched on the working surface beside the sink.

Besides those two details, nothing had changed since the days of the Black and Tans and the War of Independence, when an impeccably polite English officer sacked the house 'because he was looking for Mick'. Mick, who was Andy's half-brother, was on the run. He died in a Free State uniform in the subsequent Civil War.

It was all past history, but the idea that it had happened here, and that his people were part of it, had fascinated Pascal since he was old enough to read. One thing led back to another, and then off sideways. From the thick mud walls of this anonymous, provincial farmhouse, it was possible to trace lines of force which had invaded the whole world's history; from the rise and fall of the British Empire, to the building of America, the Revolution in France, the beginnings of popular democracy.

One idea in particular pleased him. Ballyvarren lay just outside what had once been the English Pale around Dublin. The castle and the bridge in the village had been a Tudor interface, a sally point from which Elizabethan adventurers ventured out in their raids on the Gaelic nation. He had passed the keep coming home from the funeral that day; it had family washing draped where the barons had feasted, and hens were picking among the rubble.

The kitchen was swarming with women and girls and children. They were here from all over Ireland, from Meath, and Galway and Clare, and from Donegal and Kerry. Their scents and the swirl of their skirts, and their eternal gossip seemed to fill the room. There were children rolling round on the floor; they had scrambled under the table. A dog joined in, to the general confusion. The children's shouts had an English accent, from Birmingham and Essex and London. Like Pascal himself, they'd been born in exile.

Pascal stood up, with a wry smile at an aunt from Dublin.

'Have ye eaten, Pascal?' his mother shouted. 'Are ye sure that ye had enough?'

He fled from this regiment of women. The men in the parlour were telling jokes. The smell was of drink and polish. It was hard to think of these bulky men, some of them balding, with their impeccable suits and their highly polished shoes, running round barefoot in the yard outside. Pascal himself had done that. He'd sailed matchsticks in the trough, on water from the old iron pump, before running water was heard of in Ballyvarren.

Guns in the thatch or gunmen in the attic? The birds used to nest in the thatch—how often he'd stolen their eggs!—but the thatchers had all died out. The thatch was gone, and so were the coloured birds.

A big fire blazed. There were pottery plaques, of Gladstone and Parnell, on each side of the fireplace. Parnell's plaque had been smashed by the English soldiers, but they'd saved the pieces and carefully stuck them together.

'It's valuable, that. Antique.'

What would you get for the uncrowned king of an unmade Ireland? Stuck together with glue? It couldn't be very much. All you were selling was faith.

'Are you drinking, Pascal?'

'I'll have a whiskey.'

'Begob, an' you will, an' two.'

The tobacco swirled in the air. Some of the men smoked pipes. One, a countryman, had a briar pipe with a silver cap. The light seemed to focus on that, gleaming, spreading out round the rest of the room.

The great originals were enshrined on the opposite wall. Edwardians, both of them. They looked gravely out of their photographs at an age that was not quite right, not all that they might have expected.

178

Pascal's grandfather, one of the first Catholic Irishmen for several centuries who had lived to own land in Ireland, gazed sternly down at his heirs. He was a big, fat-faced man with a walrus moustache and a golden watch-chain. An amiable eccentric. Pascal remembered him only very vaguely, stalking the yard in a billy-cock hat. He'd drunk himself almost bankrupt; but Pascal had been too young to realize why he walked in the funny way that he did.

In the frame next to him, his wife was an Irish beauty. She was wearing a frilly ball-gown—or what looked like a ball-gown to Pascal—and had challenging eyes and a small, pert nose. It was she who coped. Pascal had known her only when she was old; first, as a forthright old lady, baking flat brown bread and feeding him currants; then as a tragic invalid, bedridden, constantly praying, racked by pain and frustration.

She was the central fact of the farm's existence; fiercely possessive, practical, independent. She'd smothered everyone, of course. Kept her husband as sober as possible, educated, fed and clothed her own children and any other children who happened to need it; christianized them, insisting on rosaries, novenas and regular penance; sung to them; told stories, endlessly, about Fenian uncles who died beside General Custer; a kind of loving tyrant.

Now she was dead; and Andy, who'd worshipped her, was dead as well. The surviving sons, Jack, and Joe, and Phil, had all had children, but Andy hadn't. Pascal sat next to Jack, the only O'Loughlin who was dark and had dark brown eyes.

'Well, Pascal?' said Jack, who was sucking a pipe.

'Jack?'

'Looks black up there in the North.'

'It is.'

Jack tapped his knee. 'Get the hell out of that place, Pascal. Bring up the kids in peace.'

The North was an Irish attic, peopled with ghosts, old junk that was best forgotten. Jack had been there once, for a football game, and had never forgotten the Specials who searched his car.

'Black oul' bastards . . . better leave 'em to go to Hell.'

They were talking of football now. Andy had played at

Croke Park and they still remembered his glories. They were experts here on the art of the Gaelic game. Nobody bothered Pascal, who sat in his corner watching them all. Rather a strange young man, but Seamus, his cousin had once been like him. 'It comes from them reading books.'

He liked having such an enormous family. It made for constant entertainment. He'd tried to count them once, on his mother's and father's side, and stopped at a hundred and twenty aunts and uncles and first-degree cousins. Some, in America, he'd never met, but they wrote, and their letters were passed around. The rest he knew more or less well, a fantastic kaleidoscope of characters who all had a link with him.

A group of men in one of the corners of the room called for everyone else to be quiet. One of them started to sing, and the rest joined in at the chorus. When the song was over they could hear the clattering pots in the kitchen, where the women were putting things right.

Someone struck a match—crack—and more blue smoke appeared in the air of the parlour. 'Sing us another like that.'

Mick, who was Seamus's brother, sang a nostalgic ballad of exile. They went on to sing other songs, as they always did when they gathered together. They were sad songs, but people laughed and joked when the songs were over. Singing made everything right.

Pascal wondered, listening to them sing, if they'd recognize the North. Could they know it was part of themselves? The thought depressed him. What did they know about terror, and death, and the loss of faith? Yet the songs were made out of that.

Seamus, who'd sprung Costello and sent him to roost in a widow's attic, began singing softly. He was a lawyer now, in Dublin. A big rawboned man with intense, pale eyes.

'As I was standing on the scaffold high,
My own dear father was standing by,
My own dear father did me deny,
And the name he gave me was the Croppy Boy.'

Seamus had been shot in the shoulder on a raid on an English barracks in Northern Ireland. It happened the year

180

that Costello escaped. He'd been interned in a camp in the Irish Republic. When the party which interned him engineered the Provisional split in the Republican movement he followed neither wing. He was now inactive, or marginally active; a soldier without an Army. The vision he followed was personal.

When he had finished Jack looked round. 'Pascal! You're sittin' there quiet. Give us a song.'

'I won't,' said Pascal. The demand alarmed him. 'Don't ask me.'

'Come on, now! Sing.'

'I don't want to sing.' Did they know where the songs would lead? Yet he knew that he would. 'I've a cold,' said Pascal. 'I couldn't sing at the moment.'

But Jack insisted.

'What will I sing?'

'Whatever you like.'

Pascal looked out at the people he loved. 'I'll sing my grandmother's favourite.' They settled back in their seats. Pascal felt helpless. He closed his eyes and began lilting quietly.

'Down by the glenside, I met an old woman,
A-pluckin' young nettles, nae saw I was comin',
I listened a while to the song she was hummin'—
Glory-o, glory-o to the bold Fenian men.

'Tis fifty long years since I saw the moon beamin',
On strong manly forms and on eyes with hope gleamin',
Sure, I see them again, aye, through all my day-dreamin'—
Glory-o, glory-o to the bold Fenian men.'

Pascal loved the rhythm of this song, the strength of it, its admission of failure and its boundless hope.

'Some died by the wayside, some died 'mid the stranger,
And wise men have told us their cause was a failure,
But they stood by old Ireland and never feared danger—
Glory-o, glory-o to the bold Fenian men.'

When he'd finished he looked helplessly round in the silence. The big blond men had crossed their legs, were pulling at their pipes, or just looking at him.

181

'That was gorgeous, Pascal.' It was a girl who'd said it; Peggy, one of his cousins. Pascal couldn't bear to wait for a new performance. He had an empty image of failure; of barren farmsteads, exiles' children, ideals corrupted and courage wasted. He stood up, smiled, slouched his way out.

There was a small lobby, with a glimpse of green, between parlour and kitchen. He paused, and gazed out towards the mountains hidden in mist. Then he was back with the women. They were talking about tea and children. His mother was there, playing the queen, unconsciously but cruelly, on somebody else's hearth.

'Pascal!' she said.

'Ma?'

'Have they got enough drink in there?' she asked anxiously.

'Yes,' said Pascal. 'Plenty.'

She smiled. 'You wanted a breath of air?'

Pascal looked at her. 'Yes,' he said. 'I thought that I'd go for a walk.'

Was she nervous of him? He wanted to go to Ann, but Ann was trapped with a group of gossips behind the table.

'You'll need boots,' his mother said, placating him. 'The fields are muddy. It's started to rain.'

'Yes, ma. I'll take my coat.'

She nodded. Her hair, that had once been red, was yellow and silver now. Perhaps mostly silver. 'Why don't you take the gun?'

'No,' said Pascal. The idea shocked him. 'In the middle of a wake?'

'Go on,' she said. 'Nobody minds.' She crossed to the corner and seized Andy's shotgun. 'You might get a rabbit. Take it.'

The shells were on top of the dresser. She went and got them. Pascal took them indignantly, not wanting to make a scene. She thought that she'd pleased him. She knew how he loved to hunt. No one else in the room seemed to notice. Brandy, a fat old spaniel, followed him out of the house. Pascal was furious. The yard looked miserable, grey and wet. Even the hens had left.

'Get home to blazes!' cried Pascal. He shook his fist at the dog. 'Get out! Go on!' The big liquid eyes of the spaniel watched. 'Go on! Get home!' The dog slunk dejectedly back.

A mist was falling; you flattered it, calling it rain. In the Foxes' field, the clover was soaking wet. A wren followed him, skulking along the hedgerow. He pretended he didn't notice.

In the Golden field he passed a mechanical harrow. It had lain in a ditch and rusted there for years. The brambles had overgrown it. He remembered that harrow well. A blackbird had nested in it. A white one. Andy had shown him the nest. 'A contrary thing to nature.' Marvellous, all the same.

He was tired when the circuit was finished. He had not shot rabbits though he had seen them, and foxes, too. A thin drizzle replaced the mist, cotton-wool on the hills, rolling down like a threat. He stumbled along through the paddock. The tractor, the cattle's hooves, had rutted, corrupted the ground.

The hay-barn was full, and there were two large stacks in the corner. Winter was setting in. He did not want to go inside. More than anything else, he wanted to be alone. He was tired of everything. He wanted to get some peace.

He stopped, looked about uncertainly. With the rain that was falling, he needed shelter. He rejected the hay-barn. You could see nothing from it. He walked towards one of the ricks. There was a plantation of firs at the back of the haggard, and a view beyond that to Raheen, the Ridge, and the gentle, indifferent hills.

The nettles were full of bones. Andy had kept dogs in the haggard. A dozen dogs at a time—greyhounds, good ones. One of them won the Irish Cup, the greatest course in the calendar.

The old chewed bones lay scattered among the dock leaves, where the dogs had dropped them. He established himself, under the eaves of the hay-rick. The shotgun was in his hands. He burrowed into the hay, using his back, making a nest, getting in snugly out of the rain. He stood there and did not move. He could hear the drips from the pine trees, the creaks of branches. A few birds passed by and were hidden among the branches. A sheep had been flung for the dogs to devour. Its skin was a smear on the thorn hedge. Its skinned corpse was distended with gas, the port-coloured flesh dotted with fragments of tired grey straw.

It was a strange locale. It occurred to Pascal how sinister it was, but the still, cold air and the muted colours kept him locked inside himself, so he soon forgot that the minutes were passing. He felt outside time. It frightened him in the end. There were no limits to perceptions like these; and therefore no causes for action. They could not be improved or diminished. They left you naked.

When he woke it was exactly as though from sleep. The shadows in the pine trees were intensely green. The straw was intensely grey. Small birds, like jewels, were flying from trees to sheep and were eating the rotting flesh.

There were blue-tits, goldcrests, robins, and chaffinches. He didn't know why, but they angered him. When he fired the shot-gun the stench was sickening. The guts fell out in a welter of yellow puss. The smoke hung blue in the darkening air, the bright little feathers drifted.

He turned away, and walked slowly back to the house.

III

It was two days later. Pascal was woken by the clatter of pails in the yard outside. Paddy Timmins, the farm's dogged labourer, was giving the calves their morning feed. His ash-plant thwacked on their bony shoulders as they butted to get at the milk. A cow—one of their mothers?—lowed in sympathy in a near-by field. Paddy's angry curses drifted into the bedroom, diminished a little by distance. His temper had not worn off.

The sun was shining through thin net curtains. The little dust-motes drifted. A wasp, which had somehow got trapped in the bedroom, buzzed angrily at the window.

Pascal propped himself up on an elbow, and shook his head. The cold out of bed was icy. The farm's new wing had been built when Andy got married, and it took several winters to confirm that the builder had failed to install a damp course. It was so absurd that Andy refused to believe it.

The whole wing needed pulling down and rebuilding. Nothing could stop the mildew. The wallpaper peeled, the plaster perished, and most of the woodwork warped. The

184

expected children had failed to put in an appearance, the guilty firm had gone bankrupt, so the building stayed as it was, a satiric commentary on Irish life for the exiles returned from the English suburbs.

People made the best of it. The discomfort was never mentioned, for fear of offending Mary, but Mary accepted the decay of the bedrooms with the same ironic detachment she displayed towards everything else; her childless condition, the annual waves of invasion from England, the trials of nursing her senile mother-in-law.

Mary, in Pascal's opinion, was secretly flighty. He could see that now. It made him respect her more. The colourless fidelity imposed by life did not touch her core. He thought of the brilliant scarves which she wore to the daily Mass; of the trips to Lourdes, as much to buy French perfume as for holy water from Bernadette's well.

Pascal snuggled back down into bed, tugging the blankets till they almost covered his nose. Out in the yard, some dim-witted hen had admitted laying. It announced the news with delighted clucks, in spite of its past bereavements.

The damp discouraged him. It lay in patches and maps on the bedroom walls. It got in everywhere, even into the picture on the wall at the end of the bed, another pious image of the Sacred Heart like the one he'd grown up with in England.

How he resented that picture! The paper had warped, so that Jesus squinted. Pascal's first adolescent erections had been watched by this wall-eyed Saviour, a merciless Divinity whose reproachful gaze seemed to follow the boy round the room.

When they'd called at the farm on their honeymoon Ann was amused when he insisted on switching the light off. She couldn't understand the unsettling guilt which the icon could still inspire. 'It's only a piece of paper.'

Pascal tunnelled down next to her now. His hand lay across her belly. He nuzzled the down of her neck.

'Ann?' She twisted. 'Ann!'

The children were stirring next door. Pascal could hear them talking their baby-talk, laughing. They loved coming down to the farm. They loved playing round in the hay.

'Ann? Time to get up.' She groaned.

'Mmmh?' She came to the surface slowly, watched him through half-shut eyes. 'I was dreaming,' she muttered. 'You interrupted.'

'We have to leave early to get back North.'

Pascal lay back while Ann turned round to face him. 'Cold,' she said. She yawned. 'Far too cold to get up.'

'Two minutes more,' said Pascal.

'I could stay in this bed all day.'

'You could stay in any bed,' said Pascal. The wasp broke away from the window and buzzed round the room like a spark. 'But we have to get up.'

'You'd better go down first,' said Ann, eventually. 'I don't know if I could face her.'

'We'll go down together.'

'I'll laugh,' warned Ann. 'When I look at poor Paddy, I'll laugh.'

'It isn't a laughing matter.'

'No,' said Ann. 'But what do you want me to do?'

The rest of the mourners had all gone home, and Pascal and Ann were alone in the house with Mary. As far as Pascal knew, he would never sleep there again.

'You were all so serious,' said Ann.

Everyone knew of the terms of Andy O'Loughlin's will. He had written it years before, leaving all his property to Mary for the rest of her life, but adding the proviso that Jack should have Ballyvarren when Mary eventually died.

It wasn't going to happen like that. The twentieth century had caught up on Ireland in some spheres of life at least. Farmers' widows could no longer be treated—as they often had been in the past—as inconvenient chattels with neither rights nor feelings of their own.

Jack had no real use for the farm. He was in his sixties, far too old to return to farming. His children had been born in London and couldn't tell a bullock from a heifer.

'I think we should sell Ballyvarren,' Mary announced on the day after the funeral. 'We'll divide the money two ways. I'll buy a cottage and live a bit closer to town.'

There was a storm of protest.

'It's the family home . . .'

186

'. . . the O'Loughlin name . . .'

'You can't sell this place . . .'

But under the succession laws, she could: and faced with the prospect of living alone on an empty farmstead, under the constant financial supervision of Jack's solicitor—who, after all, would have to protect Jack's interests rather than hers—there was no doubt at all that she would. The family reunion broke up in confusion. It was the end of an era; the final episode in the O'Forsyte Saga.

'I thought your mother would have had a fit,' Ann said.

'She never did trust in-laws,' Pascal said.

Ann laughed. 'And Jack!'

'Poor old Jack,' said Pascal. 'He didn't know what to say.' Pascal glared at the picture on the wall at the end of the bed. Jesus was still reproachful, and his squint had got worse than ever. He looked like a tradesman whose honesty had suddenly been called in question.

'I didn't know what to say,' said Ann.

'It was best to say nothing.'

'And Paddy Timmins. He said Mary was worse than a Protestant.'

'A bloody Protestant,' said Pascal. 'Not just a Protestant. A bloody Protestant.'

'I suppose that he'll lose his job.'

'I suppose he will.'

She touched him. 'Jack couldn't buy Mary out?'

'With land the price that it is? Besides, what would he do when he had it?'

'He'd have to rebuild the farmhouse for starters,' Ann said. 'He couldn't ask his family to live here as it is.'

'Close the chapter,' said Pascal. 'Ballyvarren is dead.'

'It was nice while it lasted, wasn't it, Pascal?'

'Great.'

'And it's not really Mary's fault?'

Pascal turned up his nose. 'She could have tried . . .'

'No,' said Ann. Pascal swung himself out of bed. 'Anyway, Pascal . . .'

'Anyway what?'

'You were always fond of a rebel.'

187

Part Six

I

They made good time going north, and had passed through Dublin shortly after midday. The rich farm milk had given both the children diarrhoea, so much so that it ceased to be an inconvenience and became a reason for hilarity. They ran out of paper nappies for Helen, and the run between Dublin and Swords became a race against time. Eventually they found some.

'God help the Paras,' said Pascal.

Ann looked at him. 'What?'

'Can you imagine searching this car? It stinks like a public toilet.'

She laughed. 'You have to be ready for anything in war.'

'They shouldn't have joined if they can't take a joke.'

They had a picnic lunch on a pebble beach near the Dublin–Meath border. Tom, the eldest boy, was well past the toddling stage and ran around delightedly hunting for seashells.

'What are these?' asked Ann.

'That's called a pelican's foot,' said Pascal.

'Ah.'

They washed Helen's bottom for the umpteenth time, and then walked along the tideline, the baby in Pascal's arms.

'You've cheered up,' said Ann.

'Yeah.'

'You're almost human.'

He grinned.

'We should go to funerals more often,' Ann said. Pascal grabbed at her and missed. She began running along the shore, laughing at him.

'Come back here, woman!' he bellowed. He dumped Helen on a sandy patch of sand and sprinted after his wife. When he caught up with her he grabbed her round the waist and kissed her. She broke away, giggling breathlessly.

'That's no way to handle a pregnant woman,' she said.

Pascal froze. 'You're not pregnant?'

She nodded. 'I'm afraid so.'

'Jesus!' he said.

Ann burst into tears. 'I didn't want to be pregnant,' she sobbed.

'Now,' said Pascal, hugging her. 'Don't worry.' Helen screamed on her patch of sand behind them. 'I thought you couldn't,' said Pascal. 'I thought . . .'

'So did I,' sniffed Ann. She'd been fitted with an IUD after Helen was born. 'I didn't know that the coil had a failure rate,' she said tearfully; and then the tears turned into a reluctant giggle. 'The poor little bugger might be born with a ring through its nose.'

Pascal bellowed with laughter. 'You're impossible,' he said. 'Come on. Let's go and get Helen.' He smacked her on the bottom, and they walked back happily to the car.

Pascal was back at work today. The bombings and assassinations had continued unabated during his absence from the city. An elderly Catholic woman had been killed by a Provisional bullet intended for a soldier. Three Catholic men had had their kneecaps blown off for giving information about the IRA to the police. The Loyalists had murdered a barman, and erected barricades to keep the Army out of the little streets off the Shankhill.

Ann arranged for a babysitter, and came into town to meet Pascal at McGlades's.

'All dressed up to go dancing,' one of the barmen said.

'That's it,' said Pascal, who had changed at the office. 'Life is a constant round of pleasure.'

190

They clattered down the wooden stairs which led from the Old Vic Lounge and emerged into a high, narrow passage, shut off by a spiked steel gate.

'Raw oul' night, Pascal.' An old man was sitting on a beer barrel, guarding the drinkers inside. Pascal felt in his pocket for money. 'Ah, thanks, Pascal. Have a good night. Good luck.'

Library Street led from Royal Avenue, the city's major shopping street, to the Catholic outpost of Unity Flats at the bottom of the Shankhill. It was lined with tall, half-derelict Victorian buildings.

They walked towards the largest bomb site, where Pascal had left the car.

'Pascal!' protested Ann. 'My legs are shorter than yours.'

'Sorry.' He held out his hand, and she smiled and took it as they threaded across the slippery mud and half-buried bricks.

'Brrr!' shivered Ann, settling in on the passenger side. 'It's cold all right.'

Pascal looked at her face, half-hidden in the darkness.

'Come here,' he whispered.

She leaned obediently across.

'Kiss.'

It lasted a long time. It began hesitantly, almost reluctantly, and then the cold was forgotten as their mouths pressed hard and their bodies drew close together. When it was over their lips wanted to linger. They had to be peeled apart like the petals on flowers.

She buried her face in his shoulder, clutching tight while he stroked her hair.

Later they passed along the devastation of the Grosvenor Road without making any comment. But Ann shuddered when Pascal turned into Roden Street, making for Donegall Road and the motorway to Lisburn.

'This must be the most hateful place in the city,' she said, unconsciously shrinking back against the seat.

Pascal looked at her curiously as he slowed for a series of ramps across the road. 'The Army calls it an interface,' he said.

'Murder country,' said Ann.

Outside it was raining. They were among the unlit acres of

191

slums where rubbish was never collected. Behind the rows of gutted houses fronting the street was a hinterland of terror and despair.

'How can you judge them?' Pascal asked. 'I can't.'

'Hurry up, Pascal . . . drive faster.'

They passed from the Catholic to the Protestant sector. The slogans changed. The Army had erected barriers of screens in an attempt to foil the snipers from Donegall Pass. A large brown rat waddled quickly away from the headlights.

'They're as bad as each other, aren't they?' Ann exclaimed, staring nervously out at the evil landscape.

'Lovers grow like each other,' Pascal said. 'Why shouldn't haters too?'

'There is a lot of hatred here.'

'Of course. It provides an explanation.'

'For what?'

'For why things are.'

The narrow street was dark and apparently lifeless. Pascal failed to notice a ramp, and they were both thrown violently forward as the car bounced and landed with a jolt.

The only light was the feeble light of the moon. A cloud scudded across it, and it seemed like a yellow bruise.

'I don't know what to think,' said Ann. 'I'm tired of thinking.'

'Know what Benny says?'

'Who?'

'McWilliams. He said all this—' Pascal waved at the shattered street—'all this was part of an idea we haven't had.'

'It must be a bloody bad one,' Ann said. She turned her face away.

'Ann—'

'I don't think I want to talk about it, Pascal. Go speak to the widows about ideas. I suppose you must. Tell the orphans you haven't had one yet, but you'll let them know when you do.'

A wall slogan slanted grotesquely across the gable of a house. I THINK—THEREFORE I AM, I THINK. They drove in silence, eventually reaching the motorway. A black fog stretched across to the Falls, and the Falls stretched across to the mountain.

192

'I'm sorry, Pascal,' said Ann, contritely.

'No, you're right.'

'Well? So are you. Can't we both be right?'

A mile or two later, Ann spoke again: 'I don't really feel like dancing.'

'We'll have to go. I promised the Colonel. McDowell's going to be there.'

'Will he be surprised when you tell him you're leaving?'

'I expect he'll be bloody delighted.'

Ann touched his face, so softly that he had to shiver. The fleeting touch lasted only a second, a tender gesture that made him smile.

'Don't you think that I've liked it here? Almost as much as you?'

'I suppose. We had happy times.'

'Do you remember our honeymoon?'

'Mmmh.'

Ann sighed. 'Clonmel,' she said. 'What a silly place to take me.'

'The field of honey?'

'That's right. And Slievnamon by bus. And Cashel. I liked doing silly things like that.'

'They weren't so silly.'

She giggled. 'Do you remember the little boy? The one who caught all those fish? So you bought a rod, and you couldn't catch a thing?'

'Carrick-on-Suir.'

'I'd never seen a kingfisher till then. Do you remember in the mountains? When we tried to get a lift, and we couldn't get one, Pascal? We were rescued by a man from Leeds.'

'That's the Irish,' Pascal said. 'All talk and no lifts.'

'They're not so bad. But where would we go, Pascal? Supposing we really left?'

'Somewhere peaceful,' Pascal said. 'How about Beirut?'

'Explain it to me again.' She lay back, staring up at the roof of the saloon, where the children's dirty fingers had left grubby little prints. 'I'm only a woman. I feed people, occasionally give birth. I don't pretend to understand these important questions.'

'You stick to your place, then.'

'Why don't you write McDowell's story? You admit that you know it's true.'

'Only partly.'

'Even a part is better than nothing.'

'No.' He glanced across at his wife. 'Not this time.' Part of him wished to continue, go over again all the doubts that nagged him, and all the secret hatreds. His wife seemed to think that he hated England, and he wanted to tell her, again and again until at last she believed him, that he hated empires and what empires had done to people.

'People aren't such fools as you think,' said Ann. 'They can tell propaganda from truth, and they already know the Provisionals are evil.'

'People don't know what's happening here,' said Pascal. 'How could they? They hear what they want to hear, or what they're permitted to hear. The whole political process has been subject to mystification, disinformation.'

'People are bored,' said Ann.

'That's precisely the Army's intention.'

'And the Provisionals?'

'Are inexcusable.'

'Yet you excuse them.'

'Do you think it's as simple as that?'

They motored on for another mile. The time seemed to stretch like elastic, constantly threatening to snap, to produce another crisis of pain.

'Why do you hate McDowell?'

'We like each other,' said Pascal. 'We've been playing these games for years.'

'Games?'

'Manoeuvres.'

'It isn't a game. People are getting killed.'

'McDowell thinks it's a game. He wants to win it. The Provos have the same obsession.'

'He's trying to stop a civil war. The Provos are trying to start one.'

'There's been civil war since the English came here. Partition was only a truce. Let's talk about something else.'

194

'Belfast would burn,' said Ann. 'What about Jenny?' Jenny was Ann's best friend. A Protestant girl with children.

'McDowell might send a wreath. "We warned you that this would happen." '

'I'm sorry for you, Pascal.'

'Why? I'm agreeing with you. You've heard of the poem? "The beggars change places, but the lash goes on"?'

'Nothing will change,' Ann said. 'They'll continue to kill one another.'

'Conservative people.'

'Self-deluding.'

There was a rigorous search when they drove to the gates of the Barracks. They had to get out of the car while a guard went through it. In the dripping bushes military policemen with sub-machine-guns were patrolling with dogs on leashes.

'Don't step off the path,' a soldier warned them. 'There are trip-wires on the lawns.'

'There you are,' joked Ann, 'he's warned you. You mustn't stray from the straight and narrow.'

It was chilly, and as they walked Ann shivered. She pulled her coat more tightly around her shoulders and made Pascal put his arm around her waist. They followed a gloomy path through a shrubbery until another barred gate loomed out of the darkness. A soldier appeared with a shouted challenge.

'Press!' replied Pascal. 'To see Colonel Fergusson. We're expected.'

'I'll have to phone ahead, sir.'

'You frightened me,' said Ann. The soldier smiled apologetically. Ann squeezed her husband's arm. 'There's nothing like an evening out,' she said. 'Can you hear? My teeth have started to chatter.'

'You'll survive,' said Pascal. He pecked her cheek. 'I hope so, anyway.'

'It's a beggar of an evening,' said the soldier. He went to a shelter to phone.

Colonel Fergusson came to the gate to meet them. His detached, four-bedroomed house stood in an officers' estate which looked like a rich commuter suburb on the fringe of an English city. They were welcomed at the door by Susan Fergusson, the Colonel's wife. She was ten years younger than her husband, an elegant artificial blonde.

They were led to the sitting-room for sherry and *petits fours*. Susan had made a cheese dip and served the pale dry sherry in *señoritas* of Spanish gold. There was half an hour of well-bred chatter which carefully avoided any reference to current affairs. Instead they talked of holidays in Portugal and Africa, discussed the decline of War Department furnishings, and agreed that you needed children in an enormous house like this.

'We'd have preferred a flat,' said Susan. 'But unfortunately, the place goes with the job.'

They finally strolled to the Mess where the dance was starting. As they walked there was an enormous clatter and a helicopter landed nearby.

'The GOC,' remarked Colonel Adam, as the portly figure of the General got out. They entered the Mess at a respectful distance behind him, following a phalanx of immaculate subalterns whose keen, clean-cut profiles drew speculative glances from many of the women. The reception rooms were brilliantly lit, and after dropping off their coats they went to an auxiliary bar for a drink.

The Colonel struggled through the crowds, to reappear with a couple of gin-and-tonics, a whiskey for Pascal, and tomato juice for Ann. His face was boyishly amused, and he was obviously enjoying himself. Pascal and Ann found themselves relaxing too.

'Now that we're here,' Ann whispered, 'I'm looking forward to the evening.'

'I got a table somewhere,' said Colonel Adam. 'I reserved one for six, because Bill McDowell said that he'd come and join us.'

'That's only five,' said Ann.

'He's bringing his assistant,' the Colonel said. 'I think he wants to talk to you about that affair at Long Kesh.' He glanced casually at Ann. 'Did Pascal mention it?'

'He mentioned it,' said Ann. 'I can't say I understand what happened very well.'

'It was the Provisionals,' said Susan Fergusson. 'One of their people found out just what a crowd of crooks they are, so they beat him up and nearly killed him.'

'Dear me,' said Ann.

'The chap McDowell is bringing with him was at the camp that night,' Colonel Fergusson said. 'He saw them go into the hut to hold their kangaroo court, and he heard the fellow screaming and saw them drag him out.'

'You'll like him,' Susan Fergusson promised. 'He's a real old sweat.'

But Pascal had almost forgotten about Nelson by the time they entered the ballroom. The room was oblong, low and dark, with a bar at one end and a crowded dance-floor in the middle. There were candlelit tables at either side, alive with the gleam of bottles, the blur of faces, the sparkle of women's jewels. There was a frantic din from a small stage in the middle of the room, where half a dozen barbered and uniformed musicians were belting out pop-songs with a bizarre mixture of military efficiency and real enthusiasm.

'We're here,' said the Colonel, sitting them down. He leaned backwards on his chair to share a joke with some fellow officers.

There was more light chat. Colonel Fergusson suggested a dance, and Pascal shambled around awkwardly with Susan, who was laughing, while the soldier showed off his paces.

'I hope I've not damaged you too badly,' said Pascal apologetically. 'We'd better sit down, or I'll trip myself up.'

They were talking about the bandsmen's haircuts when McDowell arrived with Lance-Corporal Nelson and introduced him. 'My new assistant.'

'Albert,' said Nelson helpfully. 'No relation to the Admiral. They called me after me dad.'

He repeated the information when the Colonel came back with Ann. Ann laughed.

'You can call me Bert,' he said. 'Seein' as I'm out of uniform.'

'D'you like your new job?' asked Ann, delighted.

'Cushy number, innit, Major? I like journalists, you see, Mrs Canning.'

'Why do you like 'em, Bert?' demanded Susan.

'Keep buyin' me drinks.' Lance-Corporal Nelson folded his arms and beamed benignly at the company. 'Be learnin' photography next. Clickin' away. Gettin' spreads in the *Daily Mirror*.'

'Shall we order the wine?' asked the Colonel. 'They're starting to serve the buffet.'

'You never know, Mister Canning, do you? Reckoned I'd end up guarding a car-park, but wit me gratuity, an' all, reckon I might start a photographic shop.'

'The Beaujolais?' suggested McDowell. 'Will that do?'

'That'll be fine."

'Ann?'

Ann nodded. 'Yes.'

'Nothin' like a bit o' Beaujolais,' Nelson whispered to Pascal. 'I'm gettin' real educated in the way o' drinks.'

'There's a stampede,' said Colonel Adam. 'We better go and get our grub while there's still some left.'

'Pascal?' said Bill McDowell. 'Why don't you and Nelson stick together and have a chat?'

'I'll bring yours back,' Pascal told Ann. 'C'mon, Bert.'

'We'll be with you when we get the wine,' the Colonel shouted after them. They passed the waiter, hurrying back with a bottle, on their way towards the food.

It was not till the second bottle was almost drunk and the lamb kebabs consumed that Pascal and Nelson got round to talking about his duties at Long Kesh Camp. The seamed old soldier interested Pascal, but Ann was entirely enchanted. While McDowell chatted suavely to the Fergussons Nelson gave the Cannings a detailed analysis of the erotic arts of Hong Kong whores, hangovers experienced in Latin American hurricanes, and knavery done in the *souks*. Ann didn't want him to stop, but when Pascal finally drew him back to business he repeated his lines by rote.

'But what do you think yourself?' the reporter demanded.

Nelson shrugged. 'I told you what I seen.' His face was elastic—he contrived to both smile and sneer. 'They're all mad bastards.' He paused, as though he were thinking. 'Be better off, wouldn't they, if they didn't bother? It's all the same in the end.'

'Of course it is,' said Ann.

'It's like this, Mrs Canning. I seen it all, see? Never saw it do any good.' He absently wiped a drip from the end of his nose. 'Once you start, you can't trust anyone. Can't even trust yourself. They're all mad bastards.' He drank. 'You know I was in Kenya?'

'Were you?'

Corporal Nelson grinned. 'See the Masai? They drink warm cow's blood with milk and urine, and they still get drunk.'

Pascal wandered off by himself. He drifted to the men's room, absently read the graffiti, and then went back to the dance. He felt light-headed, forgetting—when he ordered half a dozen fresh drinks at the bar—that he would not be allowed to pay. He brought them back on a tray, having put them on Fergusson's bill.

'Find another chair,' suggested McDowell. 'Sit up with us at the end of the table.'

Pascal did what he was told and sat down to sip his whiskey.

'Did you talk to Corporal Nelson?'

'Yeah. He's quite a fellow.'

'And what do you think, Pascal?'

'I'm still not happy, Bill.' The sharp taste of the undiluted whiskey made him shiver. 'I don't like to do it on my own.'

McDowell said nothing, looked benignly curious.

'If I passed it on to the London office,' Pascal offered, 'they could send over one, or a team of reporters, and do a proper job.'

'I don't see why it's worth the bother,' said Susan Fergusson quickly. 'It seems like a perfectly straightforward piece of reporting.'

'Ah, but you see,' said Pascal, wearily, 'I'm not worried about the story. I just think that if I used it on my own, I'd ruin a lot of my contacts on the Falls.'

'Well, that's OK,' said McDowell easily. 'I'll give it to somebody else.'

'You wouldn't give it to everybody else as a release? I'd be happy to use it then.'

'Bill thought there would be more impact if we gave it to you exclusively,' said the Colonel gravely.

'Ah,' Pascal stared at his glass as though looking for portents. 'That would make things difficult for me. I'm sorry.'

'Forget about it, Pascal,' McDowell said. 'There'll be other stories.'

Pascal looked at him. 'Thanks.' A steady supply of fillers.

The next fifteen minutes was filled with desultory conversation. Pascal sat through it unhappily. Susan Fergusson was plainly fuming. If Pascal said something which called for an answer her reply was invariably sharp. In the end he gave up. He sat morosely, waiting to go home.

Finally McDowell stood up. 'Nelson and I had better be off, Colonel.' He shook hands with everyone. 'Goodnight, Ann. Be seeing you, Pascal.'

Nelson winked. 'I'll call round your office, some day,' he said. 'We can have a chat.'

'Any time,' said Pascal.

When they were gone, Ann moved up the table to sit beside the Colonel. 'What a nice man Corporal Nelson is!' he said brightly. 'Is all the business settled now?'

Pascal nodded. 'Yes.'

'I'll say it's settled!' Susan Fergusson exclaimed. 'I would never have believed it!' she added angrily.

Her husband murmured, 'Susan . . .'

'I'm sorry, Adam!' she said shrilly. 'I've got to say it!' She glared reprovingly at Pascal. 'How could you be so disloyal?'

'I beg your pardon!' said Ann.

'When I think of those barbarians outside! All the people they've killed! All the soldiers they've murdered! Why couldn't Pascal do what he was asked?'

'It's a technical problem,' said Pascal quickly.

'Technical?' Mrs Fergusson demanded. 'What's technical about it? You were asked to write a story, and you won't.' A stray wisp of hair had fallen over her eyes. 'Everyone knows where your sympathies lie!' Her voice, particularly the tone of it, carried far beyond their table. In the moment of startled silence she added defensively, 'At least you've never tried to hide those.'

'I think we've all said enough,' said Colonel Fergusson sharply. He looked back and forth between them. 'We'll regret

what we said tomorrow; let's not spoil the evening any further.'
He stood up. 'Come on,' he told his wife. 'Shall we cool off
now?'

Pascal and Ann sat silently for several minutes. Ann's
expression was stunned. Pascal reached out to her. 'I suppose
we better leave,' he said.

'No,' she said, softly. 'Why should we run away?'

The Mess, warm and dark and pleasant, was no longer
welcoming. They were strangers who had quarrelled with their
hosts. Pascal could feel how tensely she held herself when he
took his wife to dance. He squeezed her sympathetically.

'Pascal?'

'Yes?'

'You know all those trip-wires, and dogs, and fences, and
guns?'

'Yes, dear?'

Her eyes were green. She wore a rueful little smile. 'They're
only meant to stop people getting in. Do you suppose we'll be
able to get out?'

He laughed affectionately. 'The two of us? We shouldn't
have any trouble.'

II

Next evening Christopher Strickland strolled jauntily towards
Great Victoria Street, came out opposite a bombed cinema, and
looked idly across at the Europa Hotel. A light drizzle was falling, and the homebound traffic threw up a purling spray as it
sped towards the Lisburn Road, but Strickland was happy and
hardly noticed the rain.

That afternoon, while writing up the detail of the previous
night's assassinations, he had received a telephone call from
London. It was advance notice that there were promotions in
the offing at head office. It seemed to Strickland that his golden
opportunity had come, for he had been careful to acquire a
patron. His first concern had been to get in touch.

'So, you're really keen to come back home, are you, Chris?'

'I'd love to,' said Strickland fervently. 'But I'd need the right kind of job.'

'I can't promise you anything.'

'I understand that.'

'No. Well,' said Strickland's friend, 'there's going to be a shuffle in the staffing of "Searchlight", Chris. The *Tribune*'ll need some bright new talent to do some digging and come up with some fresh ideas.'

'I love in-depth reporting, mate. I'm good at it, as well.'

'I know. You've already proved it, in Belfast. But what you need now is one good scoop from Ireland. Something to really clinch it. Bow out in a blaze of glory.'

'I've got one, I think,' said Strickland eagerly.

'Spare it me.' The man on the newsdesk laughed. 'I don't want to know till you're sure. But go out and get it, eh? When the Editor looks over the list of names they give him, I want yours to leap out of the page.'

'Sure. I'm telling you, it will.'

'I want him leaning back in his moulded swivel chair,' said the London executive, 'wiping his nose on his sleeve and saying, "Eee, bah goom . . ." '

' "We 'ad a bit o' fun wi' that," ' mimicked Chris. 'The famous Northern-lad-made-good performance. I understand exactly what you mean.'

'I'll boost you up as much as I can—but it's up to you. You know there's a lot of competition so you've got to deliver—and you've got to be seen to deliver.'

'I will,' said Chris. 'I'm working on a great one.'

Thinking of this, he breathed in deeply. The air already had the chill of the coming winter. The twelve-storey Europa Hotel, a symbolic fort which overshadowed the slums of the Sandy Row and the Grosvenor Road, was lit brightly yellow against the navy of the sky. Opposite, the Hammill Hotel was a huddled ruin. A pity, that, thought Strickland. The Hammill used to be good. He went into the Crown Bar and looked around for McDowell.

A warm blast of beery air hit him in the face. The Crown was the finest bar in Belfast, the most authentic gin palace still surviving anywhere in the British Isles. It had been built in the middle of the nineteenth century, and every inch of surface had been covered with intricate decoration by a band of itinerant Italian craftsmen who had come to the country initially to ornament cathedrals.

Ireland's revenge on the bishops was much as normal. McDowell was nowhere to be seen, so Strickland took his place at the bar with a crowd of regulars. He ordered a pint of Guinness, and had the leisure to look around him.

He couldn't help thinking how wasted it all was on Northern Ireland, where one side or the other would be bound to blow it up eventually. With a place like this in Hammersmith or Chelsea you could make a fortune. The walls were lined with antique mirrors touting long-defunct distilleries. There was a series of black-and-gilt pillars, carved to resemble exotic tree-trunks, which supported a delicately traceried roof.

Seized by a sudden doubt, Strickland put down his pint and walked across to the line of snugs which ran opposite the bar. Craning over the doors, each protected by a lion and a griffon, he inspected the booths' occupants. McDowell wasn't there, either. He shrugged and went back to his drink.

'Mr Strickland!' Chris felt a tug at his sleeve. 'Is that yourself, Mr Strickland?'

He looked at the hawk-nosed, withered, weatherbeaten face.

'Paddy,' he said, with faint enthusiasm, 'it's you.'

'It is meself,' affirmed Paddy. 'All that's left of me, Mr Strickland, after them Anglicans was done.'

'Anglicans?' asked Chris.

'Royal Anglicans. Dem sodjers.'

Comprehension flooded Strickland's face. 'The Anglians. The Royal Anglians, you mean?'

'Dem's the fellas,' said Paddy, nodding violently in confirmation. 'Dey have me destroyed. Dey bet me, Mr Strickland, to within half an inch o' me very life, an' me twin brother Brendan too. I have duh doctor's testimonials to prove it.' He pulled a grubby shirt-tail from his dark-grey trousers. 'Look at me sufferin' flesh!' he exclaimed, exhibiting his withered belly. 'Look at the welts they laid on me, an' me wid all the innocent characteristics of a new-born infant in th' bedlam of the world.'

The reporter made a show of examining the old man's bruises. 'That's terrible, Paddy. I wish there was something I could do.'

'Well, you could buy me a drink,' the old man suggested. 'Me brother Brendan is up there, shootin' the pay, but I haven't the heart to listen to him. In all me born days, I never met such barbarians. Them Anglicans is worse than Protestants. They're fierce.'

'What will you have?' asked Strickland, smiling.

'That's a very generous offer. A wee whisky. Vat 69, Mister Strickland, an' thank ye.'

Chris beckoned to a barman. 'Vat 69,' he ordered.

Paddy dug him in the ribs. 'Pope Paul's phone number, eh?' He cackled with amusement. 'An' if it was, he'd be a busy man, himself. Oh, yes. Greatly in demand.'

Strickland glanced towards the door. Major Bill McDowell had just come in, with a stocky companion the reporter did not know. 'Here's my company, Paddy. You'll have your Scotch in a minute.'

'God bless you, Mr Strickland.' The old man looked at the *Tribune*'s reporter with shrewd old eyes. 'I was set to dander off into th' outer darkness, but sure, when you've a glass in your hand, conversation is easy to find.'

Major McDowell arrived, and nodded courteously to Paddy, although Strickland made no attempt at an introduction. Corporal Nelson, who had followed the Major like a damp and faithful St Bernard, beamed broadly at the company. ' 'Evenin', all,' he said.

'Still sthreamin', is it, sorr, outside?' whined Paddy, looking at the Major with calculating eyes.

McDowell shook the raindrops from his shoulders. 'It is indeed. I think it'll get worse.'

'Oh, it will,' said Paddy, quickly. 'It surely will. It's teemin' out there now, but it'll be worse before it ever does get better. There'll be floods.'

'Never rains but it pours,' said Corporal Nelson cheerily.

'You don't know each other,' McDowell said to Chris. 'This is Corporal Nelson. He's giving me a hand.'

'Albert,' said Nelson. 'As in Victoria an' Albert.'

'Albert Memorial,' said **Paddy** sagely. The barman reappeared with his Vat 69, and the old man snatched it at once from the top of the counter. '*Slainte var,*' he said, and downed it with a gulp. 'That was grand, Chris, grand. Just what the doctor ordered.'

'What will you drink, Major?' Strickland asked.

'When in Rome,' said the Major. 'I think I'll have a Guinness.'

'I'll have a Scotch,' Corporal Nelson volunteered.

'Ach, a Scotch,' declaimed Paddy, waving his empty glass. 'A Scotch'll put heat in yer bones, Corporal. A man needs somethin' warming on a night like this, it's a terrible night entirely.' He grinned, looked expectantly at Strickland.

'Scotch?' said Chris, expansively. 'Major, I want you to meet Paddy. Paddy Toner. Paddy Obituary, we call him.'

'Another Scotch?' asked Paddy hastily. 'I don't mind if I do. You'll have yer reward, Mr Strickland. If not in this valley of tears, then up there up above.'

'Paddy's our man in the ghettos,' Strickland said. 'Barman! Two Scotch, a Guinness, and a pint of single.'

That foolish little silence fell which sometimes comes when strangers find themselves together in a bar.

'So you work for Chris, then, do you?' asked Major McDowell politely.

'As, yes. Oh, I do.'

'What was that he called you?' Corporal Nelson demanded. 'Obituary? Paddy Obituary?'

'Paddy has the most original occupation in Ireland,' Strickland said, anxious to show him off. 'When somebody gets killed, Paddy gets us his picture.'

Corporal Nelson laughed.

'I do,' said the old man seriously. 'Never failed them yet. I works for all the papers, but especially for Chris.' He looked at them slyly. 'You might say business was booming.'

'Two Scotch, one Guinness, one Single-X,' the barman shouted.

'Guinness, Major. There y'are, Paddy. Corporal. And a pint of plain for me. You ever tried it?'

'What is it?'

'Porter,' Strickland said, boastfully. 'Puts hairs on a navvy's chest.'

'Pope's piss,' said Paddy. 'That's what they call it here.'

'Give us a taste,' beckoned Nelson. He drank from Strickland's glass. 'I must try a sup of that.'

'Bad for yer liver,' the old man warned.

'Listen, Major,' said Strickland. 'Why don't we find a snug and talk? We can leave Paddy here with Corporal Nelson. They can try some porter while they're waiting.'

'I'm game,' said Corporal Nelson.

'You'll get a terrible headache.'

McDowell looked at them doubtfully. 'You be all right, Nelson?'

'Certainly, sir. No problem.'

'All right,' said McDowell, grudgingly. 'We'll find a snug.'

McDowell and Strickland found the last free booth. They were walled in by solid mahogany, safe from eavesdroppers, business-like.

'What can I do for you, Chris? You said you wanted to see me.'

'I have a story,' Chris began. 'It's an odd one. I wanted your opinion.'

McDowell smiled. 'That's what I'm paid for.'

'I got this from a member of the clergy,' said Strickland, grinning. He produced a folded document which he handed to Major McDowell. It was a photostat copy of an Army Intelligence Summary, dated the previous week, and listing the names of several men 'who are not to be arrested unless seen committing a crime'.

'He's going to raise it in the House of Commons,' Strickland said. 'It's positive proof that some of the most wanted Provisionals in Ulster have been granted official immunity.'

McDowell smiled sarcastically. 'So what?'

'The Government must be negotiating terms,' said Strickland. 'They keep denying it, but they must be.'

'Of course they are.'

'The Reverend won't like that.'

'Look, Chris,' McDowell said, 'this is obviously genuine. It's an official document.'

'Don't wave the Official Secrets Act at me,' said Strickland, sharply. 'You can't censor this one, Major. I told you. He's going to read it out in the Commons.'

'Censorship?' said McDowell, smiling. 'I wouldn't dream of it. But it is an official document. So where did the reverend gentleman get hold of it?'

'How do I know?' demanded Strickland. He looked slightly nonplussed. 'He's got lots of contacts.'

'He got it from us,' said McDowell.

In the bar outside Corporal Nelson ordered two more glasses of Scotch. 'An' I'll have a pint of that Pope's piss,' he told the barman. 'The Scotch'll do for a chaser.'

'I'm warnin' you,' said Paddy. 'You'll regret it, Corporal.'

'We gave it him,' McDowell said, 'for the best of reasons.'

Strickland thought for a while. He grinned at McDowell slyly. 'You bastards.' He laughed, and then struck the table. 'You're trying to embarrass the Government. You're on the side of the Reverend Doctor. You want to scupper the negotiations.'

McDowell shook his head. 'You disappoint me, Christopher.'

Strickland was honestly bewildered. 'Isn't that what you want? To stop the Government from talking to the Provos?'

'The opposite,' McDowell said. 'We want to maintain the illusion that these negotiations are serious.'

'I don't know what you're talking about,' said Strickland. 'You say one thing one minute, and the opposite the next. If the negotiations aren't serious, what on earth is the point of having them?'

'They're giving us,' said McDowell. 'We aren't giving them.'

'What are they giving you?'

'They're keeping their men out of London.'

'Ah,' said Strickland, slyly. 'But their leadership's intact. That's what you're giving them.'

'Has it never occurred to you,' asked McDowell patiently, 'what a marvellous power is the power of selective arrest?'

'What are you talking about?' said Strickland.

'If you can choose who you arrest and who you don't arrest,' McDowell said, 'you can choose your enemies' leaders.'

'Oh, Christ!' said Strickland. 'You've got to be mad.'

'Two Scotches! Two pints of porter!' Corporal Nelson shouted.

'Yer a dacent man,' said Paddy.

'I mean, they're not very bright, Chris, are they? The present Provisional mob?'

Strickland cradled his head in his hands. 'You're saying this to stop me from using the story.'

'Not at all,' said McDowell smoothly. 'I wish to heavens you would.'

'I'll also report what you've just told me.'

'Chris,' said McDowell mockingly. 'Do you think that the *Tribune* would use it?'

'You're a bastard, Major.'

'Listen,' McDowell said. 'We're both grown up. Publish this list, if you want to. If you don't, too bad. I've got a better story, anyway. I'm looking for someone to print it.'

Strickland said, 'A better story than this?'

'Much better.'

'What is it?' asked Strickland suspiciously.

'It starts in a prison camp,' said Major McDowell. 'It goes on through blackmail, extortion, and theft. By the Provisionals. I've got facts and figures.'

'People always talk about that,' said Strickland. 'Proof is another matter.'

'I can prove it. I could give you the name of a Provisional who'll confirm what I'm saying is true.'

Strickland stared at him. 'An informer?'

'Branco Kane?' said McDowell. 'You could say he was a bit of an idealist. He helps out with their intelligence operation. He heard about this from somewhere and he's spreading the word round the Falls.'

'That's how you know?' asked Strickland.

'That's how I know.'

'Do you know where I'd get in touch?'

McDowell looked at him reprovingly. 'Shall I have him arrested for you, Chris?'

'Of course,' said Strickland, blushing, 'I'll find him easily. I just wondered if you knew, that's all.'

'Try the shebeen called the Broken Bough,' said McDowell coldly. 'If you come to my office tomorrow I'll give you all the rest of the details.'

'Thank you,' said Strickland.

'Shall we go outside?'

The two stood up. In the main saloon, Paddy Obituary and Corporal Nelson had each finished their fourth pint of porter and fifth glass of Scotch. Nelson had his arm draped round Paddy, who had amiably refused to sing *Tipperary* as Nelson requested.

'It isn't a singin' bar,' he said. 'We'd both of us get thrun out.'

'It's a drinkin' bar,' slurred Nelson.

'It is,' said Paddy.

'You know the Masai, Paddy? Them's niggers. They drink blood and piss.'

'I know them,' said Paddy. 'Them's Protestant niggers.'

McDowell strode across from the snugs. His face had gone white with anger. 'Nelson!' he hissed. 'Nelson!'

'Hello, Major Mac,' bellowed Nelson, beaming. 'Come out, then, have we? Come an' have a chat with Paddy. Lemme buy you all another little drinkie.'

III

The Strickland story on the Shamrock Mafia caused a great sensation. It made front-page lead in the *British Tribune,* with two columns over on Page Two. The night before it was published, Strickland rang Pascal to say goodbye.

'You're going to be busy tonight.'

'Have you got a story?'

'A blinder,' said Christopher Strickland. 'I thought I'd better warn you. Louis Golden's going to go berserk.'

'Thanks,' said Pascal, gratefully, 'I'll disconnect the phone tonight, or go out, or something. It's a big one, is it?'

'The biggest I've ever done.'

'What's it about?'

'Wait till you buy the paper.' Strickland laughed. 'It's so big I'm taking the next plane out.'

'Worried that they'll get you?'

'Fuck 'em,' Strickland said. 'I got offered a job in London.'

'Great,' said Pascal.

'No life for anyone here.'

'No,' said Pascal. 'I'm leaving myself.'

There was an awkward silence. 'I'll see you, Pascal.'

' 'Bye, Chris.'

' 'Bye.'

The Shamrock Mafia story was copied or quoted from the *Tribune*'s early editions by every paper in Fleet Street. The news agencies sent it across the world on telex as the day's lead story from London. By midday teams of reporters and cameramen were on their way by air to Belfast. Their rooms had been reserved at the Europa Hotel and they had instructions to question barmen, taxi-drivers and anyone else they could think of, about the incidence of graft and extortion within the Provisional IRA.

The BBC featured Strickland's story in all its bulletins for the next three days. It went out on the World Service and was discussed at length on several programmes devoted to news analysis and current affairs. The verdict of the Conservative Party's spokesman on Northern Ireland affairs was taken up and expanded by the Labour Secretary of State; a thousand people had been killed, and tens of thousands either wounded, bereaved, or arrested, as the result of the operations of a band of thieves and brigands.

A theme had been set which by constant repetition would enable the bloody war in the North to continue almost indefinitely. Peace, if it came at all, would come as the peace of exhaustion. There was no civil war in the North, and there never had been. It would only be civil war if the British Army went home. The British Government said so.

There was now no need to take any political action to bring an end to the terror. The victims themselves must 'renounce' the gunmen and bombers. If they did not they were criminals too. It sounded easy, and yet it was not.

All pretence at constructive policy would soon, it was clear, be abandoned. A Consul would rule by fiat. The politicians, of every shade, had better find other work; because nothing was really wrong.

Pascal, who had already resigned under the terms of the *Standard Reporter*'s generous redundancy scheme (the paper was heavily unionized), was working out his notice when the scandal broke. He was planning to go to France for at least a year. He was unsurprised when the chief crime correspondent, who had worked closely with the Army in Aden and Cyprus, flew in from London with special orders to milk the Mafia story for every line it was worth. It had already been decided that such reactive reportage would be the general pattern for the *Standard Reporter*'s future coverage of the war. The readership, the Editor had decided, was not interested in the bloody thicket of day-to-day events, which made it quite impossible to see the wood for the trees, or to understand what in fact was happening. It was also cheaper not to reappoint a full-time correspondent in Pascal's place.

'We can get all we want from the wires,' explained Louis Golden. 'Not that we'll want very much, because really it's terribly boring.'

Pascal's last assignment was to prepare a list of all the people who had been killed in the Province since the day he arrived. This was to be published with a little note explaining why the *Standard Repoter* was following the *British Tribune* in not replacing its full-time correspondent in the Northern Irish capital.

The headline was already written: HUNDREDS OF WASTED LIVES. The Editor thought it had balance. It was quite impartial, saying nothing that anyone could possibly disagree with. He would explain to the readership that the *Standard Reporter*'s continuing coverage of future events in Ireland would fearlessly stick to the same broad principle. 'The Paper With The Great Big Heart'—he had already set it in lead— 'Knows its responsibilities.'

Louis Golden had toyed with the idea of hiring hundreds of English models, and costuming them by sex and occupation to correspond with the legion of English and Irish dead. It

211

would make a terrific picture, Lou thought, 'the proper note to go out on'.

The Editor said no; it was too expensive to hire the models.

So Pascal laboured on. He was swamped by the differing statistics kept by various sides in the conflict. The police, the Army, the Government, the Civil Rights Association and the Women for Peace came up with conflicting totals. It all depended on where you started, where you looked, and who you agreed to count.

'It mustn't be controversial,' said Golden darkly.

'Well, Lou, what can I do?'

'Compromise,' said Lou. 'Get rid of the questionable deaths.'

'I wouldn't know how to start.'

'All this crappy propaganda people make out of crisis,' the News Editor said warmly. 'We don't want any of that.'

'But it's only a list of names.'

'Yeah,' said Lou. 'But you know the Irish. They could twist the alphabet. Some of these deaths were accidental.'

'A lot of them were,' said Pascal.

'Them people the Army ran over. I mean, they were road fatalities.'

'There's been more than fifty.'

'The assassinations. Half of them were private vendettas, Pascal.' He paused. 'Gangland slayings. Mobsters paying off scores.'

'The murder rate here was the lowest in Europe,' said Pascal. 'That was before the troubles.'

'You know what I mean,' said Golden sharply.

'I know.'

'I mean, you've got to include Bloody Sunday,' said Lou. 'Everyone knows about that. But play it down if any of these stiffs could embarrass the paper.'

'I'll try.'

'You won't get all of them anyway,' said Lou. 'There must be dozens of dead Provos we don't know about. Hundreds, probably. They get dragged away, and the Provos cover it up.'

'There must be some,' said Pascal.

Lou's wistful sigh came clearly across the line. 'There's a secret graveyard, somewhere. It would be great if we could find

212

it. It's bound to be somewhere near the Border. They've got a bent priest making secret burials at midnight. The ones they can't get down there, they just shove down sewers.'

'Yes,' said Pascal.

'If we could prove it,' said Louis Golden, 'it would be better than that *Tribune* story of Strickland's. Show we were really winning.'

'Of course it would,' said Pascal.

'Anyway,' said Golden, 'I can't sit here talking to you all day. I've got things to do.'

'Goodbye,' said Pascal.

The police reporter from London had left the office and gone to a lunch at Lisburn. He was interviewing McDowell, who had information that the Provos had hired American veterans of the Vietnam war for five thousand dollars a month. The Irish Godfathers sat around, smoking rich cheroots and robbing occasional banks, while the Yanks did the dangerous fighting. Pascal was grateful for the cynical freemasonry of veteran Belfast reporters, which had omitted to inform his London colleague that McDowell's imagination had already reinforced the Provisional IRA with cadres of Vietcong, Czechoslovakians, Lithuanians and Communist Frenchmen. It was all the fault of the foreign devils, so why should he care any more?

The going rate for killing a British soldier—McDowell had said so—was £500 per corpse. You got a bottle of whiskey for tearing off somebody's limbs. Every Provisional owned a luxury villa, a bar, or else a hotel. They went into battle secure in the faith that their children were stinking rich. They had bank accounts in Geneva which they filled by bullying widows. They even—it was so much worse—they even defrauded the State. It was done through the Social Security. They drew unemployment pay for planting their bombs in pubs. Corruption was rife. Even tots of six got fifty pence each for taking part in a riot. No wonder the thing dragged on.

'We're in the wrong profession,' said Eddie Armstrong.

Pascal looked up. 'I've stopped believing in justice.'

The telephone shrilled and Pascal answered. He scribbled some notes in shorthand. 'When? Just now? All right.'

'I wouldn't mind,' said Eddie, 'but they stay in the best hotels.' He was doing his week's expenses.

'Only in Dublin,' said Pascal.

'Even so,' said Eddie.

'That was another corpse.'

'D'you want to look at it?'

'Aye. I suppose we'd better.'

'You can put it down on your list.'

The call had come from the Catholic Upper Falls. When they got there the road was blocked by a group of about sixty spectators. The corpse lay on a traffic island, its arms and legs spreadeagled. It had been dumped from a car which had sped away in the Ballymurphy direction.

A dark green hood covered the dead boy's features. One of his shoes had come off, revealing the hole in his sock.

'You'd think his mum would have darned it,' said Eddie Armstrong.

Eddie moved around, taking pictures of the body from every angle. This was unfriendly territory, so he was careful to be obsequious. The light was fading, so for the final sequence he used a flashgun, which would make the huddle seem sinister and black.

The onlookers watched him with interest. The children had lived like this for years, and were now quite fearless. To them death was part of the game, like being 'out' when you played at tag. Pascal tapped on a small boy's shoulder. 'D'you know who he was?'

'Dunno.'

Eddie, who had taken up station at Pascal's side, said in a loud stage-whisper, 'Probably his brother.'

' 'Tis not,' protested the boy.

'Maybe his brother did it, then,' said Eddie.

'Doesn't anyone know who he was?' asked Pascal.

The boy scowled. 'He was a lousy stinking tout.'

'An informer?'

'Yeah.' The child nodded, and returned to contemplating the body. Eddie Armstrong unloaded his camera. He slipped the exposed film into Pascal's pocket in case anyone searched him later. 'Sonny?' he said, winding another reel in. 'Sonny?'

The boy glanced round. 'What?'

'Take his hood off for us. Give you half a dollar.'

The boy looked at him dumbly. He didn't say no.

'Give you twenty-five pee,' urged Eddie. 'Run over and whip it off.'

'Leave him alone,' hissed Pascal. 'You'll start a riot.'

'Twenty-five pee! Take it or leave it!'

The urchin hesitated.

'Thirty,' said Eddie flatly. 'But I'll pay in advance.' He pressed three silver florins into grubby fingers. They were immediately transferred to the little boy's pocket. 'Give it a minute or two,' hissed Eddie. 'I'll nod my head when I'm ready.'

The boy drifted off.

'Make a better picture,' said Eddie apologetically. He punched Pascal's arm. 'Haven't you heard? There's a war on.'

'Why is everyone standing around?' asked Pascal.

'Fucking sheep, that's why. Waiting to see what happens.'

The body lay on its back. It was dressed in jeans and a yellow shirt. The little boy darted out of the crowd and yanked off the hood with a single tug. There was a curious public sigh.

Eddie's flashgun exploded in the naked face. It was Branco Kane's. He'd been shot through the nostril, the traditional manner.

Eddie came striding back. 'Right,' he said. 'Let's get out before somebody smashes the camera.'

Pascal stared at the face. 'I knew him.'

'What?' said Eddie.

'He's the guy who gave Strickland that story.'

'Fucking hell,' said Eddie.

'The one Strickland quoted.'

'He didn't use any names.'

'That's him, though. Benny McWilliams told me they'd picked him up.'

'That's great,' said Eddie. 'That makes the splash for tomorrow.'

'They didn't kill him for that.'

'No?'

'For informing on somebody's brother.'

'Come on,' said Eddie, 'Let's go.'

Pascal hesitated. A woman had fallen on her knees and begun to say the rosary. Soon the whole crowd had taken it up, and a priest appeared and slipped through the kneeling figures.

'Don't hang about,' said Eddie. 'We'll miss the deadline.'

IV

The little seaside town beside Belfast Lough was bright in the wintry sunlight. Its small old buildings had the pastel washes one associates with Ireland. There was a brisk wind, trailing white horses on the corrugated sea. Some schoolboys were fishing at the pier. A few pensioners watched them closely. In the tiny harbour a coaster unloaded coal. There were lots of shoppers. The Salvation Army was giving a concert on the promenade, and the wind kept tugging at the musical scores on the bells of their silver trumpets.

Ann had decided to go shopping. She bought some tipsy cake from a bakery near the car-park, and wheeled her double pushchair towards the queue of housewives who were waiting to be searched at the gates of the security fence which was thrown round the centre of town.

A WRAC rummaged through her bags, and she was passing through the checkpoint when a male voice stopped her.

'Gonna get the tea then, are you?'

She looked up, startled. 'Geoff!'

The soldier returned her smile of recognition. 'Only got in last week. I wondered if I'd see you.'

Ann shook her head and laughed. 'I didn't know you,' she said.

'Didn't know your own first cousin? That's disgraceful, that is.'

'You look different . . . all dressed up.' She laughed. 'You look funny in that flak jacket.'

'Me steel bolero?' the soldier said. 'Got to wear it, haven't I? Case any of Pascal's lot takes a pot shot.'

'They've got special orders,' said Ann. 'They're not allowed to shoot you.' She bent down, and lifted her little girl. 'You haven't met Helen, have you?'

The infantryman tickled Helen's chin with a dirty finger. 'Adda babba?' He pulled a ridiculous face.

'I'll have to set her down,' said Ann. 'I'm expecting another.'

'You're working at it, aren't you?' He looked down at Tom, who was scowling at him. 'You shouldn't have married an Irishman.' He made a slight gesture with his rifle towards the little boy. 'He looks a nasty beggar.'

'You mustn't mind Tom,' Ann said. 'He's always frightened of soldiers.'

'Bleedin' Sinn Feiner. I bet you he smiles for the nuns.' He looked suddenly at Ann. 'Your eyes are as green as ever.'

'So are yours,' she said.

'Yeah,' said the soldier, grinning. 'The rest of it's not so pretty.' He patted the children's heads. 'You better move these Fenians. The sergeant'll say that they're blocking the traffic.'

'Goodbye,' said Ann.

'See you, kid. Give all me best to your mother.'

'Keep safe,' said Ann.

The encounter had cheered her up. She took special pleasure in buying some shoes for Helen. She was toddling now, and she needed the ankle support. The shoes were red, and she thought they looked rather French.

France. The thought of it thrilled her. She knew that Pascal would do well in Paris. He was worried about money, but she knew that they'd make out somehow. It was a pity it wasn't the Spring.

'Shall we go and see the band play, shall we?'

They could hear the band as soon as they stepped from the shoeshop. It was playing *Onward Christian Soldiers*, which sounded very martial. Bangor was a Protestant town, and a knot of onlookers had stopped to enjoy the music. They were mostly old, the women with scarves or dilapidated fox-furs round their necks, a lot of the men with sticks.

The little boy Tom begged his mother to pick him up. He stood on the seat of the pushchair, looking urgently up at

217

Ann. A seagull was standing on the corroded sandstone of the sea wall. It had bright yellow eyes and a cruel beak. It looked rather comical, with its feathers ruffled and its head cocked sideways, as though it were listening closely to Salvation Army hymns.

'All right?' asked Ann. Tom nodded, clinging tightly round her neck, and staring with fascination at the red-faced bandsmen. 'I'll put you down now,' said Ann. 'We've got all that shopping to finish.'

It was hard work getting the pushchair even half-way up the main shopping street. The children were getting heavy, and the hill seemed steeper with every visit she made. She wished Pascal was there to help her, and then cheered herself up by thinking that Paris was probably flatter.

'We'll have a little drink, later on,' she told the children. 'We'll find a café and have a nice sit-down.'

The Loyalist para-militaries had called a one-day strike, and the power was off, and the shops were gloomy and un-welcoming. Ann went into a small department store and bought groceries from the supermarket section. When she got the children out into the sunshine she decided to go for that drink.

She was trudging up the hill when a bomb went off in the shop she had only just left. It exploded with a deafening whoosh! and an arc of blazing petrol was thrown halfway across the street. There were screams and shouts from inside the shop, and a man ran out of the smoke with his hair and clothing on fire.

Ann halted, stunned. A continual rattle of small explosions was coming from inside the store. The paints department was at the front of the building.

In the street below her a man was wrestling with the wretch who'd been doused in petrol. The burning man was shrieking and lashing out. Fat clouds of black smoke were billowing out of the shop. The street was alive with people. Some were running away from the shop, while others were running towards it.

The pushchair, which was hung with groceries, was heavier now than ever. She pushed it uphill as fast as possible. The

218

children were still bewildered, and neither had started to cry. She talked to them softly, panting with effort because of the heavy pram.

A few yards in front of them a shop front exploded outwards. The hot blast of it almost threw her backwards. At the same instant she screamed as a fragment of glass shrapnel shattered on the handle of the pushchair, slashing her finger and showering the children with tiny pieces.

Sucking her finger, and sobbing with pain and shock, she frantically checked them for cuts. Neither was injured, but Tom had become hysterical and was screaming loudly. Helen had her thumb in her mouth and was watching her brother with interest.

She knelt down and was hugging her son when another two bombs went off. Both exploded close to the top of the hill. There was smoke everywhere, stinging and acrid, and Helen was crying as well.

One look was enough to tell that the top of the street was cut off. The winter sunlight made the billowing smoke look solid. It was lit from inside by flames.

Ann twisted the pushchair and ran, the hill helping her now, in the direction from which she had come. The department store had become an inferno. The wind off the sea was helping the flames to spread.

She hesitated, for there were still explosions from somewhere inside the store. She became conscious of shouts and screams as other shoppers came face to face with the same dilemma. There were crowds of people trapped in the space between fires.

She had no way of knowing what other explosions might happen at any minute. The waves of heat from the burning store made her feel she was trapped in an oven. She took a deep breath and ran as fast as she could to the other side of the road. The smoke loomed in front of her, as thick as a solid wall. The children were screaming in terror. She ran headlong into it, clamping her eyes tight shut.

She knew at once when she'd broken through. The cool, clean wind still blew from the sparkling sea. She had a heavy stitch in her side, had to stop while she gasped for breath.

Herds of people were milling on the promenade, for there had been other explosions on parallel streets and nobody knew where to run. She unhooked the shopping bags and flung them into a doorway. They were slowing her down. The roof of the store behind her collapsed in a shower of sparks.

At last she got on to the promenade. She looked desperately around her, trying to find a way out of the ruck and away from the danger. She remembered Pascal's advice: *'Find an empty street and get yourself into a doorway'*. But that was advice for car bombs; if you saw a car you ran from it. That was simple enough.

There had never been an incendiary attack like this. The Provos burnt buildings one at a time. They didn't dismember whole towns.

Ann chewed on her lower lip, blinking down tears, her head swivelling. She stood on tiptoe, trying to see over the crowds. How had the Provos done it? How had they got through the fence?

Her hand hurt. The glass had gashed at the base of her little finger. The push-chair's handle was sticky with blood. She went round to the children and tried to calm them, but she couldn't think how. She was sobbing herself. A huge column of smoke, uniting the ruin from all the fires, had spread like a giant umbrella above their heads.

There was panic everywhere. She could see them all pushing and shouting. Someone blundered into her, kicking her ankle so hard that she yelped with pain. She began to limp, sobbing with outrage, in the direction of the headland where the children went swimming in summer. People were clambering over the sea-wall to shelter on the narrow strip of beach, and one woman was standing waist-deep in the water, holding her cheeks and screaming.

There were more explosions. She counted three. Ann snatched up Helen, grabbed Tom by the hand, and abandoned the push-chair. She began to elbow her way through the milling people, to move as far away as possible from buildings.

Someone was shouting in the street in front of her. She couldn't make out what he said. Then there were cries all round her; 'Car bomb! Car bomb!' and the people turned in a mad stampede.

Ann knew that it couldn't be true. Nothing so big as a car bomb could have got through the soldiers' cordon. But she had no choice but to turn and run before the mob of people. She was frightened of tearing Tom's arm from its socket, but she ran like a wild thing, dragging him through his stumbles with the strength of hysteria and fear.

The small grey town was completely blanketed in smoke. Isolated fires, as rich as cherries, cast a flickering, infernal light. Compelled by the pressure behind her, Ann stumbled forward, only to be halted by an immovable wall of bodies. The people here were pointing, and shouting, waving the others to stop.

The town gasometer was stencilled in leaping flame. Ann could hear fire engines, and see jets of water being played on its steaming sides.

'It's going to explode,' came a cry. 'It'll kill us all!'

The crowd heaved back like a panicked monster. Ann was pressed backwards, shoved, her son almost torn from her grasp. She yelled, spitting like a cat at the men who did it. The black smoke pillar pressed like a monstrous thumb while she scrambled to pick up Tom. She remembered seeing the sun, its face black through smoke, and then heard another explosion.

It was another small bomb which the Provos had placed in a shop. What looked like a ball made of fire and glass floated lazily towards the crowd. The people went mad like stampeding cattle. Ann tried to stand steady, but was overwhelmed. She stumbled and then collapsed, in a strange dark forest of frantic legs. She thought to protect the children. She writhed and twisted, trying to grab at Helen. Someone stamped on her stomach. Something burst inside her with a terrible, tearing pain. She felt wet on her legs, but her screams choked off when she fainted.

It was just too late to interest the *Standard Reporter*. They never carried a line.

V

Ann and Pascal never did get to live in Paris. They talked it over while Ann was recovering in hospital. They went into the question very thoroughly indeed. They enjoyed it.

'It's supposed to be nice in the spring,' Ann said. 'Everyone talks about April in Paris.'

'I was once there in August,' Pascal said. 'They charge a lot for ice-cream in August. We couldn't afford it. And you know how you like ice-cream.'

Ann, who was very pale, leaned dreamily back on the pillow. 'I heard bad reports about Paris in November,' she observed.

'I believe it rains.'

'Pascal, it doesn't just rain. It freezes.'

'And the Métro smells, you know,' said Pascal.

'I heard that the Métro stinks.'

'They push you about. People in Paris are rude.'

'Famous for being rude,' said Ann. 'Not like the Irish at all.'

'Unfriendly.'

'An aggressive race,' said Ann, and giggled.

'Picasso put up with it,' Pascal said.

'He was a Spaniard.'

'Anyway, he could paint.'

'Hemingway lived in Paris,' said Ann. 'Look what happened to him.'

'Look what happened to Joyce.'

'Dead,' said Ann, with a doleful smile.

'Where shall we live, then?'

'Spain. Somewhere sunny.'

'I can't speak Spanish.'

'Italy?' said Ann. 'It's very sunny in Rome.'

'Not in the winter.'

'No?'

'It's worse than Paris in the winter.'

'Ah, well,' said Ann. 'It'll have to be Cannes. Or possibly Monte Carlo.'

They finally settled for Nice. When the house was sold they had sufficient money to stake themselves for a year. 'Two,' said Ann, with determination. It turned out that she was right.

The customs officer who met them at Calais was as black as the ace of spades. He came from the French West Indies. He looked them over carefully when they announced their intention of coming to live in France. He seemed doubtful about it. They had all the papers from the Consulate, so there was nothing that he could do.

'Anglais?' he said, eventually.

Ann could speak better French than Pascal. *'Mon mari est irlandais,'* she said stoutly.

The Customs man shrugged. *'C'est la même chose.'* He eventually let them through.

In Nice they fell among journalists. The French reporters didn't seem very different from the crowd that they'd left behind. They had a finely developed sense of humour.

'Ira ou ira pas?' The one called André used to ask every time he saw them. 'Is everything going to be all right, or not?'

'Ira,' Pascal was supposed to reply. And when he did so— it was, after all, expected of him—André would burst into gales of Gallic laughter.

'Well, what's so funny?' whispered Ann.

'Ira,' replied Pascal. 'A pun.'

They were usually happy. The first time Ann saw the Battle of the Flowers she burst into tears. Pascal, alarmed, tried to soothe her. He didn't know what was wrong. They were watching a long parade of bands and dancers as it passed through the Place Masséna. The local majorettes had just gone by, kicking their legs in the air, and a phalanx of Swiss blowing green tin trumpets were following them. Both of the children seemed to be enjoying themselves.

'What's the matter?' he asked.

'I was looking at them,' sobbed Ann.

A group of Italians dressed up in Renaissance costume were flinging flags in the air and catching them. It looked very impressive.

223

'Who?' said Pascal.

'Just them,' sniffed Ann. She smiled at him tearfully. 'Do you know what day this is?' Pascal hesitated. 'What date?' said Ann.

'It's July 12th,' said Pascal.

Ann nodded. 'Yes,' she said. 'It's July 12th.'

They found out later that two more people had died that day, when the Provos put bombs near the Orange Parade in Belfast.